Also by J.A. Gates

Selendria Book 1: Legacy of Power

Contents

Dedicated to all those who have lost that which they can never get back. May your heart be filled and your hope renewed.

Northern Forest
Northern Backbone Ranges
Twilfell Basin
Milliger Pass
Snowmelt
Resahil
Umethrion
Kamde Forest
Monkwich Lake
Milliger River
Na Aethel
Amathnore
Vafanas
Chelmsman Iles
Estathemar
Ifellean
Selendria
Omel Orthelad
Roguevale
Krodon's Fortress

Hope is a waking dream.

Aristotle

Chapter One

Jacek, also known as The Red Hunter, the most feared assassin and mercenary in all of Selendria, was the one being hunted.

Years of experience had honed his senses, and they were screaming at him now that someone was following the caravan he guarded. They were nearly at the western edge of the Kamde forest on one side of the road. An icy breeze stalking down from the northern Backbone ranges dropped the occasional clump of snow from the thick evergreen trees of the forest, escorting the icy cold down the back of Jacek's neck and under his leather armor.

He halted his horse and cocked his head to listen. Nothing. He was sure he had seen movement from the corner of his eye. They were in the forest. He just couldn't pinpoint exactly where. They moved fast, and there was more than one person.

Overhead, the sky was clouded over, blotting out the sun. The air had a scent to it that usually heralded snow. It was the most normal smell in Selendria.

He nudged his horse on ahead again, moving alongside the plain carriage in the middle of the caravan. Knocking on the wooden siding, he waited until they pulled a curtain back to reveal a gloved hand. The arm was clothed in a baggy sleeve that formed part of a black robe; the face lost in the interior's gloom.

"We need to pick up the pace. Someone may follow us," Jacek said.

A dry male voice spoke out of the shadows. "And your job is to protect us, Red Hunter. I'm sure we will be fine. You have brought enough men with you?"

Jacek glanced around at the four other people who rode with the group, providing security. He had hired them after asking around for reliable mercenaries in Amathnore. These four, along with a few others, had been recommended. Testing them had been fun, he admitted to himself, whittling the candidates down to this small group. They were capable enough for the job - protection of the High Deacon and his monks of the Creed of Redemption on a trip to Resahil.

With the Creed's rise in the vacuum of power left by Krodon and his father, they were now a target from various factions. Jacek wasn't sure if it was a sign of their wealth or paranoia that had them seek him out.

He turned back to the carriage. "We'll keep you safe. Whatever happens, stay in the carriage." He kicked his horse to move ahead to where the lead mercenary rode.

The woman turned her head to greet him quietly with a nod. She was solidly built, with her ebony hair cropped short against her head. A sword hung at her waist on the left, with a knife on her right hip. The piebald gelding she rode matched the patches of pale skin visible on her face against the darker tan shades. Jacek guessed she felt some affinity with the animal because of her condition.

"Keep your eyes on a swivel, Solel."

"You expecting trouble?" Her voice was deep for a woman.

"Possibly. Just stay alert."

Solel scoffed. "What made you think I'd stopped?"

He wouldn't answer that. It was probably a trap, and he didn't have time to work it out with her. Woman or not, he needed her. Not that he had a problem with woman fighters. Aleni, his elven adopted daughter, could now keep up with him in training. He had been so proud when she'd disarmed him finally one day.

No, he just had a problem with fighters who had something to prove. They made mistakes. And with Selendria being mostly full of male fighters, any female ones felt they had more to prove to keep up with the men. In his eyes, they didn't. But whenever another fighter came up either against him, or even just near him, they often tried to challenge him. Having a reputation like his meant being the standard that others were judged by. He had to be wary of every fighter. It could mean a knife in the back. These mercenaries were simply swords for hire; not to be relied upon.

Jacek wheeled his horse around and cantered to the back of the line. He passed the red-haired Dunvern on the way, giving him a keep-a-look-out signal with two fingers. The young man straightened and nodded gravely, gripping the reins in his left hand and placing the other on one of his two swords.

Blond-haired Rilaiz and dark-skinned Mular, stationed aside the four other monks in the group, caught the silent communication as well and shifted to a more readied position on their horses' backs. Jacek took his place again at the back of the caravan, waiting for any movement from behind.

When the attack started, it came not from behind, but from the front. He had credited whoever it was with more intelligence than they deserved. However, it didn't matter. Jacek counted fifteen of the attackers, riding out from both sides of the road with weapons held aloft. They vastly outnumbered him and his crew. Jacek cursed and dug his heels into his mount's side.

Racing along the caravan's line, he freed his axe from the loop in his belt and clenched the handle in anticipation. His heart sped up almost in time with his horses' hooves. Tingles ran across his skin in anticipation of a fight. His crew drew their weapons as he passed them and spurred their horses into action.

Solel, having pulled her piebald to a stop, already had her sword drawn and pointed at the men galloping toward them. Dunvern, Rilaiz and Mular drew up alongside them in a line facing the attackers, spaced out just enough to not hit each other with their weapons.

"Hold this line as long as you can!" Jacek steadied his horse as he slowed it. They spread out along the width of the road. Mular, a tall man with a large build, drew his long axe and swung it around his head experimentally. It was an intimidating move.

Jacek turned his upper body and looked back at the monks clustering around the carriage. "Draw your weapons! This will get ugly." The monks were all trained in basic combat, almost a prerequisite for survival in Selendria. He hoped he had been wrong before and there wasn't another group behind them. So far, the road behind was empty. He couldn't spare the people to guard the back right now. They would all have their hands full with the numbers coming at them.

He turned back to face the oncoming threat. Normally he would favor riding forward and getting momentum to meet them, but they had to stay close to the carriage to protect the Deacon. Jacek hated these kinds of odds.

Breathing in and out slowly, he focused in on the rider coming right at him, assessing the man. He carried a sword and held it reasonably confidently in his left hand. The distance closed between them in only a few seconds; the sword coming across to slice at Jacek's neck.

Jacek ducked and parried the blow, flicking the sword away to the side. Because of the man's momentum, he barreled on past Jacek, forcing Jacek to deal with the woman coming in behind him. A clash of metal rang out as swords and axes met along the width of the road. Horses screamed and snorted as the two sides engaged in battle.

Ducking under another sword swipe, Jacek swung his axe up to bite into the armpit of his opponent, nearly taking the arm off at the shoulder. The woman screamed and dropped her weapon. He yanked the axe out and the woman clutched the deep wound, falling slowly from her horse.

Jacek moved his horse to the next person, pulling his knife out as he went, stabbing it into a man's side up to the hilt. The man cried out and swung his sword in Jacek's direction, who leaned back to avoid the blade.

With one massive swing, Jacek's axe took off the man's head. Dodging the resultant spray of blood, he spurred his horse to the right to move on to the next person.

He came near Solel, who was holding her own in the fray, trading blows with a man who looked to Jacek like it insulted him to be fighting against a woman. Jacek allowed himself a small smile, his thoughts going immediately to Aleni. He was glad she was not with him today. He had ordered her to stay home in the cabin they shared deep in the Kamde forest.

Movement to his left pulled his thoughts from him. Another man attempting to break through the line. As he fought, he turned his horse so he could look back at the carriage carrying the old Deacon. The man who had first engaged Jacek was now fighting two monks who guarded the carriage. He was holding his own. The monks looked tired. They weren't used to fighting in extended combat like this. Jacek would have to get in there soon, or they would be in trouble.

His attention divided, he almost missed blocking a swing from the right. He caught the long blade with his knife just in time, the hand guard stopping it from cutting into his hand. He pushed away with all his strength, but the man pushed back. For a few seconds, they stared at each other, trying to best their opponent with muscle alone.

Finally, Jacek swung his axe around with the other hand and knocked him on the side of the head with the flat of his weapon. The man's eyes rolled up in his head, and he toppled from his mount. Despite only using the side of the weapon, he knew it would be a killing blow. This way, there was less blood. It covered him enough as it was.

Grunting with satisfaction, Jacek looked around to assess the battle. Each of his mercenaries struggled with an enemy. More were piling up around the carriage on horseback, overwhelming the monks there. Jacek moved his horse toward it and started attacking the enemy from behind. As soon as he did, they turned to defend. He was now fighting three men at once. On horseback. Not good. He needed to back up to make some space. But the men crowded him in. It was all he could do to dodge and parry each strike.

Just then, he heard barking. A dog. It sounded familiar. Was that...?

The man attacking him grunted suddenly as a weight landed on his back. Jacek glanced up between strikes to see a small, hooded figure with their arms wrapped around the man's throat, pulling back. Strands of stray white hair hung out of the bottom of the hood.

Aleni.

Her opponent grabbed at her, but she held on fast, using her weight to pull him off his horse.

Jacek's heart did a somersault at seeing her. How did she get here? Had she been the one following them? Forced to push back on his attackers, he turned his back on her, his heart beating so hard in his chest it hurt. And it wasn't the battle causing it.

He leaped from his horse and crashed into one man, taking him down to the ground. The man's breath came out in a whoosh as Jacek's weight landed on top of him. He didn't have time to breathe back in as Jacek's knife buried itself in his throat.

Screams and cries could be heard in the tumult, and now Bandur's barking was added to it. The smell of sweat and blood hung in the air. Jacek got to his feet and turned back to see his dog biting down on the arm of the person Aleni was fighting with. She slashed down on an angle with a short sword. The man screamed, and tried weakly to hit back, but Aleni danced back out of reach. The young girl stepped back in to stab her sword through her opponent when Jacek saw another man coming up behind her, his sword raised to strike.

Chapter Two

He raced through the throng of fighting bodies, launching himself at the bandit just before the man ran Aleni through with his sword. They both tumbled to the ground. The man grunted in pain as they rolled. Once they'd come to a stop, they both scurried to get their limbs under control and strike first. Jacek was faster, not even bothering to get to his feet. He chopped down with his axe, but the man dodged his head to the side, the weapon just missing his ear and biting into the slush underneath. He threw an elbow at the Red Hunter's head. The bony elbow wrapped in animal hide scraped multiple layers of skin off his cheek, drawing blood.

As Jacek shook his head to clear the pain, he caught movement and saw the man's other hand coming down toward his chest with a knife. He dropped his axe and caught the wrist with one hand, pushing back with everything he had. He brought his own knife hand up to bolster the attempt, using the position to cut into the bandit's hand. Blood flowed, and a cry of pain went out.

Jacek brought his knee up under the bandit and pushed out, using his momentum to roll him over onto his back. Within a second, Jacek's blade slashed across the exposed throat.

Rolling to his feet, he wiped his blade on his leather pants. He looked around for Aleni. She was standing over a dead bandit, Bandur close beside her. The numbers of the enemy had thinned out by now, his mercenaries getting a hold of the fight. Jacek stomped over to where Aleni was and grabbed her by the arm.

"What are you doing here? I told you to stay at home."

Despite him holding her arm, she shrugged. "Home was boring. You're lucky I did leave. You obviously needed the help." She gestured to the man at her feet.

"You almost cost us this fight. Because I saw movement in the forest behind us, which was you, I thought an attack was coming from behind. And I just had to rescue you from being skewered. I don't need that distraction right now!" His voice had an edge of growl to it. He glanced up at the carriage. Two bandits were trying to get into the cabin. Jacek let go of Aleni and took two steps toward them.

He rammed his knife into the back of one man's neck, between two bones. The other man next to him startled and looked over at his mate in horror. He took one quick look at Jacek and ran off down the road.

Sighing, Jacek let the dead man fall, holding on to his knife. He watched the other run off down the road and wondered if he should get his horse and follow.

Before he decided, Aleni took off after the man.

"Aleni!" He made for his horse, swearing. It would pay to question the man. He had to get to him before she took him out. Leaping onto his mount, he took off at a gallop, Bandur hot on his heels.

Being an elf, Aleni's speed was faster than the bandit's. She leaped onto the man from an angle off to the side, pushing him to the ground. Punching him in the face, she reached for the knife at her hip.

"Aleni, no!" Jacek barked. He had almost reached them. He dismounted before the horse had even stopped. He grabbed her arm just in time to stop her from plunging the knife into the man.

"What? Why?" She looked up at him, anger and confusion on her face.

"Because I need to question him." Jacek trained his gaze back on the fight around the carriage. His team had put everyone else down. Two monks lay also on the ground, unmoving. "He's probably the last one left alive."

Aleni grumbled, but got up off the man. When the bandit went to move, Jacek placed a boot on his chest, pushing him back down.

"Stay."

The bandit, who had dark close-cropped hair and small dark eyes, tried to scowl, but fear fought for precedence on his face. His distinctive eyes gave him away as one of the Lontar, a race of people who specialized in the healing arts. He wasn't a big man, and not well dressed. Only just enough to stave off the freezing temperatures of Selendria, but not enough to protect him much in a fight.

"Why did you attack us?" Jacek asked.

The man clamped his mouth shut and tried for a look of defiance. Amusing.

Aleni placed the tip of her knife at the man's groin. Jacek stifled a smile. She was probably relishing that.

The man gasped as the point bit through his clothes. "Okay, okay." He put his hands out in surrender. "Deacon Sesk. I want him dead. He is the reason my wife is dead."

"Don't care." Jacek pushed harder on his chest.

He coughed against the added pressure. "He must pay for what happened to her! His teachings are poison! Now my daughter is gone too."

Jacek hesitated. He knew that fear. He looked down at Aleni, still so small even though she was thirteen now. He didn't know what he'd do if she went missing. Yes, he did, actually. He would rip the world apart looking for her. She wasn't his flesh and blood, nor was she even the same race as him, but she may as well be now. Her safety was all that mattered to him.

Could the Deacon know something about this man's daughter? What could he have been up to? He looked back at the caravan down the road. But even if he did, did it matter? Jacek was being paid to protect him. That was his priority right now. He took his contracts seriously.

He looked down at the bandit. Was that what he really was? Or just a father on a mission? Whatever the case, Jacek felt a little pity for the man. Even if he would not admit it out loud.

He drew his knife. Gripping the handle in a fist, he swung in an arc across the man's head. The butt of the handle hit his temple, and the man went out cold.

Dragging the man to the side of the road, he left him in the snow. Once that was done, he turned on Aleni.

"I told you to stay at home!" Anger and fear fought for a place in the pit of his belly.

"How come you get to go out on jobs while I have to stay at the cabin?" Aleni gave him an accusing look.

He kept his voice low. "Because I'm not a young, naïve elf that needs protecting from the dangers of this world."

Aleni's white hair was mostly tucked away under her hood, her pointed ears safely hidden from sight. No one but Jacek knew what she was. The last of an extinct race, and probably the only one in the world with magic. She could be a valuable commodity to the highest bidder. Jacek would do everything in his power to prevent that from happening. If it meant she had to stay hidden away in their forest home, then so be it.

"I don't need protecting!" She thrust her chin up, her icy-blue eyes boring into Jacek's.

"Yes. You do." He pointed a finger at her. "You don't watch your surroundings, and you're too emotional when you fight. It will get you killed. You're not immortal. Not even your people could cheat death."

She narrowed her eyes. "Thanks for the reminder." Her tone was dry.

Heat flooded through Jacek's face as he realized what he'd said. He lowered his gaze from hers. Why was he always putting his foot in his mouth?

"Why didn't you kill him?" Aleni pointed at the man unconscious in the ditch behind them.

"He was unarmed, Aleni. Beaten. He was no threat. I have a rule."

"Since when?" She accused him.

"It's new." He tipped his head sideways ruefully.

"You took pity on him."

He raised his gaze back up to hers, his brow furrowed. "What has gotten into you? Since when have you been so enTusiastic about killing? What did he do to you?"

The young girl clamped her mouth shut. She shifted her foot slightly before replying. "Nothing. But you're the most feared assassin in the world. Now you're just knocking people out and walking on? I could ask you what's gotten into you!"

He stared at her, taking in her diminutive size, her pale skin and extraordinary blue eyes. She was who had gotten into him. He now

had another reason for living. Looking after this orphan, an en-
dangered being, was his new life's purpose. Since she had healed
him from the illness that would have taken his life and wormed
her way into his heart, everything he did now was to protect and
care for her. As a father would.

"Go home, Aleni. Please."

She was silent for a beat, her mouth set firm and her eyes
blazing. She had such a fire inside. Jacek's heart burned with pride
at it. Not that he'd had anything to do with it.

Finally, she clicked her fingers toward Bandur and spun away,
moving off toward the forest without another word.

Letting out a heavy sigh, Jacek watched her go. She moved at a
normal human pace until she went beyond the tree line. Then she
sped up, Bandur matching pace with her. In only a few seconds,
she disappeared from sight.

Checking once again that the bandit was out cold, Jacek re-
mounted his horse and rode back to the caravan and his crew.
After a report from Solel, he found that two monks had died. Only
minor injuries for the other monks. His crew were unharmed. All
the other bandits were dead.

He dismounted then and checked in on the Deacon.

"I am fine, thank you." The elderly man replied to his enquiry.
"A little shaken, but uninjured. My thanks to you and your team
for keeping me safe."

"Two of your men are dead."

"And they will be welcomed by the gods into eternity as mar-
tyrs."

Jacek clenched his jaw and didn't reply.

"Was that your daughter?" The gloved hand gestured back
toward the woods.

Jacek stared down the road at the spot where she had disappeared into the trees.

"She's a wild one, isn't she? Did you teach her those skills?"

He thought again about her desire to kill. He had been careful in her training not to teach killing blows. The last thing he needed was her turning into someone like him. "Not all of them. We need to keep moving if we want to reach Resahil by nightfall." He gestured to his team. "Move these bodies off the road and we'll get going." He moved off before the Deacon could ask any more questions.

Chapter Three

Aleni wasn't going back to the cabin. With Bandur bounding along beside her, she flew through the forest, along the side of the road, heading to Amathnore. She'd been cooped up in the cabin for so long, she couldn't stand the thought of going back there alone now. She craved human interaction. She also craved elven interaction, but she wasn't getting any of that, no matter how much she tried.

Human would have to do.

Jacek got to go off and have an adventure while she was kept in isolation like a criminal. She was the only one in this world that wasn't descended from a prisoner. Selendria had become a penal colony after her people had been summarily wiped out. With no elves around, the seasons had become unbalanced, which left Selendria with an almost year-long winter. So instead of taking over themselves, the humans from another world exiled their prisoners here through a magical portal.

Krodon, the former warlord that had terrorized everyone, including his own father, had planned to rebuild the elven nation under his own control, with Aleni as his brood mare. Being only twelve, it hadn't worked out well biologically for him.

It also hadn't worked out physically for him. Aleni and Jacek had left him in a puddle of broken bones and crushed organs under the mountain that had been the seat of power for the elves.

Aleni sometimes wondered if he had gotten out of there. Or if he had eventually succumbed to his injuries and died like a warlord should. Recently, she had regretted her decision to not kill him outright and had spent a probably unreasonable amount of time fantasizing about driving a sword through the man's heart.

So Jacek wondered what had gotten into her? Hindsight. She gritted her teeth as she ran, putting on a burst of speed. Bandur fell behind, even running at full pelt. He barked at her. Sighing, she slowed to allow the animal to catch up.

"I'm sorry, Bandur." She slowed right down and came to a stop, only slightly out of breath. The dog stepped into her arms as she closed them around his sleek brown and tan fur. A tingle of his emotions crept into her mind through their connection. Confusion, but then happiness. Jacek had grumbled sometimes that Bandur liked her more than him.

"Sometimes I feel you're the only one who gets me, boy." She pressed her face into the back of his neck. Apart from Jacek, Bandur was the only other one she loved. To her, he was the equal of any human. Sometimes more than equal. "Shall we go to town? Find some adventure?"

Bandur whined, stepping back.

"I'll take that as a yes. Come on, let's go."

Amathnore was a large city. The largest in Selendria. From Aleni's memory, back when she was with her parents three hundred years before, it was the closest city to the portals that opened and let the humans into the world. After the war, once all the elves were dead, the prisoners of the other world were exiled through those portals, settling in the closest area with buildings still standing.

Not all of them were still standing, however. Most of the tall towers Aleni remembered were gone. Her people had been excellent builders, crafting monuments to their legacy that stood for thousands of years without crumbling. Then the humans came and destroyed them with their powerful weapons that exploded. The technology they had was astounding to the elves, and they could only counter them with magic.

Aleni had once been angry at the humans that were left, but she eventually realized that these people were not to blame for the tragedy that happened here. They were just as much victims of that war as she. They were left here to die by their own people, evicted because they took up too much space. And none of those original people still lived. She had been surprised to find that humans had much shorter lives than elves.

Aleni did not look forward to the day Jacek's lifespan ended while hers carried on for centuries.

As they walked into Amathnore, Aleni took in the bustling pace of the busy town. The rich who were too busy to look down. Too busy to pay any attention to a young girl and her dog.

Nearing the center of the city, she passed the grand arena. It had been an amphitheater the elves had built for cultural and theatrical performances. Now it was the home of gladiatorial fights that people bet on. Aleni had once been disgusted with the concept, but now she listened to the crowd with fascination, wondering what it would be like to fight there. Jacek used to fight there to earn money between jobs. But that was long before she had met him.

Moving on past the Arena, she came close to the market square. Crowds of people milled about and walked through the area, buying food and supplies from the vendors. There was no merry chatter, however. No laughing. Just business.

It saddened Aleni. In her time, her people had been very different. Everyone was friendly and helpful. There was little distrust, although they weren't exempt completely. Her father, the king, had run the kingdom smoothly.

She was a long way from the princess she had been.

Looking down at the furs covering her body, she wrinkled her nose slightly. While they kept her warm, there was nothing elegant about them. Jacek had fashioned them from animals he hunted. To her eyes, it was as if she'd had a goblin for a dressmaker. Instead, necessity had been her tailor. While she didn't suffer from the cold like humans did, it would certainly make her stand out if she walked into town in a light cotton dress.

As she walked, she noticed a couple of children milling about aimlessly. One looked similar in age to her, the other a lot younger. One was a boy, and the other a girl with silky black hair and warm bronze skin. Poorly dressed and skinny, they stood out from the rich mercantile class. Aleni stepped to the side of the street, hugging the corner of a building to watch. She clicked her fingers for Bandur to move to her side. The dog obediently padded over.

The girl, who looked about seven or eight, slipped her hand in a man's coat pocket as she bumped into him. The hand came back out in a flash as she looked up into his face with an apology on her own. The man frowned, but kept moving. A small smile broke out on the girl's face as she opened her palm to reveal a couple of blackened olon coins.

Aleni took a breath in, surprised at the little girl's adeptness. The movement had been so smooth, and the man hadn't even noticed. She must do this a lot. Aleni wondered if she could learn this from the girl. It was an intriguing skill. She had seen nothing like it.

As the girl moved off into the crowd, Aleni followed. The child weaved through the crowd; her hand slipping occasionally into more pockets or small bags. Aleni marveled no one noticed her. Was it because she was a child, therefore of no consequence? Or was it something else?

On the other side of the market, the girl met with two boys. The one Aleni had seen earlier, and the other someone new. The new one looked about fifteen, quite tall and thin, with messy brown hair. The three youths moved swiftly off down the street. Aleni followed at a distance.

Winding through the streets and down alleyways they went, feet sinking deep into the slush made by the snow and dirt, making them easy to follow. Jacek had taught Aleni much about tracking over the last year.

Finally, the group stopped in a little closed off alley between two buildings. The snow had built up along the sides, which the children had shaped and flattened off and covered with boards to sit on. Five other youths were already waiting, a mixture of girls and boys. Aleni spied on them from further down the street behind a stand of crates. The younger girl with the black hair that fascinated Aleni gave over her coins to the older, tall boy. There must be a hierarchy in this group, and the little girl was not at the top. Still, the injustice of the action galled Aleni, knowing the little girl probably needed the coins more than the older one. She was so tiny.

Aleni stepped out from behind the crates and walked down to the group, checking to make sure her headscarf covering her ears was in place.

"Hello." Aleni put a hand on Bandur's scruff to keep him in place. He was not great with strangers. She sent calming thoughts to him.

The children turned to her, their eyes narrowed in suspicion. Nobody replied.

"My name is Aleni, and I noticed you in the marketplace." She looked down at the younger girl. "You are very talented. The way you took those coins without being noticed."

"Hey!" The taller boy stepped forward. "What are you all about, coming in here and accusing us of stealing?"

Aleni raised her hands, palms out toward him. "I don't mean to accuse you of anything. I was just admiring. I have never seen anyone do that."

The boy's face scrunched into a question. "You've seen no one steal? Have you lived under a rock all your life?"

Did living under a mountain in the hidden city count? Maybe a little too much information there. "I, uh, I'm not from around here. I'm from up north."

"Hah, you do sound funny. I've never heard an accent like that." The older boy relaxed a little, but folded his arms over his chest, his feet set widely.

Aleni had tried to work the accent out of her speech, practicing with Jacek, but she had never quite got rid of it. It wasn't as thick as when she had first woken up in this time period, but it was still there.

"Yes, well I was wondering if you would teach me how to do that."

The boy laughed. "Why would we do that?"

That was a good question, now that it was put to Aleni. She pondered the answer, studying the group of children. When her eyes rested on the younger girl, who seemed to be the youngest of the lot, she noticed the girl now gripped a small white stone.

She gestured to the stone. "Can I see that, please?"

The girl enclosed it tighter in both hands, covering it completely. She looked up at the bigger boy.

"I won't steal it, I promise. I believe I can help you with it."

Both the boy and the little girl looked puzzled. After opening her hands and staring down at the small stone, the little girl eventually passed it to Aleni, who studied it carefully.

"It was my mother's." The little girl said quietly.

It was an elven power stone. Not activated, of course, but the rune carved into it meant a mountain. On a hunch, Aleni pulled out her knife. The kids all took a step back cautiously. The oldest boy went for a knife at his own waist, his hand resting on the handle.

"It's ok, I'm not here to hurt you." She dug into the stone with the point of her knife, grating out a few additions to the rune. After about a minute, she blew away the powdery fragments and viewed her work. It now meant fire.

"Hold this, please." She handed the stone back to the little girl, who took it and stared at the defaced memento. A pinched expression screwed up her little face, but she kept her silence.

Next, Aleni sliced into her palm with her knife, waiting for the beads of blood to evolve into a solid line. Then she gestured to take back the stone. The little girl hesitantly gave it to her, her eyes alight with curiosity.

The stone fit into her bloody palm, her fingers closing over it. Nothing happened straight away, but after a few seconds, the stone glowed brightly. The children all let out a gasp. Aleni opened her hand after a bit and the stone continued to glow. It grew warm suddenly, and the white glow turned to a deep red. The air around the alleyway suddenly went up in temperature, and the feeling came back into Aleni's nose with a prickly sensation.

She smiled at the group, using a handful of snow to wipe the blood off the stone. She handed the stone back to the little girl. It wasn't hot to touch, just warm. The girl's face lit up with a beatific smile, her small frame visibly relaxing.

"Thank you!" she said in a tiny voice.

"You're welcome."

"How did you do that?" The older boy had a look on his face that was a cross between awe and disturbed.

"Just a gift I was born with." She hedged around it. Had it been a mistake? Should she have shown her ability to these kids? She had been so caught up in wanting to help that she didn't even think about the fact she'd just given away some of her secret to these strangers. She hoped it worked in making them trust her.

"Right." He looked suspicious, but he said no more.

"What's your name?" Aleni asked the little girl.

"Thiri."

"How old are you?"

"Eight and three quarters." The pride in her voice seemed out of place in their current surroundings. Aleni smiled warmly.

"Where's your home?"

Thiri pressed her lips together and looked up at the older boy.

"We have no home," the boy said.

"What? Why do you have no home?" Aleni couldn't imagine living on these streets, in this cold. How did they survive?

The boy scoffed. "You really aren't from around here are you?"

"No, I'm not."

"Dato looks after us," Thiri said.

"Thiri," Dato stressed the last syllable of her name. "Why did you have to tell her my name?"

"But you do look after us."

"That's not the point." He sighed.

"Will you teach me how to do what you do?" Aleni didn't know the word for it. While she knew that it involved stealing, she had an idea there might be other uses for the skill she could incorporate into fighting. If nothing else, it trained deftness with the fingers that could always come in handy.

Thiri looked up at Dato as if for permission. The older boy shrugged and turned away to sit down on the makeshift seat against the wall of the next building. "Do whatever you want, Thiri."

The little girl gave a small smile and turned back to Aleni. For the next couple of hours, she showed Aleni the basics of pick-pocketing. How to use distraction and misdirection to focus someone's attention on something while the hand was lifting elsewhere. Cutting a purse string to take off with a purse. Or slicing open the bottom of the purse to get at the contents. She showed many times using one of her fellow street kids to be the mark.

It wasn't long before Aleni was doing it herself. She watched carefully and mimicked the girl's movements perfectly. With her elven swiftness and enhanced senses, she picked up the skill extremely quickly. The other children were amazed at her ability to move silently and quickly without being noticed. Even Thiri herself couldn't match Aleni's silence.

"You are very special, Aleni." Thiri said, her deep smile revealing tiny dimples on her olive-skinned cheek.

Dato was watching with his arms crossed and his eyes narrowed. Aleni got the feeling he still didn't entirely trust her. She was not one of them.

Another boy ran up, panting, and approached Dato.

"Obal?" Dato straightened and frowned, loosening his arms. "What's wrong?"

The boy took a moment to catch his breath, then spoke. "Amik is missing."

"What?"

"We were out in the marketplace, doing the rounds. When he didn't show up at the meeting spot, I got worried. I waited and waited, but he didn't show. I looked all over for him, but he seems to be gone. Do you think -?"

Dato held up a hand. "We'll find him."

"But he's the third one now!" Obal wrung his hands.

"The third what?" Aleni butted in.

"Some other street kids have gone missing," Thiri whispered, giving Dato a worried look.

"Missing?" Aleni frowned. "Why?"

The little girl shrugged. "We don't know." She looked around at the other kids, five in all, who nodded silently.

"Maybe I can help. My... father could help." It was strange saying that word, but that's who Jacek had become to her.

"You have a father?" Dato asked. "You're not an orphan?"

Aleni hesitated. Technically, she was an orphan since her birth parents died three hundred years ago. She had been magically frozen for all that time, only being awoken by an explorer working for a ruthless warlord.

"Well, he's my adopted father. My real parents died. But he's the Red Hunter, he can help."

Dato laughed. He slapped his thigh with mirth and then shook his head. "Oh, now I really know you're full of shit. You've probably got rich parents waiting at home for you right now, especially by the looks of those clothes." He gestured at her in derision.

"I'm telling the truth!" Aleni's face flushed. "Why don't you believe me?"

"Because every kid says his father is the Red Hunter when he wants to scare people. He's the one parents threaten their kids with when they want them to obey." He went into a singsong voice, imitating an adult. "'If you don't do this, I'll get the Red Hunter to come and visit you and then you'll be sorry!'" He laughed again. "At least we don't have to hear that anymore. Get out of here! You're not one of us, we don't need your help!"

Gritting her teeth, Aleni backed away. Dato moved toward her, swinging his arms in a shooing motion. "Get lost, rich girl!" She stopped herself short of an instinctive block as his long arms swung at her. She just jumped back out of the way, silently fuming. Bandur growled.

Thiri looked close to tears as she watched her new friend leave. Aleni wished she could help the little girl, but it seemed she already had a protector. One who wasn't tolerant of outsiders. Not wanting to hurt anyone, she fled.

Chapter Four

Resahil was a much smaller town than Amathnore. It had been built to service the pit farms in the area. During the colder months of the year, food was grown in great pits dug into the ground and covered with a sheer cloth to keep the snow off. The produce was then traded to Amathnore for supplies needed for the town.

Resahil was a more close-knit community, since it comprised only a few large family units who ran the farms. Over the years those family units had inter-joined to create one big, related community. It was a joke among other cities in Selendria that the inbreeding in Resahil made for a village full of idiots. Jacek wondered if that was why the Deacon wanted to go there now to spread his message. Maybe the people would actually believe it. Not that Jacek cared. He was just here for the coin. Although the fight earlier had certainly sweetened the deal. His veins still sang with the buzz of battle.

He wasn't the only one feeling the exhilaration after the scuffle. Solel was also riding straighter and lighter, her face open and content.

As the caravan rolled into town, Jacek noted the citizens who stopped and stared at them. Bristling with weapons, he and his crew were probably not the typical visitors to Resahil. Traders from Amathnore were too cheap to hire muscle to protect them on the road. They relied on moving swiftly and bribing any bandits to leave them alone.

The snow had held off so far, and they made their way into the center of the town, where a circular open space was situated. The aroma of a meat stew cooking over a smoky fire wafted past Jacek's nose, making his stomach rumble. The houses surrounding the area spoke to a level of care in their construction, which surprised him. They must have a skilled builder here.

The carriage, driven by a monk, pulled into the open space and came to a stop. Deacon Sesk finally stepped out.

The man was in his sixties at least and wore a cowl over his head that hid most of his face. When he stepped out into the open air, he pulled back the cowl. A lean, weathered face revealed itself, with dark piercing eyes that took in everything in their surroundings. But the thing that caught Jacek's eye the most was the shriveled skin covering one side of his neck and up onto his left cheek. It looked like he had been in a fire in the past. Jacek had to admit that made him slightly more interesting.

Over the next hour, the Deacon and the monks that remained set up a small stage using wooden boxes they'd brought with them in the square. Jacek thought it odd they weren't mourning their colleagues, but he just shrugged and left them to it. Instead, he and his crew took up positions around the gathering area, monitoring the growing crowd. Only what he was being paid for, no more.

The monastic order had grown in popularity in the last year. When a family had bought one of their 'atonement' stones, they discovered after a fire in their home that the stone actually worked. It put a shield up around them, protecting them from the flames. When Jacek had learned of this, he idly wondered if it was the same one Aleni had held in the marketplace that day they had passed through over a year ago. With the cut she'd had on her hand, it may have been enough to activate the stone without her realizing.

Since then, demand for the stones had grown in popularity. However, only the rich could afford them once demand increased. How was the Creed convincing people the stones were all working, since they weren't all activated? But that wasn't his problem.

As he leaned against a building with his hands resting on his weapons to encourage people to stay away from him, a small child with dirty hair and even dirtier face walked up with a bundle of goods in a woven basket. Obviously, looking mean and unapproachable wasn't working.

"Excuse me, sir." The little boy looked up at him with hope in his eyes. "Do you want to buy some jewelry?"

"No. Go away." *Don't make eye contact.* Ever since Aleni had come into his life, he had found it harder and harder to say no to kids on the streets.

"M-maybe a gift for someone special?" In the corner of his eye, he saw the kid hold something up. He couldn't help himself. He glanced down. It was a small handmade woven bracelet. Aleni immediately came to his mind. Maybe she would like it, since she couldn't leave the house while he was away. It might be useful to smooth things over with her. Maybe he had spoken a little too harshly.

He reached down and took the bracelet from the boy's hand. He ran his thumb over the texture of the woven thread interlaced with green painted wooden beads.

"How much?" he asked.

"A-a quarter olon, sir." The boy gulped air down, stumbling over his words slightly. He looked away, wiping his hands down the front of his tunic. Someone was probably watching, making sure he made some money.

Jacek fished inside his leather jacket for his coin bag and pulled out a quarter, flicking it to the boy. The kid gave a grin and ran off. Jacek suspected he wasn't as scared as he had made out to be. Probably sucked in many people with the sympathy vote. Wait, it had worked on him. Giving a sigh, he wondered if he was going soft.

Pocketing the bracelet, he went back to watching the crowd.

Staring into a bowl of gelatinous goop the proprietor of the local inn had cooked up, Jacek decided the term 'cooked' was too generous. The odor wafting up from it was not encouraging. He pushed it away from him and pulled out some pieces of dried meat from his pouch he had wrapped up for just such occasions. It was evening and the Deacon's public meeting had been uneventful. It was now time to relax while the Deacon sat safely upstairs in his room.

His team were all drinking heavily, laughing and talking together at the table. Jacek took another tangy gulp of his Dire Sip and watched them. Outside, the wind banged against the shutters of the inn, demanding to be let in. The room was warmed by a large open fireplace, which had drawn many locals in from the frigid outdoors.

"So, Jacek, you gonna actually join us in drinking? 'Cos that sludge ain't gonna get you there." Rilaiz raised his mug of ale, along with his eyebrows.

Jacek stared at him. "No." He took another drink. Dire Sip had no alcohol in it, but it was warming and full of healthy herbs. Or so they said. Maybe it *was* just sludge. It wasn't the most popular of drinks, but Jacek had developed a taste for it over the years. Getting drunk wasn't a good idea for him. He'd given up drinking nearly thirty years before, when he was a teenager. One night of a drunken stupor had gotten him robbed and nearly killed. Never again.

"Oh, come on, boss! Maybe you'll feel better!"

Jacek frowned at him.

"There's nothing wrong with him," Solel offered. "He's like that all the time." One side of her mouth curved up at him as she raised her own mug in an imitation of a toast.

"How would you know?" Rilaiz replied. "You just met him two days ago, like the rest of us." He leaned in toward her, his eyes gleaming. "Or have you two known each other longer?"

Even Mular raised questioning eyebrows at this. He said little, but he was a good fighter. Two good reasons for Jacek to hire him.

Solel gave Rilaiz a withering look and leaned back with her drink. "Please. He's not my type."

"Oh yeah? Am I your type?" He pursed his mouth at her in a kissing motion.

"You're nobody's type." Dunvern's thick accent made him barely understandable, but Rilaiz seemed to get his meaning.

"You've probably never even bedded a woman yet. Women prefer someone who can actually grow something on their face." Rilaiz patted his scraggly beard.

"What, like a venereal disease?" Dunvern said with a smirk.

Rilaiz pointed at the young redhead. "You're gonna pay for that comment later! I know which room is yours."

"Please, you're not my type either, Rilaiz." He spoke into his mug before taking a swig of his own drink.

Rilaiz spluttered. "I didn't mean... ugh!"

Laughter rang out around the table. Jacek ignored them. He was watching the monks on the other side of the room. Deacon Sesk had retired to his room early with his dinner. The two monks left were sitting quietly eating their 'meal' without complaint.

One of them had a carved wooden horse sitting next to him on the table. As he ate, he would pick it up and run his thumb over it, commenting on it to his fellow monk. Possibly it was something he had newly attained. It looked like something a child would play with. Perhaps he'd bought it from the boy that had sold Jacek the bracelet earlier.

Thinking of it, he took the bracelet out from his pocket and held it discreetly in his left hand under the table. He wished she was here. She brightened any room she was in with her smile. He often marveled that she could smile at all, considering what she'd been through. Losing her parents to the war three hundred years ago, waking up from a magical sleep only to find her entire race was extinct.

Then to be treated like a sack of potatoes - worse than a sack of potatoes actually, after she woke up. Krodon had raped her repeatedly in order to re-start the elven race, not realizing that Elves weren't particularly fertile. She had been only twelve. The trauma from that alone still haunted her. Although she was a positive and hopeful girl, he still recognized the darkness that sat behind her eyes. However, she didn't have as many nightmares as she used to, and she seemed more confident since she'd learned to fight competently.

She was incredibly gifted in that area. Jacek didn't know if it was her innate elven abilities of speed and dexterity, but she seemed born to move like that. And she enjoyed it. Movement with purpose seemed to exhilarate her, and her fears disappeared. He just wished she would be more aware of her surroundings. Her emotions gave her blinders. And lately she seemed more angry, as opposed to the despondence she had displayed a year ago.

He was just glad she had Bandur with her. The two had bonded quickly. He suspected she had some ability to communicate with the dog telepathically, although she had never spoken of it. He swore the dog knew what she wanted before she said anything. Bandur had never been like that with him. He still had an understanding with the dog, but not like those two.

He continued to watch the monks. Something about them didn't sit well with him. Maybe because they were con men. But that wasn't uncommon in Selendria. Everyone was out to get for themselves. It was almost expected. No, there was something else. Something that left a pit in Jacek's stomach. But he couldn't put his finger on it. Even though he was being paid by them, by their boss, it didn't mean he trusted them.

Chapter Five

Two days later, the group rode back into Amathnore. Jacek and his team escorted Deacon Sesk and his monks to their 'monastery', which was the recently vacated stone fortress that Krodon's father had built many years before. Krodon had killed Tarken and taken it over briefly before going 'missing' in the north. Only Jacek and Aleni knew what happened to him.

His lieutenant, Traslek, took a handful of men and retreated to Krodon's original fortress on the southern continent. He had disbanded the rest, leaving the old fortress abandoned. The Creed of Redemption brotherhood had taken it over not long after.

With their rise in power and influence, they had become a beacon of hope for many people. Their benevolence was in stark contrast to the former power, making people follow them by the droves. Jacek had never understood why people felt the need to follow someone at all.

His team sat on their horses outside the gates of the fortress. Deacon Sesk had exited his carriage and was handing over a medium-sized bag of coins to Jacek.

"Thank you for your services, Red Hunter. We might not have survived if you hadn't been along."

Jacek didn't bother replying to that, merely taking the bag silently and nodding. He kept his expression blank.

"Maybe next time you could bring along your daughter. She was most useful." He had a gleam in his eye that gave rise to some primitive part of Jacek's brain.

"Don't you ever speak of her again," he growled. "She is not my business partner, she's my daughter. You will have no contact with her." With that, he turned his horse away and rode back to his team, who sat a small distance away.

After doling out their share of the money, he let them disperse. But not before Rilaiz commented they were available any time he needed them for another job.

"Don't hold your breath," Jacek said, kicking his horse into action to ride off. He wasn't here to make friends. If he made it a habit to hire the same people, he would be in danger of doing just that. Even if they were a useful team.

"I think he likes me," he heard Rilaiz comment to the others as he left them behind.

* * *

Back in the central part of town, Jacek dismounted and led his horse through the growing throng of people. He needed some supplies for home, but going to the market made his jaw ache. He would get in and out as quick as possible.

Spotting a vendor for cheeses, he made his way there. Voices grumbled on his way through the crowd at the bulky body of his horse getting in their way, but he ignored them. No one was stupid enough to pick a fight with him. They either recognized him and knew better, or the sight of his axe and sword were enough to discourage any malcontent.

After choosing a truckle of cheese, he stowed it away safely in the bags strapped to his horse. Over the horse's back, he suddenly glimpsed something familiar. Long white hair. He wouldn't normally take any notice, but long hair wasn't so common. And white hair was even less so. Was that Aleni?

He hadn't even considered the possibility she might have disobeyed him. She was a good girl. Not that he disciplined her or anything. He guided her. Even if she was technically over three hundred years old, she was still so inexperienced in life.

She had been a princess in her past life. Probably pampered and looked after carefully. Everything in Selendria had changed so dramatically, she still had problems understanding it. She wanted to believe the best in people, despite what had happened to her. It was part of her nature. He loved that about her, but it made her naïve.

So when he saw the back of a small person with a headscarf on and white hair poking out the bottom, he went after them.

Leaving the horse behind, he moved through the crowd like a boat plowing through the sea. His stature made for an effective deterrent. People took one look at him and moved out of the way.

But she moved fast, weaving in between people instead of cutting through them. Being small, she disappeared behind people easily. It forced Jacek to stop and turn his head around to find her. He stood half a head taller than everyone else, but what he was looking for was not above the crowd. It didn't help in this situation.

There. A flash of white. Northern side. He pushed his way through again, ignoring the cries of indignation that cut off as soon as they saw him.

The tiny figure ran off down a side street. Jacek pursued. It certainly looked like Aleni. What was she doing here? By the time he got to the much emptier street, there was no sign of her. He looked down all the alleyways off it, but she was gone.

Letting out a huff of frustration, he made his way back to the central market square to retrieve his horse and finish his supply run. He would have to just go home and wait for her there. There was nothing else he could do. He just hoped she would return.

As the light faded from the day and the shadows lengthened under the trees of Kamde forest, Jacek arrived back at the little cabin they called home. Constructed of the very wood that surrounded them, Jacek had to admit that while he was sure it was sturdy, it was not a thing of beauty. A skilled carpenter, he was not. To be fair, Aleni had been the one to do a lot of the heavy lifting. With her power to move things with her magic, she could lift and maneuver the wood into place while Jacek hammered them together. In doing it this way, they could put it together quicker than most.

The cabin consisted of one large room with a circular fireplace in the center, a metal chimney reaching up through the roof hanging over the top. Aleni had shaped the metal easily with her magic. Jacek wagered no one in Selendria had anything like it, as it had been her idea, inspired by her people's design.

When Jacek had designed a couple of beds for them on paper, Aleni had crossed her one out when he wasn't looking. He asked her about it, and she mumbled something about never wanting to sleep in a bed again. She had been happy with thick furs laid down by the fire each night. Sighing, Jacek had followed suit and slept on the other side of the fire.

It was a cozy room. Certainly the fanciest house Jacek had ever lived in. Not that he had lived in many houses. Indeed, he had lived in a cave for the last ten years at least. It had served him well. Sometimes he missed that cave.

A small shed sat outside the cabin to store firewood and hang meat for drying and smoking. Out the front was a table where Jacek had taught Aleni how to butcher her hunt. To the right of the little cabin, Aleni had planted a small herb garden. Under the protection of the trees and with her careful nurturing, the plants had grown well.

Stepping into the cabin, Jacek glanced around before removing his leather jacket and hanging it on the hook behind the door. Normally, if she had been there, her dirty boots would be haphazardly thrown somewhere close to the door. Jacek would call her out on it every time and there would have been a half-hearted argument. He often suspected she did it on purpose just to promote a verbal exchange with him. It was almost a joke between them. There was no sign of the boots. The fireplace was cold and there were no wet boot prints on the floor. His heart sank.

He had never been one to worry, but now he had a daughter the thoughts came unbidden. Where was she? Was she safe? Could she be hurt somewhere in a ditch? What if a warlord had kidnapped her and locked her in his dungeon? Could a troll have eaten her?

Probably things all fathers worried about.

He took a deep breath and determined to act normally. To calm himself, he pictured facing a horde of goblins with his sword at the ready. His heartbeat slowed right down and his mind calmed like a frozen sea.

On to some chores. He checked the box by the door. They needed more firewood. Back on his jacket went.

Well after dark, and once a giant's torso of firewood was heaped next to him, Jacek finally put the axe down. His muscles burned from the exertion, but he felt much better. Carting arm loads of wood in, he filled the box to overflowing in short time. Then he stood next to the still giant pile of wood and suddenly realized the wood shed was already full.

Giving up on that, he went back indoors and lit the fire. He spent the evening putting together a simple meal before rolling out his furs to sleep on. As he lay next to the fire, all he could think of was Aleni and if she was warm and safe. Tossing and turning for hours, he finally fell into a restless sleep.

Dawn brought with it a fresh layer of snow. A bleary-eyed Jacek got up and fetched some crisp snow in a pot to melt over the fire. After a quick breakfast, he potted around the cabin, tidying and making an inventory of supplies.

It was early afternoon, and he was curing skins when he spotted Aleni coming through the trees with Bandur in tow.

⁓

The stones of the old fortress in the east quarter of Amathnore held the cold in like ice cubes. Icas, a man of few scruples and many nefarious skills, had a fire going in the hearth of his office. But the heat of the flames didn't exactly reach where he sat at his desk. The wood in the fireplace was too soft and a little damp. He would have to order better fuel. He noted that down on a piece of parchment before going back to reading a report on merchant activity in Amathnore. He pulled his cloak tighter around himself.

Various paper sheets with reports, lists, manifests and dossiers littered his desk. Only Icas knew where everything was. To the outside observer it must look like chaos, but to the lean spy there was a certain order.

His network of spies had reported two merchants who were up to some sort of strange activity. Meeting in secret and buying up large stocks of woven material. What were they up to?

The second page had him completely puzzled when his door opened and Deacon Sesk stepped in. Icas looked up into the scarred face of the old man and kept his expression blank. Sesk probably knew he didn't like him, but it didn't pay to be open about it when he was his employer.

"Icas, I need your services."

"That is what you pay me for."

"Yes, but I need you to actually do something for me."

Icas slowly put the paper down and interlinked his fingers on the desk. He met Sesk's eyes. What did Sesk think he did all day? "I am doing something."

"Fine, fine, whatever. I have a new job for you."

Icas gave him a bland look and waited. He had little patience for beating around the bush and wasn't interested in small talk.

"The Red Hunter," Sesk finally said.

"I've heard of him."

"Of course you have, everyone has."

Icas crossed his ankles and sat back in his chair. Would he get to the point already?

"Does he have a daughter? Any family?" Sesk wrung his hands, his eyes alight with eagerness.

"Not to my knowledge. Although, he was spotted passing through Amathnore about a year ago with a young girl." He got up and went over to a shelf on the right. He rummaged through some scrolls until he picked one out and opened it up. "Yes, that's right. My sources told me he stole her from Krodon's fortress in the south. Krodon sent out his entire force looking for them, eventually leaving to go on the trail himself. This precipitated him usurping his father and killing him. It might be connected somehow, although I'm not sure." He looked up from the scroll. "Why do you ask?"

"I need to know who she is. There's something different about her. She turned up on the road to Resahil, joining The Red Hunter and helped us fend off some bandits. She looked to be in her early teens, perhaps thirteen or fourteen. I got the feeling she wasn't supposed to be seen by us. Why would he hide her away?" He lowered his chin to rest on his hand.

Icas shrugged. "Well, he stole her from Krodon."

"But Krodon is dead, his men disbanded."

"Is he?"

Sesk snapped his head up. "Why? What have you heard?"

Icas put his hands up, palms out. "Nothing. I just... well, we never heard what happened. All we know is that he followed The Red Hunter up north and didn't come back. His men said he was dead, but we've never seen a body. You would think they would at least make a public burning of his body, considering what a tyrant he was."

"You credit people with too much intelligence, Icas. The common man only needs to be told something, and if it coincides with what they want to hear, they will believe it. No evidence is needed."

"Yes, I can see that works well in your favor," Icas said. No, stop. It was none of his business how Sesk made his money. As long as a decent amount of it came his way.

Sesk shot him a pointed look but didn't comment on it. "So who is she then? Why did Krodon have her in the first place? Who was she to him? She was obviously important, enough so that he spent exorbitant resources just to get her back. She's not Krodon's daughter, is she?"

"Krodon had a daughter, but the age doesn't fit. You said she was a teen? Krodon's daughter was much younger. Is much younger. I assume she's still alive." Icas started rifling through the papers on his desk, looking for a report. It was here somewhere.

Behind him, Sesk paced the room, tucking his hands up into his wide sleeves. "Alright, so she's not Krodon's daughter, so who is she? I must know, Icas. I need you to investigate. Talk to any men who used to work for Krodon, see if you can find out more. I need to know everything. Leave no stone unturned."

Ah, here it was. Activity reported at Krodon's old fortress in the south, but no sign of Krodon himself or his daughter. He looked up from the paper. "Fine, I'll get started right away. But I may have to charge extra for this. The Red Hunter is nobody to trifle with. He's slippery. My past attempts to gather information on him have fallen short."

"Very well. Let's hope the girl is not so cautious."

Chapter Six

At the sight of her, Jacek's heart pumped faster and feeling returned to his extremities. They stood facing each other, the wind rustling the trees above. Not trusting himself, he waited for her to say something first. Anger bubbled up in his gut now that the worry was gone.

She had a boar over her shoulders, the tusks only half grown, but it was sizeable considering she wasn't very big.

Then he noticed the blood.

Her left leg, sheathed in fur-lined leather, had a deep slash running round from her calf to her shin on a downward angle.

"What happened?" He dropped the knife he was holding onto the table and moved toward her, wiping his hands on a cloth at his belt.

She put out her palm to stop him. "I'm fine, it's just a hunting accident. The boar's tusk, that's all." She dumped the boar on the butchering table and limped over to the steps of the cabin to sit down.

"Let me see."

"No, leave it alone. I'll be fine. You know I heal quickly."

"It still needs to be tended, or you'll have a massive scar."

"You have scars." Her eyes went to the one bisecting his face.

"That's not the point. You don't need them. Let me see."

Sighing, she straightened her leg and pulled out her knife, handing it to him. "The pants are ruined, anyway."

Jacek detected something in her voice but decided not to comment. Now was not the time for an argument. He took the knife and kneeled in front of her. Carefully, he placed the blade inside the slashed leather and cut the pant leg open to her ankle to reveal the wound. It stained the fur lining a dark red and was sticking to the wound. He gently pulled it away. Aleni gritted her teeth and gripped her thigh with both hands.

"Sorry." Jacek hated he was causing her pain, but it had to be done.

"Just do it," she said between her teeth.

Finally, he pulled the last of the fur away. Aleni let out her breath and loosened her grip on her thigh. It was a deep wound. Jacek frowned. It didn't look wide enough to have been gouged by a boar's tusk. It was too clean for that. The edges were cut with something sharp. Like a sword.

He looked back up at Aleni. She was concentrating on the wound and not looking him in the eye. There was some reason she wasn't telling him the truth. He wasn't going to get it out of her if she didn't want to talk. She wasn't one of his torture victims. Maybe when she felt safe enough, she would tell him the truth.

"I'll get a needle and thread and a bandage." Jacek got to his feet and went inside the cabin. As soon as he was alone, he put out a hand on a chair back to steady himself, letting out a slow breath. What had she gotten into? Had bandits stopped her on the way home? What about the person he'd seen in Amathnore that looked like her? He had to at least ask if she'd been there.

He retrieved the wound supplies and returned to Aleni.

"Did I see you in Amathnore yesterday?" He busied himself with threading the needle and didn't meet her eye.

"What? Of course not. I've been out hunting."

"I swear I saw someone that looked just like you in Amathnore when I was at the market."

"It could have been anyone." She stared intently over his shoulder.

He gave her a bland look and flicked her long snowy hair flowing out from under her headscarf. "It's such a common color."

"It. Wasn't. Me."

"Right." He shook his head and went back to stitching her leg. She hissed as he pulled it tight.

"Sorry." He'd barely said that word in the last twenty-five years and today he'd already said it twice. How things had changed.

Once he'd finished tending to her leg, he wiped it clean of blood with a handful of fresh snow. The cold would help with the pain and swelling too. He held a clean clump of it against the stitched wound.

"I can do it." Her words were curt.

"Fine." Jacek put his hands up in surrender, letting the snow drop. "I'll be inside."

He left her sitting there and shut the door behind him. She probably needed some space. Something was up with her, and his hovering would not help. He watched her from the window.

She pulled her headscarf off and dumped it on the porch next to her. Bandur had curled up on the wooden planks, tired from their journey. Aleni could outrun the dog any day. She probably had barely stopped on the way home.

He watched as she limped to the boar on the table and picked up the knife he'd been using. She cleared the skins off and went to work on the carcass. At first, her slices were precise and deliberate, but it wasn't long before she started slashing into the beast haphazardly. Her movements became stiff and jerky, charged with emotion.

Why was she so angry? Jacek watched with a broken heart as she lay into the beast like it was Krodon himself. Wait, was that it? Was she still suffering the aftereffects of what that man had done to her? Perhaps this was just another stage.

He gripped the edge of the bench top under the window. How could he help her? He thought maybe learning how to fight would make her feel less afraid and help her heal. But he also knew from his time on the streets that the girls there who had been raped were never the same.

The carcass was becoming unrecognizable so Jacek felt it was time to intervene. They didn't need mincemeat. He rushed outside and reached her quickly, grabbing the knife hand and holding it firm.

With a wordless cry she dropped her weight and locked her legs around his knees, swinging around to force him to let go of her and catch himself on the ground. They both tumbled to the lightly snowed forest floor, Aleni slightly more graceful than Jacek. She caught herself on all fours and stood facing Jacek, her stance telling him she was priming for a fight.

Fine, he'd give her a fight. She obviously needed something to get some anger out. He rolled to his feet and faced her. Immediately she surged in with a punch to his face. Dodging his head to the side, he lashed out with his own fist. She blocked him easily, as he knew she would, and kicked out at his knee with her good leg. If she'd gone at full strength, which wasn't anything to sneer at considering her size, he might have lost his kneecap. But she pulled back at the last second, only scraping the top of his knee. Just enough to push it awkwardly to the side and make him stumble.

Before she could take advantage of that, he pushed off with the other leg and tackled her to the ground, pinning her under him. He wouldn't have done this move a year ago, as it would have triggered her, but they had practiced many times until it conditioned her to the stress. She said it still triggered her, but she could push past it now and rely on her training.

Because of this, he knew exactly what she was going to do. She wrapped her hands in a lock around his neck and pulled him down toward her. He pushed back on the ground, resisting. Her small body lifted off the ground, hanging from his neck.

She leaned in closer and bit down on his ear.

He roared with pain. In training they had only mimicked this so as not to hurt each other. She was throwing that out and doing it for real now. It wasn't hard enough to bite through the flesh of his ear, but it certainly hurt. The pain made his blood boil, and he pulled back to get away instinctively. She let go and dropped on her back on the ground. Tucking her legs up, she kicked out with the flat of her feet and pushed at his chest. He flew back and hit the snow on his butt, surprised.

"What the -" he started, feeling his ear to make sure she hadn't ripped it off. "That's not how we train!"

"Consider me trained." Her voice was hard, the words clipped. She came at him with a flurry of punches to his chest, making full contact. He tensed his muscles, taking the hits. He wondered why she was bothering to hit him there at all. It took more effort for her, and he was conditioned to take the blows. He trained her only to go for the weaker spots on a body: knees, groin and eyes. Perhaps she just needed something to hit?

With each blow, she got weaker and weaker, her energy flagging. At this point, she was probably hurting her knuckles on the hard leather of his jacket more than him.

"Alright, stop." He wrapped his arms around her to trap her, engulfing her in a bear hug. She continued to struggle against him for a few seconds, letting out another wordless cry. "Shhh." Jacek crooned, pressing his chin on the top of her head, rocking slightly.

Eventually she stilled, going completely limp. Soon he felt her body shudder as she cried. Together they sank down in the snow, Jacek still holding her tight, but more comforting than controlling. She cried for some time until there was a danger of her tears freezing to her face.

If it weren't for the fact Aleni had had these breakdowns before, Jacek would have felt like a deer in the bow sights. Experience had taught him not to say anything. She just wanted to be held. To feel safe. That was enough.

And that he could do. It didn't require him to have the right words at the right time. The gods knew he was terrible at that. He was a man of action, and this was an action.

Finally, Aleni squirmed, and he let her go. She got to her feet, wiping at her face. "Sorry if I took your ear off."

He smiled faintly at the accidental turn of phrase, rubbing at his ear. "It'll be fine. It nearly got taken off by a wolf once." He felt at a small scar on the top of his ear. "If it survived that, it'll survive you."

She smiled. "I almost wish I could scar. It can at least remind you of times in your life when you survived. Help you remember and keep going."

He frowned at that. What did that mean? Did she struggle to keep going sometimes? The thought terrified him, so he didn't press any further. He got to his feet. "Come on, let's go inside where it's warm. The fire's going." He looked over at the mangled carcass of the boar. "We'll deal with that later."

Hot. It was too hot. Had they built the fire up too high? Sweat caused Aleni's hair to slick to her head, beading down her forehead and neck. Where was Jacek? Something felt wrong. Her heart hammered in her chest, beating out a rhythm like heavy footsteps running toward her. And he was there. The monster. Krodon. He was still alive. Still hunting her. She could hear him coming.

She tried to run. In the distance she could see Jacek, standing with his axe in his hand. He was small from this far away. He hadn't seen her yet. She tried to cry out to him, but her voice wouldn't work.

Neither would her feet.

Behind her, amongst some trees, she could hear growling. Krodon had turned into a beast of some kind. And he was huge. Somehow, she knew this without seeing him. Trying to run toward Jacek, her feet moved sluggishly, as though she was knee deep in a bog. The progress was slow and agonizing. She had to escape. She must. But it was futile. Surely Krodon would catch her soon. It was too hot.

She gasped at the heat growing in her body. Feeling like she had too many layers on, she pulled at the laces on her jerkin. But if she took her clothes off, she would be vulnerable. Too easy for Krodon to get at her then. She would have to keep them on.

Her body trembled, and the panic rose in her chest. She tried again to call out to Jacek in the distance, but her throat constricted and her voice came out in a weak garble. The monster would get her. She could feel his breath on her neck...

"Aleni! Wake up!" She was suddenly shaken awake. Her eyes took a few moments to clear, then Jacek's worried face came into view hovering over her. "There you are. It was just a dream."

Aleni took a few more breaths to slow her racing heart. She could feel its beat in her head. "It felt so real." She hated the sound of the weakness in her voice.

"I know, baby girl." He rested his large, calloused hand on her sweating forehead. "You're burning up." He shifted himself to his feet and crouched to drag her sleeping furs away from the fire burning slowly in the little cabin. He then grabbed a scrap of thin leather and, after putting his boots on, stepped outside, letting the freezing night air into the room. It felt amazing on her burning face.

Bandur sat close by, watching her intently. She reached out to him through their emotional link, sending him calming vibes. His eyes drooped in response, and he lowered himself to lie next to her on the floor. His wet nose sat inches from her head.

Jacek returned a minute later with the leather scrap filled with a lump of what she guessed was snow, wrapped up into a ball and pulled together with a thong at the top. He closed the door behind him and removed his boots. Sitting himself between her and the fire, he gently placed the ball of wrapped snow on her forehead. It took a few moments for her to feel the cold seeping through the leather, but soon enough it cooled her burning skin.

She closed her weary eyes and let the chill sink into her head. When she opened them again, she sensed some time had passed. She was shivering. Jacek had pulled his sleeping furs around from the other side of the fire to be next to her. He lay with the little leather ball, now wet and sagging with the melted snow, loosely held in his grip as he slept.

Still feeling light-headed but cold now rather than the hot flush of before, she rolled to her knees and slowly got to her feet. Bandur was by her side in an instant. Holding on to his fur for stability, she walked around Jacek to the fire to stoke it up. Once the flames were crackling again, Aleni retrieved an extra blanket and wrapped it around herself.

Her heartbeat still pounded in her ears. The room spun suddenly, and the ground came up to meet her. She caught herself on her hands and knees, but she still felt unsteady.

Bandur barked. Jacek jerked awake, sitting bolt upright. He looked around, saw Aleni and rushed to her.

"What are you doing up?"

"I was cold."

"You have a fever, that's what happens. You should have woken me."

"You were lying with a melted snowball in your hand, you obviously needed the rest."

He shook off the water on his hand and wiped it on his pant leg. "That's besides the point. Come on, let's get you back to bed." He pulled her to her feet and guided her back. Arranging the blanket and her furs over her, the warmth grew. But her body still shook.

"I don't understand what's happening," she said. "I never get sick."

"I'm not sure either. Unless it's something to do with your normal growth cycle. Do you remember any other elves your age going through anything like this?"

She thought for a second, then shook her head. "Not that I remember, but that doesn't mean it didn't happen."

Jacek looked away, thinking. "What else do you feel? Does anything hurt?"

"No, nothing hurts. Occasionally my hands feel tingly, and my blood pounds in my ears, but the fever is the biggest one." Her eyelids suddenly felt heavy, and she let them close.

His large hand rested on her head, smoothing her hair back. "Just rest, my girl."

Once more the monster was close. Aleni stumbled along a narrow corridor. Putting out a hand to steady herself, she pulled back immediately as the shock of burning pain seared her palm. The walls were burning from the other side. Soon the fire would break through and engulf her. She had to get out before that happened.

Stomping footsteps echoed from somewhere behind her. The monster. Krodon. She knew it, but didn't know how she knew it. How could he be here? She had broken almost every bone in his body. Her logical mind couldn't figure it out.

The path ahead was dark and she could barely see her hand in front of her face. It was fear alone that prompted her to put one foot in front of the other. As the footsteps neared, she sped up to get away faster. It didn't seem to make any difference. Her heart clamored in her chest, pumping blood around her body with fervor. Sweat poured down her face and neck, drenching her clothes and leaving her skin prickly in places. It was not a sensation she enjoyed.

The corridor seemed to go on forever, with little sign of it ending. Nothing changed, there were no windows or breaks in the walls. Steam hissed off the sides, and the heat pressed in from all angles.

The monster let out a roar, and she cried out in fear without thinking. How could this be? How had he found her? Where was Jacek? If she could only find him, she would be safe.

Something brushed her back. A shock ran through her, her spine going rigid. She stopped moving, finding herself frozen to the spot. Her breathing increased in pace. Something big breathed on the back of her neck. Her palms dripped with sweat.

A clawed finger pulled her hair back over her shoulder and off her neck to the side. She felt light-headed and everything in her wanted to scream and flee. But she couldn't move. Couldn't do anything. It was all over. He would take her and rape her again and again until she fell pregnant and carried on his crazy plan to re-populate the world with elves.

A hand gripped her neck, and she screamed.

"Aleni!"

She opened her eyes to the voice. Her vision blurred with the tears and sweat. In her fear and confusion, she exploded with power. A wave of kinetic force and flame surged out from her toward the voice.

She blinked, and her vision finally cleared. She watched in shock as Jacek went flying across the room. He crashed hard into the wooden timbers of the cabin wall and slumped down onto his side.

The fire in the hearth suddenly flared, lighting up the room. Her hands were hot. Extremely hot. She looked down at her open palms and saw fire licking at the ends of her fingers.

Did *she* do that? What was this? Was she still hallucinating? The heat in her body was coalescing to her fingers. Yet they didn't burn. She flicked her eyes back up to Jacek and her chest tightened. He seemed to be conscious but wasn't moving much.

She curled her hands inwards, and the flames flickered out. What had she done? She'd hurt him now, and she couldn't take it back.

Getting to her feet, Aleni rushed over to Jacek, wanting to help, but not wanting to touch him. What if she hurt him again?

He groaned and slowly raised himself to a sitting position.

"Jacek, I -" she didn't know what to say to him.

"Aleni. I'm ok." He panted, reaching to touch the back of his head. His hand came away with blood on it.

Her breathing shortened as she realized it was worse than she initially thought. She knew the pain of a head injury.

"Are you all right?" He asked.

"Am I all right?" She couldn't handle this. It was too much. She was guilty of hurting the only person who cared about her in this world.

She did the only thing she could. She ran.

Chapter Seven

T he room was still spinning long after she left. Jacek shook his head to make it stop, but that only made it worse. Pain lanced through his skull, terminating in a fist behind his right eye. In addition, his face felt scorched. He gingerly touched it, but there didn't seem to be much damage. Were his eyebrows shorter?

It took a few minutes to get his bearings and get himself off the floor. He moved unsteadily to the still-open door and peered out into the night. No sign of Aleni. He had little chance of finding her if he went out there. Not that he was in any condition to do so.

Bandur whined at him from his position by the fire. He probably knew something was wrong, but might be confused about whom to stay with.

Sighing, he shut the door quietly and stumbled to his bedroll next to the fire, patting Bandur reassuringly.

"Thank you for staying with me old friend, but maybe it might have been better to go with her. She needs the company right now."

The dog cocked his head and lay back down with his head on Jacek's leg. Oh well, Bandur probably wouldn't have been able to keep up with her, anyway. When she was in a mood like that, she ran at full speed. Not even the dog could run that fast.

He dabbed at his wound with a clean cloth. It wasn't that bad. It had already stopped bleeding. He wouldn't even need stitching up. He sighed to himself and closed his eyes. Aleni needn't have worried. It wasn't her fault.

The nightmares had returned. He wasn't surprised after the day she'd had. And with the fever combined, she would have been extra confused and fearful.

However, he was sure he'd seen flames as he flew across the room. Had the fire gotten out of control? He stared at the flames in the hearth. They seemed sedate and perfectly normal now. Could Aleni's power have done something to fuel the fire? It didn't make sense. It had never happened before.

He lay down on his bedroll, being careful with his head. He needed to rest, but his mind wouldn't stop thinking about Aleni. Her powers, although they came in handy, were also a burden to her. Being the sole bearer of magic in Selendria, she took the responsibility seriously. She had spent the last year practicing controlling it so she wouldn't hurt anyone. Jacek often wondered if what she had done to Krodon weighed heavily on her.

If it had been him, he would have killed him, but that was not in Aleni. Could she be regretting that now?

Maybe she feared him coming to find her after all this time? Surely she had all the skills to fight him off by now? Between her magic and her fight training, she could certainly deal with him. He had been careful to only train her in defense, however. He didn't want her turning into him. Assassination was a dirty business, and it left a stain on the soul that never washed out. It had eaten away at his humanity over the years. That was the last thing he wanted for Aleni. She was so pure and naïve.

Despite what had happened to her, she still sought to find the best in people. That still surprised him. She didn't trust them, but she gave people a chance to prove themselves, believing wholeheartedly that they would. Something Jacek never bothered with. And yet, it was one thing he loved about her. It was because of this he had taken a chance hiring the crew for the job with the Deacon. In only a year, she had changed him that much already.

With the throbbing in his head drumming a beat without a rhythm, he eventually fell asleep to the crackle of the fire.

It took two days for Aleni to return. Jacek's head was a lot better by then, and he was left with only a mild headache. The dizziness had completely passed. He spent the time doing various chores around the cabin, tidying and preparing for the coming months. He harvested honey from a nearby hive and stored it in jars on a shelf. Aleni loved honey, it was one of her favorite things to eat, so Jacek always made sure they had a good stock.

He made up a few loaves of the special elven bread Aleni had taught him to make. It was unlike any bread he had eaten before. The loaves were small, but dense. Sweeter than any other bread, it filled the stomach quickly and was good for traveling, as it stayed fresh for longer. Honey was a key ingredient.

He wrapped up the pieces of the boar carcass Aleni had decimated, deciding to keep them for Bandur. The dog got the choicest bits first, and the rest Jacek put in the shed wrapped in clean cloth and buried in snow. It would keep for some time.

When Aleni appeared, Jacek was not prepared for the sight. She was covered in blood almost from head to toe. And yet, she looked no more injured than she had been when she arrived the other day. And she was no longer limping.

Jacek had been trying again to cure the hides outside on the butchering table, but at the sight of her stomping into their home, he forgot immediately.

"What happened?" This felt far too familiar.

"I don't want to talk about it. But I'm not hurt. It's not my blood, and it was just from a hunt. That's all you need to know." She stomped into the cabin and slammed the door behind her.

Great. In a mood again and covered in blood. Jacek hoped this would not become a teenage habit. Blood he could handle, but the moods on top of it? Just might prove too much for his nerves. Being a parent was not as easy as he thought it would be. Especially a parent of a three hundred-year-old teenage elf with burgeoning magical powers and teenage angst.

He gave her some time to clean herself up and then knocked on the door.

There was silence for a second and then a quiet "Come in."

He entered, taking a second for his sight to adjust to the dim interior of the cabin. Aleni was sitting on one of their two wooden chairs at the table in a corner of the room, spinning her knife on the table-top. A bowl of water and a cloth sat in front of her, dyed red. A small puddle of stained water decorated the wooden floorboards near her feet.

Jacek just stared at her silently.

"I'm sorry."

He waved the apology away. "I'm not looking for that."

She got to her feet and faced him. "But I need to say it. I really am sorry I hurt you. Are you all right?"

"I'm fine. My head is harder than that wall. It wasn't your fault. It was those darn nightmares. And the fever."

She raised her hand, palm down in a placating gesture. "Which is gone." She took a deep breath. "Still, I need to have better control over my emotions. I know you've said it to me lots of times, particularly about fighting, but I guess these dreams are like a battle. They certainly feel like a battle. In my mind." She pointed to her temple.

"What do you dream about?" He leaned back on the bench next to the door, his arms crossed.

"A monster. I think it's Krodon, but I never see his face. He's chasing me."

Jacek's chest tightened, his organs twisting. He had to push the anger back down at the mention of that name. "Come here." He put his arms out to her.

She rushed into them, allowing him to enfold her in his embrace. He held her for a few seconds, his chin resting on the top of her head. He then remembered something from the other night.

"I'm mostly sure I didn't imagine this, but did you throw a fireball at me the other night?"

She stiffened. He loosened his grip and stepped back, holding her at arm's length, bending down to try to meet her eyes.

She stared down at her open palms. "I think this is a new power of mine. Producing fire from my hands. I'm not sure yet what triggers it. I've tried to do it again, but it doesn't work like my normal power."

"Could it be triggered by a specific emotion?"

She shrugged. "Possibly. I don't know which one though."

"Well, we must work on that."

He moved over to his travel bag. "I almost forgot." He pulled out the beaded bracelet and presented it to her. "This is for you."

Her eyes lit up at the sight of the jewelry. She took it with careful hands, like she didn't want to break it.

"It's beautiful," she whispered. She slid it over her slender hand and onto her wrist, holding it out in front of her to admire it. "Thank you, Jacek."

He gave a crisp nod, patting her on the shoulder. The warmth that filled his body escorted the cold out.

The moon waxed and waned, monitoring them from above. Aleni watched it every night through a clearing in the trees, as it was one constant from her time. She thought often of her parents, long dead now. There had been times she wished she could join them, but then thinking of Jacek kept her going. He needed her as much as she needed him. She wasn't so young that she didn't see that.

He sometimes seemed almost as broken as she was. She knew he didn't know what to say to her, especially when she was struggling. But in his own way, he often said just what she needed to hear, probably without realizing it. While he hadn't experienced what she had at the hands of Krodon, he had become an orphan at a young age. Even younger than her, and witnessing the state of his parents' bodies, it must have been traumatizing. Unlike her, he had had no one to help him navigate the world at that age, being forced to live on the streets like the children she had met in Amathnore.

Little Thiri had wormed her way into Aleni's heart. Even though the children had run her off, she had thought of her often since. Maybe she could try to find her on her own next time they went to Amathnore. She still wanted to help them somehow.

Bandur sat with her every night she was out under the stars, keeping a silent but comforting vigil. She kept one hand on his sleek coat, reassured she wasn't alone.

One afternoon, after a morning of training, Jacek stuffed a sack with hay and propped it up on a stout stick in their training area.

Aleni stepped closer, curious. "What's that for?"

"For you to light on fire."

She glanced at the open cabin door where the fire burned perpetually.

"Not through normal means." He held up his hands and wiggled his fingers. "Magically." His voice took on a dramatic tone.

She slumped her shoulders. "You know I can't pull it out at will."

"Yes, but we need to know what the trigger is. We can't have you setting Amathnore on fire the next time we visit."

"Thanks for the vote of confidence." She rolled her eyes.

"Call me a pragmatist." He folded his arms and planted his feet, waiting.

She took a deep breath and let it out. Surely she could do this. How hard could it be? She'd done it before, albeit while in a fevered dream state. Positioning herself ten feet in front of the target, she automatically went into a fight stance.

"Think back to what you were feeling the night it first appeared."

"I don't know what I was thinking! I was delirious!"

"You were dreaming. Screaming. I was trying to wake you up. What were you dreaming about?"

The breath on her neck... hair brushed away.

Fear. That's what she felt. Raising her hand, she dredged up the feeling. It wasn't hard; it sat just below the surface every moment of every day. Her heartbeat increased. Adrenaline shot through her, heightening her senses. She held her hand shakily, palm out to the sack.

The world closed in. She needed to survive. That was the only thought running through her head.

Power rushed through her body and funneled out through her hand. A force wave hit the sack and rocked it on its tether.

But that was it.

Disappointed, she lowered her hand. Breathing heavily, she turned back to Jacek.

"It's all right, kiddo. This is just the start. You can keep practicing." Jacek patted her shoulder gently and stepped to the side again. "Now, again."

She tried for another hour, but all she got was a force wave and exhaustion. Jacek must have seen her energy flagging, because he eventually stepped in and stopped her.

"I want to keep trying!" She was a little dizzy, but she would not admit that to him.

"You're exhausted. Try again later. Or tomorrow. You need to rest."

"I'm fine." She made sure she looked him directly in the eye. He could never say no to her eyes. Something about them either unnerved him or enchanted him. She wasn't sure which.

He held up his hands in surrender. "Fine. I'll be inside."

She breathed out slowly, focusing in on the sack again. She would get this. If she didn't, she could be a danger to everyone, including Jacek. And she couldn't live with that.

Chapter Eight

Jacek watched her from the window as he prepared their evening meal. The focus on her face showed she was taking this seriously. Which was good, but he didn't want her pushing too hard. They still didn't know the nature of this new ability. It could be destructive to her and others. Considering it first manifested through a fever, and it was fire, he feared how it could affect her. Nevertheless, she had to learn how to control it.

As he cut up the strips of meat from the boar into cubes, he pondered on their relationship. She was like a daughter to him, but she didn't call him father. Which was fine. He had no desire to fill the sizeable shoes of her elven king father. He had often wondered what the man had been like. Aleni only spoke of him in minor stories from her childhood. Not much of his character. Although, he seemed at least benevolent. He had to be, otherwise Aleni wouldn't be who she was.

Hearing a frustrated cry from outside, Jacek looked up to see Aleni running and punching the straw target. She hit it until it was flat on the ground in the snow. As she stepped back, she stumbled slightly, only just catching herself. She was well past exhausted now.

Jacek dropped the knife and stepped back outside. "That's enough. Come in for dinner."

Aleni stared up at him for a moment, her mouth hanging open as she panted. Puffs of breath froze as they hit the frigid air. She looked for a moment like she might argue, but then lowered her eyes and stumbled toward the cabin.

* * *

The days moved on and so did their training. Aleni, frustrated with herself, left the sack alone. Jacek had her sparring every day, drilling her in both hand to hand and weapons. Her muscles ached from the constant movement, but she appreciated the distraction.

"You're dropping your right hand again." He swung at her with his left to demonstrate where she was open. She was forced to move quickly and bring her right arm up to block and almost didn't make it.

"See? If I'd been any faster, you'd have taken a blow to the head."

"You? Faster?" Aleni grinned.

His leg suddenly swung out and swiped hers from under her. In a split second she was on her back in the snow.

"Cheeky." He smiled back down at her, offering his hand to lift her up.

She took it with humility and tried to keep in her mind to keep her right hand raised.

"Will you teach me some assassin skills?" She had asked this before but hoped that maybe now he might have changed his mind.

"No." He got back into a fight stance. "Now, again. Block and hit together."

She sighed. "Please Jacek."

"I said no. No matter how many times you ask me, my answer will not change. I'm not turning you into an assassin."

"But then I can earn money like you."

"I earn enough for the both of us. There's no need for you to. Just keep being a kid as long as you can."

"I hate being a kid! I can't do anything fun." She crossed her arms over her chest and glared at him.

"I'm teaching you to defend yourself. That should be enough."

"And I'm grateful. But I'm also bored."

"Boredom is not a reason for you to become a killer."

It did sound silly when he put it like that. "Could you at least teach me how to fight a group of people at once?"

He watched her with thoughtful eyes, then finally nodded. "Alright, sounds fair. Not everyone who attacks you will be alone. In fact, most won't be."

"Right."

"Bandur! Come!" Jacek pointed to the ground beside him. The dog lifted himself from the porch in front of the cabin with a long-suffering sigh and trotted over. However, Aleni felt the loyalty in his mind as he followed his old friends' request. Jacek made it sound like a command, but Aleni knew Bandur saw it as a request. He was always happy to comply.

The dog stood quietly in the space Jacek had pointed to. The old assassin then moved a few feet away and stood in an attacking stance with his hands out in front of him. He rolled his shoulders before speaking.

"Alright, pretend Bandur and I are attacking you. How many people can you fight at once?"

"Well, I'm pretty fas-"

Jacek held up a finger. "You can't rely on that. What if that's taken away somehow?"

She sighed, remembering his training. "Only one."

"Correct. So, you need to even it up by moving." He pointed to the far side of where Bandur stood. "If you shift over to the right and face Bandur, I'm now behind him." She did so and was amazed at the simplicity of it. "I can't get to you now."

"What's stopping you from moving?"

"Nothing. You just keep moving so I'm always behind him until you've taken him out. Bandur, stay." He moved to get closer to her. She moved, putting Bandur between them again.

They practiced this for a while longer, Jacek moving constantly, forcing her to block him with the dog. Bandur looked at them both like they were crazy, but he stayed where he was.

It was so simple and now stuck firmly in her mind. She hoped she would get to use it in a real fight.

As soon as they took a break, Bandur lay down and rolled over on his back. A belly rub was fair payment. She laughed, kneeling in the snow to give it to him. All the while he stared at Jacek, as if to say, 'you too'.

"He wants payment for the help," Aleni told him.

Jacek bent down and obliged. "Well, he sells himself too cheap then. A good mercenary knows his worth."

"He's a simple creature. Probably the best of us."

"He is indeed."

Just then, Aleni's horse Beinn wandered close by, looking for patches of grass to eat. A few tufts poked through the thin layer of snow. Aleni got to her feet and met the white mare. She ran her hand over the wide belly, the winter coat rough under her hand.

"How far along do you think she is?" She asked Jacek.

He joined her, feeling along the flank, then reached under and palpated the mare's udder. "Not long now. Maybe a couple of weeks."

Aleni grinned. "It'll be so exciting!" Some of her former glee re-surged. She hadn't felt that in a long time. She patted Beinn's nose, connecting with the mare's quiet nature. A sense of calm fell over her.

Jacek watched her. "I'll need to go into town soon. Get supplies."

Aleni straightened, her body tensing. Could she go with him this time? She would have to tread carefully here. Try to sound as mature as possible. Then maybe he might trust her. She raised her eyes to meet his. He looked thoughtful. Could he be considering taking her?

"You know I want to go with you." She kept her voice quiet, almost scared to say it too loud.

He nodded, patting Beinn's back. "You can't ride her."

It was true, and she hadn't ridden her for a few months now, since her pregnancy was so far along. "I can run."

"What, and draw attention to yourself?"

She sucked in a breath. Wrong thing to say. He surely didn't trust her now. She stared at her feet, not wanting to meet his eyes.

"You can ride with me."

She slumped her shoulders before she realized what he'd said. He was letting her go! Her gaze shot back up to Jacek's face, her mouth splitting open in a grin.

He put a finger up in warning. "You keep your head covered at all times." He flicked her ear gently. "Those stay out of sight."

She played a finger over the point on the top of her ear. They were a dead giveaway she wasn't human. But also no one had ever seen an elf in living memory, so who knew what they would think? It was always a risk whenever she left the safety of the forest.

But she was sick of hiding. And Jacek was responsible for that. She had to prove to him he could trust her training and skills.

Chapter Nine

Icas trudged through the snow, mumbling to himself. He wasn't sure what to do with the information he'd gained. This was the first time in his career he believed the report but couldn't process it. The implications were astounding. He had to tell Sesk straight away.

His network had informed him the Deacon was near the center of town, preparing to speak to a crowd. As he headed there, other people came out of their houses and walked in the same direction. He sensed an excitement about them. Something that was rare in Selendria. That couldn't be good.

He hurried on, finally reaching the small building Sesk used for his preparations. Inside, he found the Deacon and one of his assistant monks.

"Whatever it is, it will have to wait, Icas." Sesk waved him off. "I'm about to address the people."

He sighed and sat down on a chair in the corner. A window near him looked out into the market square where people were gathered.

A wooden stage sat on the other side, where someone could address people from a height and be seen by everyone.

The spy watched as Sesk took to the stage, his assistant behind him. Sesk smiled a terrifying smile and started to speak. Icas could hear him from where he sat. He spoke of love for them and blessings from the gods.

Icas could see how easy it was to get the crowd in his hands. No one had ever addressed these people like this. For as long as they could all remember, Selendria had been a cold, uncaring world. Their ancestors had been criminals. And criminals made for a poor society for the most part. A very untrusting one. With Sesk treating people as if they had worth, he got extremely loyal followers. Instead of the heavy-handed leadership they had experienced from the tyrannical warlords of the past, his soft approach seemed to be more compelling. He didn't need a powerful army to capture a city. Just a few choice words here and there, sprinkled with a few 'miracles' and they were his.

He went on to tell the story of the creation of all the worlds by the gods, how it was divine will that had brought them from their original world through the portals to Selendria. That their ancestors were playing into the hands of the gods in exiling them. They had the chance to remake themselves, to become more than they had been. This excited the crowd who muttered their approval to each other.

Sesk then reached into the folds of his robe and produced a power stone. These white stones had been left behind by the elves, but over time they had gone dormant. Icas used one in his office as a paper weight. But that's all they were good for. Except this one.

Sesk had acquired the stone after a report of a family that had miraculously survived a house fire unscathed. They had been trapped in the house during the inferno, and were found in the ruins after the flames had died down, huddled together under a table. Not a singed hair between them. The father had been holding the stone.

When Sesk had bought it off the family, he had ordered Icas to investigate where it had come from. He'd tracked it back to one of Sesk's own monks who sold it to the family. Upon questioning, it was revealed that the only thing of note was that the monk had recognized the Red Hunter passing through Amathnore with the young girl. The girl had been curious about the stone, but they hadn't bought it. Icas didn't know what to make of the information, so he'd just noted it down and filed it away. It may have just been a coincidence, but Icas was beginning to think not.

Holding it up in his hand, Sesk made sure the crowd could all see the stone before he nodded to one of his assistants. The monk drew his sword. It was huge and vicious looking. All part of the drama.

Sesk lowered his hand. "You too can have this protection of the gods. But it requires faith." He held up the index finger of his other hand. "If you have enough faith, it will protect you." Of course, that would be enough to stop people questioning the validity of the stones. Probably the only real one was in Sesk's hands.

"The gods require your devotion and belief. Otherwise it will not work. You need to prove yourselves worthy to be protected by them. And you can do that by giving your monetary gift to their temples."

And there it was. The call to give money. Icas sat back, shaking his head. It was none of his business what Sesk did, but there was something about it that grated on him. It was a manipulative way to get people's money. What happened to good old-fashioned theft?

In public, Sesk had no connection to the various temples set up for the different gods around the city. He and his monks just sold the stones. But secretly he controlled the temples, with the priests reporting to him. It was all a clever money making business.

Sesk finished up his address and left the stage with his assistant in tow. After a minute, they entered the little house again. Sesk met Icas's eyes and ordered his assistant to leave them.

Once the monk left, Sesk turned back to Icas. "Report."

"I found a guard who worked for Krodon in his southern fortress around the time the girl was there. He says he didn't have direct access to her, that only Traslek and Krodon himself did. But there were rumors among the guards."

"Yes?"

"That the girl might not have been human." This was what Icas had trouble processing.

"What? How could that be?"

"There were stories she was an elf."

"Preposterous. The elves are long gone. Everyone knows that."

"Well, this is what he said. That she had been found in some sort of ancient chamber, frozen in magic and brought back to life by an incantation. Then Krodon held her captive. For what purpose, no one knows. But they did know he used her as a whore."

Sesk walked over to a table with a plate of fruit and picked up a pear. "I knew he was a strange one, but I didn't know his tastes ran to children." He sniffed the pear and then picked up a knife and began to slice into it.

Icas shrugged. "Whatever. I'm not sure I believe the story about her being an elf, but she was definitely held captive for Krodon's tastes alone."

"Why would they make that up?" Sesk's eyebrows furrowed in thought.

Icas stood, walking to the window to stare out into the market. The people were dispersing slowly. Some lined up in front of the monks selling the stones. Sesk would make a lot of money from this little show. "When it comes to something that is kept secret and little of the details are known, men are wont to embellish and make it more intriguing than it really is. Especially when they're bored. When really, it's just a perverted man in power. That's all there is to it, in my opinion."

"Well, I don't pay you for your opinion. I pay for facts. What else did you find out?" He crunched down on a slice of pear, the juices running down his chin.

Icas turned back to Sesk, pushing his irritation down. "I took your description of the girl and spread it out through my network. The white hair is distinctive enough. One of my men spotted her with a group of street children."

"Street children? That's odd. Was the Red Hunter with her?" The Deacon's scarred face twitched. Where and when did he get those scars? Sesk had never spoken of them.

Icas shook his head. "He wasn't. My man followed her around for a bit, watching from a distance. She seemed to be practicing pick pocketing. He got the sense that the children were teaching her."

"Hmmm." Sesk stared at the floor, his dark eyes lost in thought.

There was something else he needed to mention. "We learned one more interesting thing."

"What's that?"

"One of the children has a power stone. A real one."

Sesk's eyes shot up to meet Icas's, alight with interest. "Get me that child."

***

"You really should name your horse."

The sun was nearly at its zenith when Jacek and Aleni rode into Amathnore the next day. It was turning into one of the warmer months of the year. The snow covering the ground was thin, and the air was almost warm. Almost. Aleni pulled her fur-lined leather coat closer around her neck. The cold seemed to find any gap and burrow in. Although the climate didn't affect her like it did with humans, she still felt it on her skin and didn't like it. The world had not been like this when she was growing up.

Bandur trotted along beside them while Aleni rode behind Jacek on his tall black stallion.

"I don't need to name it." He shifted in his seat.

"It's a he." She patted the horse's rump. "And he's beautiful. He needs a name."

"He's survived without one so far."

"Oh, come on, Jacek. How about Salmir? It means starlight in elvish. Because his white forelock looks like a star in the night."

He scoffed but didn't reply.

"Or what about Dai? That means shadow. Ooh, or Estil. Hope. In the hope you'll actually get attached to him one day." She rolled her eyes at his back.

"I didn't let you come along so you can talk my ear off."

"You know, you're grumpy when you know you're wrong." She smiled at his back.

"I'm not naming the horse. That's final."

Aleni grinned, but let it go. He'd come around, eventually.

They both fell into silence as they rode through the streets teeming with people. Jacek found a spot to tie up their horse between a farrier and an inn. The farrier lounged outside his front door on a stool, smoking a pipe and watching the people pass by.

"Hey. You." Jacek addressed the farrier.

The man startled at the interruption, staring at Jacek strapping on his weapons. The farrier pointed to his own chest, his eyes wide.

"Yes, you. If this horse," he pointed to the black beast beside him, "isn't here when I return, I will hunt you down and take layers of your skin off. Do you get me?" The scar on his face twitched. He flicked an olon at the man, who caught it with both hands. The farrier nodded readily, his eyes even wider. Recognition sparked in them.

Aleni bit her bottom lip, trying not to laugh. Jacek's reputation served them well sometimes. It amused her greatly at other times. He was so different when they were alone.

As they walked away, she spoke quietly. "You're so warm and cuddly, you know that right?"

He gave her a sidelong glance and grunted.

She stifled a giggle, only because the farrier would hear her.

The market was busy as usual. The constant crowd moving through the main square turned the snow and dirt underfoot into muddy slush. Aleni's boots squished into the thick sludge, weighing them down. The sound of vendors calling out their wares mingled with the susurrus of the people moving past. Rich merchant's wives looked down their noses at any poor scum of Amathnore that happened to pass by. Aleni watched them, wondering what their lives were like.

Just as they walked through the thickest part of the crowd, Jacek snatched the wrist of a young boy who was trying to get at his coin bag. The boy struggled against his hold, but Jacek wouldn't let go.

Aleni recognized him. It was one of the boys from Thiri's street gang. Aleni didn't know his name, but he was one she'd seen with the little girl.

"That's not yours," she said. How could she talk to him without Jacek knowing she'd been here before? "Let him go."

Jacek narrowed his eyes at the boy, maintaining his grip on the skinny wrist.

"Please father, he didn't do any harm." She said in a slightly higher-pitched voice than normal. She had never called Jacek father before, and she wouldn't, but this boy probably assumed he was her father. She grabbed at Jacek's other forearm, trying to pull his attention away. "Let him go."

"I could take his hand off and no one would blame me." Jacek turned his head slowly to look at her.

"Yes, but then there would be a mess. And you would draw attention to us."

There was amusement in his eyes as he let the wrist go. The boy was off in an instant, weaving through the crowd.

Aleni took off after him, Bandur closely in tow.

"Hey! Where are you going?" Jacek called after her.

"I'll meet you later!" She called back over her shoulder. Hopefully, he wouldn't be too mad. But she had to find out if Thiri was all right.

She followed the boy through the crowd before it thinned out on the other side of the market. Finally, she caught up with him and grabbed his shoulder. Bandur stayed close to her side.

"Hey, can you take me to Thiri?"

The boy stopped, turning. "You know Thiri? Wait, you're that girl that came a while ago and wanted to learn thieving!"

"I didn't want to learn thieving. I wanted to learn to have light fingers. There's a difference."

The boy scoffed. "No, there isn't."

"Will you take me to her?"

"Why?"

Aleni turned her head to look over her shoulder toward Jacek. The crowd of people blocked her view, but she knew he wasn't far.

How angry would he be for her running off? Probably a lot. But she could talk him down, she was sure of it. Better to ask forgiveness than permission. She was craving interaction with other kids after all their time in the forest.

She turned back to the boy. "Because she is my friend and will want to see me."

The boy thought for a few seconds, then sighed. "Fine. Follow me."

Jacek's heart sank as he watched the crowd swallow Aleni. He would never be able to keep up with her. He had hoped she would stay with him here in the city, but he hadn't explicitly forbidden going off on her own. Maybe he should have.

He let out a heavy breath. What was he to do about her? She was still keeping something from him, and he had no idea how to find out. He almost wished he could use enforced interrogation. But he knew the worst he could do to her was a tickle. He could never hurt her.

He would just have to go to their prearranged meeting spot. An alehouse on the southern end of Amathnore. One that was at least marginally clean and had food that didn't have to be swallowed whole.

He finished up getting the supplies, then headed for his horse. Mercifully, the beast was still there. The farrier watched him with wide eyes as he unhitched the animal and mounted. Jacek flicked him another olon before riding off. Whatever anyone said about him, he made sure he always paid what he owed. He might be a monster, but he was a fair monster.

He lumbered through the snow scudded streets, watching as always for any sudden movements in his direction. He was almost always on guard, even at home, but Aleni had helped him to relax more over the last year. It certainly helped to have someone that had your back.

The alehouse was near the docks, and the salt smell of the sea hit him before he saw the masts of the ships. Outside the sturdy wooden taproom, he dismounted and gave his horse to an ostler to take around the back.

Entering the dim main room, he took a moment for his eyes to adjust. It was around noon now, and the room was almost full of sailors taking their shore leave seriously. The grog was flowing well by the looks of some people in the room.

Jacek found a table in one corner of the room and sat facing everyone, his back to the corner. The barkeep made his way over with a cup and a jug of ale. He plonked the cup down on the table in front of the assassin and went to pour the ale.

Jacek put his hand over the cup. "No ale. Do you have any Dire Sip?"

The barkeep screwed up his nose at him. "You're one of those, are you?"

Jacek gave him a bland look. Which he'd been told by Aleni was very similar to his 'do you want a knife in your gullet' look.

The barkeep took a step back and raised his free hand in a gesture of peace. "I'm not judging, sir. I - I think I have some in an urn out the back. I'll go have a look."

"You do that." He let a little more growl into his voice. He dismissed the barkeep from his mind and immediately Aleni entered it again. How long would she be? Would she remember to come here?

After the barkeep had returned with a jug of dire sip and left without comment, Jacek sat back in the shadows and watched the room. A few more sailors entered, either joining their shipmates or going straight to the bar. It wasn't long before a familiar face appeared in the doorway. Not Aleni, but the ship captain Deems. The man who had taken them from the southern continent to Amathnore a year ago. Aleni had taken a liking to him. Even saved his life. The man scoured the room with his eyes, finally alighting on Jacek. His face lit up, and he sauntered over.

"Well I'll be, is that you old friend?"

Jacek took another sip of his drink and stared at him pointedly. "You must have me mistaken with someone else. I'm not your friend."

"I'm not mistaken, but fine, we don't have to be friends." Deems took a seat at the table, waving the barkeep over and ordering a mug of ale.

Deems wrinkled his nose at Jacek's mug. "You still drink that gods-awful stuff?"

Jacek let an irritated frown form on his face. "I don't need that from you too."

"I only know a handful of people who drink the stuff, but you're definitely the crankiest of all of them."

Jacek didn't bother to deign that with a response.

"So," Deems took a swig of ale. "What have you been up to since I last saw you? You had a girl with you last time if I remember rightly. What happened to her?"

"You'll probably see her soon. She'll be meeting me here any minute." He hoped.

Deems raised his eyebrows. "She a regular client or something?"

"Or something. She lives with me now."

"She's a bit young for you, isn't she?"

Jacek's temper flared. "Not like that!" he growled.

Deems was unperturbed. "My mistake. I'm sorry, but I just didn't take you for the father type."

"Neither did I."

"Well, congratulations then." He raised his drink to Jacek. "To being a father."

Despite himself, Jacek clinked his cup with Deems and drank.

"I'm a father myself, you know, and it's not a straightforward job my friend."

Jacek let out a huff of breath. "That's putting it lightly."

"Trouble?" Deems had an amused look in his eye.

"You could say that. Not that I would take it all back, but I have no idea what I'm doing."

"Tell me."

Jacek soon found himself telling Deems most of it. He left out the part about her being an elf, and the details of her imprisonment with Krodon. But he did mention that she had been hurt by someone and was still dealing with the consequences. Deems nodded sagely throughout the telling, refraining from saying anything until Jacek had finished.

Jacek was surprised at himself for opening up so much. Perhaps the barkeep had slipped a little ale in his drink after all. Or maybe it was the fact that for the first time in his life he felt out of his depth and desperately needed some advice. He couldn't afford to get this wrong.

"Well, it certainly sounds like you have your hands full with that one." Deems sat back in his chair and took another gulp of ale before going on. "Unfortunately, this is a common thing that happens to girls. I have noticed they are often disturbed afterwards. My woman, the mother of my children, had it happen to her. She often said it was worse than murder, because you survived the attack, but your soul died. She was a wise woman."

"Was?"

"She passed away a number of years ago now. Taken by the cold sickness."

Jacek nodded. It was common enough. Not many people lived through until their later years. Someone like Deacon Sesk was a rarity. Which was probably another reason why people followed him.

"Does she talk about it much?" Deems asked.

Jacek shook his head. In a way, he was glad she didn't, but in another way he knew she probably needed to. "She has dreams about it. She had been good for a while, but recently they've started coming back."

Deems nodded then. "Aye, my Addie often had dreams."

"What did you do to help her?"

"Well, there was naught I could do, was there?" He took another swig. "All I could do was hold her while she cried."

Jacek had not suspected there was a soft side to this weathered sailor. Deems had always been unusually fair in his dealings with him, but he had only ever seen the hard sea captain side. This surprised him, but he said nothing.

"She was a broken soul." Deems stared at the table, one finger tracing the knots in the wood. "But, she was a good woman. And that's a rarity. She was kind to others and to me. She raised four boys for me. They now help me run the ship."

"Did you worry about them? When they were children?" Jacek asked.

Deems gave a little laugh. "Of course I did. That's part of being a parent. You worry about everything with them. Whether they will fall off a high beam or go overboard, or if they'll live to be thirty."

Jacek considered this. He didn't worry about those things with Aleni. There was less risk of her falling off something, or not living to be thirty. She would probably long outlive him. Elves lived for generations. He more worried that someone would take her and use her to their advantage. Or do what Krodon had been doing to her.

With her magic harnessed by someone else, she would bring un-rivaled power.

But he couldn't divulge this to Deems. He simply nodded slowly and took another drink. Frustration still raged inside him. It was a mistake to confide in Deems. He wanted some way to help Aleni, but from what Deems said, there was no way to fix her. Mentally, he kicked himself.

"So have you heard what's going on in town?" Deems raised an eyebrow at him.

"I'm sure you're going to tell me."

"Aye. So the men have been telling me about a bunch of murders been happenin' the last few weeks. Latest one just this after-noon. Got everyone mightily unsettled. Brutal they were. Cut to ribbons, and their junk cut off to boot."

At that, Jacek raised his brows. That usually indicated a sexual component. He hadn't seen it a lot, but over the years there were a few. Mostly perpetrated on women, but on men was even rarer.

"We got some sort of serial killer on the loose."

"So what's new?" Jacek shook his head, trying to hide his rising anxiety. Aleni was out there on her own somewhere.

"Alright, alright. But three a week apart? And cut up like that? That ain't so common."

"True." Jacek had to give it that. Honestly, it intrigued him. Something about it niggled at his mind.

"Where did they happen?"

"The first one was over on the east side, near the old butcher on fourth street. In an alleyway."

"Of course." Most murders happened in alleyways late at night. It was almost a given.

"The others were a few streets away from that." "But the weird thing was, these were done in the daytime. And no one saw or heard anything."

Jacek narrowed his eyes. Or nobody wanted to see or hear anything. There was a difference. But still, it was unusual. It took some skill to pull off a murder like that and not get found out. In Amathnore, there was no authority to stop them, but if people were fearful enough and stayed in their homes, some rich merchant might pay for a mercenary to hunt them down so his patrons would buy from him again. Then the townspeople would most likely lynch the murderer. Or send him to the Arena to be fodder for some fighter.

"Anything else?"

Deems thought for a second, then placed a finger in the air. "Oh yes, they were monks."

"Monks?"

"Yeah, you know, from the Creed of Redemption."

Now that was an interesting piece of the puzzle. Why would they be targeted? They were annoying, but surely that didn't warrant murdering them.

Wait, Aleni had been bugging him about learning assassin skills a lot. He had turned her down each time, of course, but what if she had taken things into her own hands? Decided to teach herself? She had gone off on her own a few times over the last month. He couldn't remember when exactly, but could she have been going off to do some extra-curricular practice? The blood drained from his face and he sat up a little straighter.

"You alright there, friend?" Deems peered at him through ale-fuzzed eyes.

"I'm not your friend," he repeated with less enthusiasm than before.

Deems patted the air placatingly. "Sure, sure. But you look like you've seen a spirit of the dead."

Jacek leaned back again and breathed slowly to calm himself. Could Aleni be the murderer? She had been very angry lately. Maybe she was taking it out on monks. Not to mention the cutting off of their sex. Could she be angry enough to do that?

Chapter Ten

T he boy, who introduced himself as Tol, led Aleni through the streets haphazardly. They cut through alleyways, across streets, through a shop and out the other side and even doubled back around a block at one point. Aleni had no idea where she was anymore or where they were going. Could he be leading her into a trap? Why was it taking so long? Bandur trotted loyally along beside her, so she felt safe enough. But serious doubts about Tol's intentions were growing when suddenly, they were there.

A group of children sat in the alley next to a tavern, huddling against the back wall of a brick chimney. High above them, smoke poured from the flue. Presumably, the bricks of the fireplace had warmed up from the fire roaring inside the tavern. Aleni didn't feel the cold as much as humans, but she had pity for the children with their meagre layers of clothing.

Thiri sat in the middle of the group, her back pushed up against the brick, her hands holding the little stone the elf had activated. On seeing Aleni, she broke out in a pleased grin and got to her feet.

"Aleni!" She came toward her with her arms out wide. Aleni took her in an embrace, returning the smile.

"Hello Thiri, it's good to see you. How are you?"

"Oh, I'm alright. It's a lot easier to stay warm now, thanks to you." She held up the stone, which pulsed slightly with light. The surrounding area warmed a little.

"I'm glad I could help."

"Where have you been? I haven't seen you for ages. And is this your dog?" Thiri grinned at Bandur and went to pat him. Bandur growled until Aleni put a hand on his head and told him it was alright. The dog then sat and allowed himself to be petted. Thiri giggled as she felt his soft fur.

"I've been out of town. I just arrived this afternoon. We happened to run into Tol and I asked him to bring me here." She shot Tol a small smile. He straightened at the sudden attention.

"Well, you're just in time," Thiri said. "I'm about to do a little job. You could help me with it."

"What kind of job?"

"One where we steal from a rich, horrible merchant." The young girl gave a cheeky grin.

Aleni hesitated in answering. Could she do that? Actually steal from someone? Jacek stole from people. If he was getting paid to. For these kids, the payment was the thing they stole.

"Why is he horrible?" She needed more information.

"He's nasty to us on the streets. He's caught some of us and cut off hands. Thiri motioned to a boy who sat at the end of the line of children. He held up his right arm to display a stump at the end instead of a hand. It was covered in a woven woolen garment.

Aleni sucked in a horrified breath, unconsciously wrapping one hand around the other wrist. That was horrible.

"So I'm going to break into his house and take some of his stuff." Thiri smirked.

The other kids all nodded in ready agreement. "Since I'm small, I can fit through a little window he has on his upper floor. It has an easy latch. You might fit too."

"How will you not get caught?"

An older boy piped up. "We know he's out at the moment at some rich people's party."

"So we have to go now." Thiri waved her arm in an inclusive motion.

"Alright, I'll join you." This might actually be fun. Almost like going on a job with Jacek. Not that he had ever let her go.

There was no sign of the oldest boy, Dato. She wondered if he was around, he might object to her involvement. But Thiri seemed to trust Aleni. Something Jacek would have frowned at. Well, Aleni's parents had always taught her that people were trustworthy. Of course, they meant elves, who were eminently more trustworthy than humans in her experience. But how could one earn trust if there was never a chance to?

Thiri led the way through the streets to a stately two-story home in a wealthy suburb. This one was constructed of thick wooden framing filled in with wattle and daub. And it was painted, which Aleni hadn't seen in this town before. It was a nice blue color with green trim around the windows and doors. A few other houses around were also painted. Aleni stood in the wide alley next to it, admiring it for some time.

Thiri scouted around, looking in the windows and checking the doors. She finally returned to Aleni and put her hands on her hips. "Well, it's all locked up, but it seems no one's home." She looked up at the second story. Aleni followed her gaze and spotted a small window.

"Is that it?"

"Yep. We need to climb up the piping there and get it open."

"How?"

"A knife slid underneath will do."

"Alright. Shall I lead?" Aleni loosened her knife in its sheath.

Thiri looked around to see if anyone was watching. Aleni checked as well. No one was walking around, and all the houses nearby seemed shut up. Maybe they were all at the same party. The sun had gone behind the clouds, leaving a darkened grimness to the day. She ordered Bandur to stay and keep watch. The dog obediently took up a position at the opening of the little gap between the merchant's house and the next building.

Aleni started up the side of the house. It was an easy climb. Not only was there the piping, but the wooden beams stuck out, framing the walls and making convenient places to put her small feet. She got up to the window swiftly and pulled out her knife. After a quick inspection of the window, she could see what Thiri had meant. The catch on the inside could be pushed aside with something long and thin. Her knife was perfect. With a small nudge, the catch opened.

She put her knife away and slid the window up. It created a gap two feet by two feet. Plenty of space for her to slide in. She had to be careful not to catch her clothing on the latch on the way in, but she eventually found herself inside the house. She leaned out and waved to Thiri below, who began her own climb.

Aleni scanned the room. It was a small office with a desk and chair up against one wall and a softer armchair in another corner. A large rug covered the middle of the wooden floor, creating a cozy feel. Aleni was reminded a little of her home growing up under the mountain in Y'ha Taesi. It left her with an uneasy feeling. Why did it feel wrong for a bad man to live in a beautiful and cozy house?

Thiri soon joined her in the office. "He is bound to have a safe somewhere here. It will be where he keeps his expensive stuff. All the rich people have them."

Aleni nodded and looked around the room, pulling open the drawers in the desk and lifting papers and other junk. Thiri pulled aside paintings on the wall. They went through the whole room and came up with nothing but some boring business contracts.

"Let's try another room," Thiri suggested. As they walked along a hallway, the floorboards creaked slightly. Thiri hugged one wall as she walked. "If you walk on the floor closest to the wall, the boards won't creak." She flashed a brilliant grin.

Aleni followed her instruction and together they made their way down the hallway to the first room off it. It was a large living room. Richly decorated in reds and blues, the floor was fully covered in a sort of rug. From wall to wall, a thick woven fabric covered the floor. Aleni had seen nothing like it. It felt soft and spongy under her booted feet. She kneeled and felt it with her hands. The thick woven fibers felt luscious and unfamiliar.

Thiri watched her. "It's called carpet. I've seen a few houses with it, but only in the really rich ones."

"It must keep the room warm."

"Yes, nice for some. Come on, we need to keep looking."

They made their way around the room methodically, looking in cupboards, drawers and behind furniture. Finally, after climbing on a chair and reaching as high as she could, Thiri pulled back a painting over the fireplace and a small metal door revealed itself. It had a circular mechanism on the front, which Aleni guessed to be the lock.

"Oh, man!" Thiri looked defeated.

"What's wrong?"

"I was hoping it would be a lock I could pick."

"How does it work?" Aleni stepped closer.

"You turn the dial back and forward until it unlocks. I don't know how to open them. I've only heard of them. They're new." She jumped back down off the chair. "Something built with knowledge from the old world our ancestors came from."

Aleni took her place and reached up to rest her palm on the metal next to the dial. She closed her eyes and went inward for her magic. It tingled up her arm and out through her palm. Warm and calming. In her mind's eye, she saw the internal mechanism. It didn't take long for her to understand how it worked. With her power, she nudged the wheel inside around until it stopped in an empty slot on the wheel behind it. She then turned the next wheel until it too slotted into the next wheel. There was a slight click. Around again until there was another click. A piece of metal fell into a newly created gap with a louder clunk and the door loosened under her palm. She leaned back and lowered her hand. The door swung free.

She turned back to look at Thiri, who had her mouth dropped open in astonishment.

"How did you do that?"

Aleni blinked. It took a few seconds to realize Thiri didn't know who she was or what she could do. She hadn't explained with the power stone, and Thiri hadn't pressed further.

Aleni had felt so comfortable with Thiri, she hadn't even thought about not using her power. She used it all the time with Jacek, mostly to practice. It was normal for them, and it came easily to her now. Would Thiri tell the others?

"Um, you have to keep this a secret, Thiri." Aleni bit at her bottom lip.

"It is that magic, correct? Like what you did with the stone?" Thiri's eyes lit up.

"It's a little different than with the stone, but yes, it's magic." She kneeled in front of the little girl, grabbing her cold hands and holding them firmly. "You can't tell anyone, Thiri. People might hurt me if they knew what I could do. They might want it for themselves, or use me to get rich and powerful. Please promise me you won't tell." She held her breath.

The white's of Thiri's eyes were large, staring at Aleni. She was still for a few seconds, then eventually, she nodded. Aleni let go of her breath.

"Thank you."

"Of course! You are my friend, I would not hurt you." The little girl grinned and climbed up on the chair to get at the contents of the safe.

If only Jacek could see this. He was adamant everyone lived only for themselves, and at the first chance they got, would stab you in the back. But Aleni could tell this little girl would never dream of betraying a friend. Maybe times had changed since Jacek lived on the streets. Or he just needed to stop making grandiose broad statements. What happened to him as a child was sad, but it didn't mean it was going to happen to her.

The sound of clinking metal snapped her back to the room. Thiri had found a bag of coins and was running her hand through it with a grin.

"It feels amazing! Do you want to try?" The little girl's dark eyes were wide with delight.

Thiri's pleasure was contagious, making Aleni smile, but she shook her head. "We should get out of here. Have you got what you came for?"

Thiri nodded vigorously and jumped down from the chair, the large coin bag in hand. She tied it back up with the leather thong sewn onto the top of it.

Just then, they heard a bang downstairs. The two girls froze. It sounded like the front door being shut. Was the merchant home? They caught each other's eyes and shared a silent warning between them. Aleni jerked her head at the door to the room. Time to go.

Thiri led the way and crept toward the door. She held the large bag in both hands, being careful not to let it jingle. Aleni followed on silent feet.

As they reached the hallway, they could hear footsteps clomping up the staircase. The merchant was coming. They wouldn't reach the room at the end of the hallway before he saw them.

Aleni grabbed Thiri's collar and pulled her back into the sitting room. They hid behind the open door, waiting with held breath. Aleni had her arms around Thiri, pulling her close. The little girl held the coin bag carefully by the top, not risking her other hand underneath unless it made a noise.

Aleni wondered if she should take the bag from her. It had to be heavy, and she was much stronger than the younger girl. Holding it like she was would put a strain on her arms before long. But even transferring the bag between them was risking making a noise.

The heavy footsteps came closer in the hallway, passing outside the sitting room and carrying on down the hall. Aleni listened carefully, trying to find out where he was in the house. It sounded like he was in the room at the end of the hall, moving around slowly, opening a drawer, then placing something on the desk. She heard the scratch of an inked nib, then paper being folded. He crossed the room. She held her breath.

The window made a scraping sound as it was closed.

Aleni's heart sank. That would make escaping much harder. She sighed inwardly. Why had she followed Thiri here? What did she really think she could gain by breaking into a man's house? She didn't need the money. Not like Thiri. But another part of her knew if she didn't come, this man would probably catch and kill Thiri.

Maybe they should sneak out while he was down there? Too late now, he made his way back down the hallway. Did he suspect he had uninvited visitors? Or would he think he'd left the window open?

He entered the sitting room, crossing to the fireplace. Aleni gripped her arm tighter across Thiri's chest. He would surely see the open safe and start looking for them. She had to distract him. Closing her eyes, she looked around the room with her inner sight. A vase sat on a small side table under a window on the other side of the room. Aleni pushed it with a little magic.

The vase didn't break as it hit the soft carpet. There was a muffled Tud, and the man spun toward it. Aleni let go of Thiri and nudged her forward. The girl stepped carefully on the balls of her feet out from behind the door.

Aleni followed, watching the man over her shoulder, her heart pounding in her ears. He was a corpulent man, going bald on the top of his head. He looked to be in his early fifties. His clothing matched the opulence of the room; well-tailored with expensive cloth. He moved over to the vase, crouching to pick it up.

The two girls snuck out into the hallway. In their rush, however, the bag of coins brushed against the doorway.

The coins inside shifted. Aleni's heart jumped. She looked back and her eyes met the merchant's. His widened in shock and he opened his mouth to shout.

"Run!" said Aleni as she pushed Thiri forward. Thiri of course turned toward the end room. She didn't know the window was now closed. Aleni would have just gone for the front door downstairs. Too late now.

There was a shout and a Tumping of heavy running footsteps behind them as they rushed down the hall to the little room. Thiri gave a wordless cry as she saw the closed window.

Aleni used a little magic and tried to push the window up. It didn't move. She tried again. It moved only a little. Thiri reached the window and tried to push it up the rest of the way, but the coin bag hampered her efforts.

Aleni turned to face the merchant. She needed to buy them some time. He slowed in the hallway as he saw he had trapped them. A small smile played on his face.

"Well, who are you two now? Thieves?"

Aleni froze, the fear building in her chest. What would this man do to them? An image of Krodon came to her mind unbidden. Would he just try to kill them? The possibilities ran through her head in quick succession. Her muscles locked and her stomach lurched as the scenario played out in her mind. They were doomed.

The merchant reached behind his back and produced a large knife that must have been sitting in his belt. "I'm going to take your hands off for this." His eyes fell on the coin bag in Thiri's hand.

The little girl gave up on the stubborn window and hid behind Aleni.

"How did you get my safe open?" He looked back up at Aleni's face, his own furrowed in puzzlement. "I was assured it was unbreakable. But here I have two children with the contents in their hands." His voice was a smooth tenor, modulated to a soothing tone. As if he wanted to placate them. Put them at ease.

Aleni was certainly not at ease. He terrified her. All her trauma came to mind in front of this man with the knife. She couldn't even reach her magic. If only Jacek was here.

That thought snapped the spell. Thinking of Jacek reminded Aleni of all the training he'd done with her. The hours and hours of drills. Her hand went to her own knife at her hip. Her mind went blank, and the training took over.

She moved to the side as she waited for the large merchant to come to her. He lunged at her with his knife. She leaped back and slashed her knife across the top of his hand. He cried out and let go of the knife. It clattered to the floor as he cradled his bleeding hand in the other. She then leaped up into the air toward him, her elbow held up high above her head. As she came down over him, she dropped her arm and crashed her elbow onto the top of his head. She dropped silently to the floor, light on her feet.

The merchant dropped to one knee, his head hanging, half conscious. He must have a hard head, because that move would have knocked most people out cold. Aleni finished up with a swinging kick with her right leg across the side of his head. The large man finally fell onto his side, unconscious.

Aleni turned back to Thiri, who crouched underneath the window, the bag of coins between her feet. She stared at Aleni with wide eyes.

Aleni reached out her hand for Thiri's. "Come on, let's get out of here."

"Is he dead?" The little girl asked, staring now at the merchant.

Aleni eyed the trickle of blood dripping down the side of the man's head. "No, but he'll wish he was when he wakes up."

Thiri gulped down air and got to her feet. She took Aleni's hand and together they ran from the large house.

Chapter Eleven

A musician was playing a stringed instrument for the evening's entertainment by the time Aleni and Bandur turned up at the alehouse. Jacek sat up in his seat and made a gesture to get her attention. She strode over to the table in the corner, showing her confidence with every step. A small spring of pride bubbled in Jacek's chest at seeing how she held herself. Her pale and otherworldly face caught the attention of a few men in the room, but she brushed past them like they didn't exist.

Anger soon pushed aside the pride as Jacek remembered she had kept him waiting, and worrying, for the entire afternoon. She looked unhurt, but she had a grim and determined look on her face. Could she be coming back from having murdered a monk? He scanned her for signs of blood spatter. There was nothing. It didn't prove she wasn't the killer, but he allowed himself some relief.

Deems still sat with Jacek at the table, and on seeing Aleni, he broke out in a smile.

"Well, look at you!" Deems stood to greet her. Jacek wondered for a second if he was going to hug her, but he kept his arms to himself. Aleni stopped in her tracks and stared at him. Bandur almost crashed into the back of her legs.

"Captain Deems?"

"It is I." He gave a grand, wide gesture with his arms. "At your service, my dear." Deems made a deep formal bow.

She gave him a small smile. It had been because of Deems she had discovered her magic. When a beam broke on his ship during a storm, Aleni had reached out instinctively and held the beam in place over his head with her mind. Thankfully, he hadn't even been aware of it because of the darkness and the noise of the storm. Jacek suspected she had a soft spot for the old sea dog.

"It's good to see you, Captain." She bowed her head back at him in respect. She moved to the chair next to Jacek, opposite Deems. Bandur came to lie down wearily between them.

He offered the dog some strips of dried meat from his pouch before turning back to his adopted daughter. "Where have you been?" Jacek couldn't quite keep the annoyance out of his voice. He didn't really want to, anyway. She needed to know she had upset him by running off.

"I met some street children. I followed the boy who tried to steal from you."

"Why?"

She hesitated. "I wanted to meet other children my age. Is that so bad?"

"Yes." Besides, she was lying. She was never good at it. Avoiding him, yes, but not lying.

"Do you really expect me to go throughout my life only talking to you?" She looked him dead in the eyes with those icy blues. The intensity forced him to look away. There was always something a little unsettling about that gaze. Something that reminded him she wasn't human. He had warned her not to look people in the eye too much. It would give her away.

"I suppose not. But street kids are not a good place to start. They'll sell you out first chance they get. I forbid you to go back to them."

Her nostrils flared suddenly, and she stared at him. "Don't do this." She lowered her voice, flicking her gaze from Deems back to him. "Please. They need our help. Kids are going missing."

"Not our problem." Jacek took another sip of his drink. "Street kids go missing all the time."

"Please Jacek."

"Leave it, Aleni."

She huffed out a breath, sat back in the chair and crossed her arms. Let her sulk then. As long as she was safe. Jacek glanced at Deems, who was trying to look interested in the musician on the other side of the alehouse.

Jacek ordered some food for them all and a warm drink for Aleni. She looked tired. They ate without speaking and eventually took their leave from Deems. Next door was a small boarding house they had used before. Jacek paid for a room with two single beds. It was small with a little table and two chairs at one end. A dirty window looked out over the harbor.

Aleni never spoke a word as they settled in and went to bed. Which was fine with Jacek; he wasn't interested in conversation.

In the morning, after a fitful night of sleep from Aleni, Jacek got up at dawn and ordered breakfast from the house madam. She was a large, stern lady who took no nonsense. But her cooking was good. Jacek paid her extra just to get her meals each time they stayed.

After eating, Jacek decided he needed to get more information. He needed to know for certain if Aleni was this killer. He had to inspect the bodies. If she was the killer, he had to remove any evidence linking them to her. Then they would sit down for a long talk.

When Aleni woke, Jacek had their breakfast out on the table in their room. The house madam provided a hot meal of sausages, bread, cheese and gruel. He had gone next door and acquired two steaming mugs of mulled wine and dire sip. He gave Bandur a couple of sausages as well. The madam had been reluctant to part with them for a dog, but Jacek paid a little more for the treats.

Aleni was quiet as she ate, but she seemed a little less obstinate at least.

"I'm going out today. Got some things to attend to," Jacek announced once he finished his drink. "I want you to stay here."

Aleni gave him a long-suffering look. "Why can't I come with you?"

"Because you ran off yesterday on your own, and now you're going to stay here. That's final."

Her bottom lip popped out, but she had no reply.

"I'm taking Bandur as well."

Her mouth dropped open in protest, her brows knitted.

"You can stay here and think about the wisdom of running off on your own. Hopefully, I won't be long. We can be on our way by midday."

"Can you at least braid my hair?" She spoke in elven and gave him one of her innocent pleading looks. Those he had trouble resisting.

She had been teaching him her language. "It's always better when you do it."

He sighed heavily. "Alright." He replied in elven and pointed a finger at her. "But you stay."

She smiled. "Of course." She switched back to the common tongue. "Your pronunciation isn't too bad, by the way. But it still needs some work. You need to put more of a lilt on the consonants."

He repeated the words until she nodded. "I'll keep working on that." He moved behind her chair and ran his fingers through her hair to get the knots out. It hung halfway down her back, fine and pure, like fresh snow. He had to admit he enjoyed doing it for her. And she seemed to get pleasure out of it too. For some reason, she still couldn't braid it straight on her own. Which seemed strange since she was so adept at everything else to do with her hands.

When he finished braiding it and had tied it off with a strip of leather, he patted her shoulders and went to get his gear. He strapped on his weapons and clicked his fingers for Bandur to follow. With a final nod to Aleni, he left.

Out in the cold, Jacek pulled his gloves on and moved off toward the east side. His gut roiled at the thought of what he could find. Not because of the dead bodies, but more because of how they could have got there.

They made their way to fourth street, looking for the butcher Deems mentioned. He had been here at least once before. The houses here were more run down, the faces of the people peering out of the doors grubbier and leaner. Life expectancy around here wasn't high to start with. The smell of fish and cabbage hung in the air like a miasma.

The butcher shop appeared finally on his right.

"Bandur, search. Body." The dog set off with his nose to the ground. Jacek hoped the smell of a decomposing body would be stronger than the dead fish in the air. It was a slim chance, but Bandur's nose hadn't failed him yet.

After a couple of minutes and some false starts, the dog gave a little bark and headed into an alleyway a few doors down. Jacek joined him and spotted a mound of fresh snow with a telltale hand sticking out the side. He gave Bandur a pat, and a dried strip of meat as a treat for his work. He stepped in closer and kneeled beside the body.

Brushing the thin layer of snow off a dark robe, he uncovered a grisly sight. The monk looked to have been in his mid-twenties. Little cuts covered his face. All made with a small knife. One about the size of Aleni's.

He inspected the body, pulling back ripped bits of fabric. There weren't many layers under the robe. Jacek wondered how he had kept warm enough. Maybe they were under a vow of suffering? More slashes and stab wounds dotted the body. But nothing fatal. The man must have bled to death. The image of the shredded boar came to mind suddenly. The cuts seemed haphazard and unplanned. Not precise and measured. Like the person was angry.

The robe had soaked with blood and then dried. More had soaked into the snow underneath him. The cuts had been done over some time. He scanned the walls of the buildings that made up the alleyway. A few spots of blood decorated the wood in places. There was no way this was all done here. There wasn't enough blood. Most of this had been done elsewhere and then finished here. But not dumped already deceased.

That would make sense if it was Aleni. She couldn't have carried a grown man here by herself, even with her added strength. And someone would notice it in the daylight. Possibly she had forced him here under duress and then finished him. No, he had to stop thinking it was her. Innocent until proven otherwise.

Bandur gave a whine from behind him. Jacek pivoted to find the dog sniffing at something under the snow. He unsheathed his knife and carefully wiped the snow away. Pink flesh appeared and Jacek winced. That would have hurt. In an unconscious move, he closed his legs protectively.

Turning back to the body, he couldn't help but lift the robe in the pelvis area with the tip of his knife and inspect the damage. Ouch. Somebody had been mad. Could it be Aleni? Could she inflict that kind of pain on someone? He thought he knew her enough that she wouldn't. But anger and fear did strange things to people. Maybe it was even stronger in elves? She was a teenager, after all. They were more driven by emotions than adults.

He let the cloth drop and got to his feet. This disturbed him. And he had been putting bodies in the snow for twenty years. But whether it was the nature of the death, or the possibility it could be Aleni, Jacek couldn't decide.

He let his gaze wander around the street at the end of the alley. People had to have seen something. Or heard something. He straightened and led Bandur out of the alley. The house across the street had a family in it. Two young boys played in the hovel's doorway. He walked over.

The two boys looked up at him, their mouths open in a silent 'o'. They froze.

"Hey! Get away from them!" An older girl ran toward him from farther back in the house, holding a broom like she was going to sweep him away. Her face was a storm of anger and fear. Jacek wasn't sure what she intended to do with the broom, but he stopped and took a few steps back. He didn't want to inadvertently hurt her if she swiped at him.

He raised his hands in the air to show he wasn't holding any weapons. "I'm not here to hurt you. I just want to ask you some questions."

The girl shooed the boys inside the house and stood in the doorway with the broom held out in front of her with both hands. Her mouth sat in a tight line. "We're not interested. You won't get anything out of us!"

Jacek sighed. There was little point in pushing for answers here. He would not interrogate her for information. She was just a kid. Not much older than Aleni. He waved a dismissing hand at her and walked on to the next house.

"What do you want?" The woman who answered his knock peered at him through rheumy eyes. She probably wasn't a good eyewitness.

"I'm investigating the murder that happened in the alley yesterday. Did you hear anything?" Jacek tried to sound as friendly as he could, but with his deep gravely tones he wasn't sure he'd achieved it. Aleni would have got her talking in no time.

"Didn't hear anything." She slammed the door in his face.

So much for that. If she had heard anything, she was probably too afraid or too smart to say anything. He tried the house next to the alley.

A thin dark man answered the door, eyeballing Jacek up and down with a wary look. "You selling something? I don't know you, do I?" He narrowed his eyes at the assassin.

Jacek sighed again. He hated talking to people. "No, you don't know me. And I'm not selling anything."

"Then why would you knock on my door? You here to kill me?" He took a step back ready to close it.

Jacek put out a hand on the door to stop him. "No! I'm just looking for information. Did you hear or see anything to do with the murder yesterday in the alley?"

The man looked like he was about to object, but then he paused. "Heard some screaming."

"Did you look out when this was happening?"

"Why would I do a stupid thing like that?" The man gave him an incredulous look. "Do I look suicidal to you?" He pointed to himself. "That sort of thing happens around here, and anyone who sticks their nose in, gets it cut off!"

Jacek gritted his teeth. The man was right, not many people would have investigated screaming. They would have shut their doors and waited for it to be over. Safer that way. "So you didn't hear any voices?"

"No." The man gave him another once over with his beady gaze. "It wasn't you, was it?"

Jacek shook his head in frustration and let go of the door. He walked back out into the street, moving north. Bandur trotted along beside him. He gave the dog a pat, glad for his company. He hadn't spent as much time with the mutt lately since Aleni was so attached to him. He sometimes missed the times it was just them. Not that he would change having Aleni around. But it had been simpler with just the two of them. Not necessarily better though.

He sent Bandur on the hunt again, and they scouted the area, looking for the other bodies. It took time, but they eventually came upon another one in an alley a few blocks away.

This body had been killed earlier than the last and had frozen solid in the snow. Jacek wondered if anyone would come to claim it. It seemed the brotherhood of the Creed of Redemption weren't very loyal to their constituents. No surprise there. From what he'd seen on the road to Resahil, they shed no tears for the two monks who had died.

Similar cuts marked this man, the blood soaking further around the body here. However, there were not as many, and some looked a lot deeper than the ones on the other body. This man had died quicker. The murderer had learned something from this one and escalated with the latest body. They were torturing them. But for what? Information? Pleasure? Practice?

If he answered that question, he might know who did it for sure. Could Aleni be practicing advanced interrogation on these people? Something he refused to teach her. Maybe she'd taken matters into her own hands. How would he deal with that? He did not know.

Again, the man's sex had been cut off and discarded to the side. Jacek didn't even bother looking for it. Bandur was sitting at the entrance to the alley, keeping watch. He was probably sick of sticking his nose in dead bodies.

Time to go. That was all he was going to get from here. There were no footprints or clues left by the killer to identify them. They weren't in it for the fame.

It was late morning by now. A light snow had begun, leaving the streets somewhat emptier. What else could he do to figure out what was going on? He pulled his collar closer and set off to find a monk.

Chapter Twelve

Only a few statues remained in Amathnore left over from the elven empire. The war had badly damaged most of them, but four endured. Selendria's current inhabitants weren't particularly inclined toward artistic expression. Most of the poorer denizens spent their energy on surviving in any way they could, while the richer ones spent their time getting richer. The four surviving elven statues comprised all the art in the city. One of those pieces sat in the east ward - a sleek, scaled dragon curving skyward. Carved from stone, the locals had smoothed the ancient artwork's lines over the years by touching it as they passed. It was believed it would bring them luck.

Jacek wasn't standing behind it for luck, however. At over seven and a half feet tall, the statue provided just enough cover to keep him out of plain sight. He was watching a monk standing on a street corner across from him. The man, wrapped well in a cowled habit, the hood up, was trying to get people's attention as they walked by in order to preach his message. He had had little luck so far. Maybe he needed to rub the dragon first. Jacek eyed the statue ruefully.

The monk shivered on his street corner. Few people were passing as the snow fell harder. Jacek pulled his fur-lined hood up over his head. Finally, after no one had come near in quite some time, the monk gave up and headed for home. Jacek hoped it was home, anyway. Now, with the streets mostly empty, would be a perfect time for the killer to act. Jacek followed at a distance.

The monk, a younger man with thin dark hair and a slight build, wore his cowl up over his head, which made following him a lot easier. No peripheral vision. As it was, Jacek had put his hood back down to make sure he wasn't being followed. He was used to the snow and cold on his head. Better than being dead.

With Bandur beside him, he tracked through the growing snow, trying not to make too much noise. He kept his head down, as though he was just on his way home. Fur around his collar kept the snow from falling down his leather jerkin.

They moved steadily east, heading toward the large citadel that used to belong to Krodon's father. The monk turned down a right-of-way between two buildings as a shortcut to the next street over. When he was halfway through, Jacek turned in as well.

At the other end of the right-of-way, a figure appeared. A man, just under six feet tall, paused as if he was turning in. Jacek caught his eye, and the man tipped his fingers at his forehead toward Jacek in acknowledgment. He looked vaguely familiar to the assassin, but he couldn't place him.

The man moved on after a moment. Was he the killer? Or could he just have been about to use the same right-of-way but decided not to because it was already busy with two other people? Impossible to tell. Where had he seen the man before?

Jacek couldn't remember. His memory wasn't what it used to be. He was getting older, he knew it. Even with his new lease on life since the healing elven stone had magically cured him, he was still ageing. There was no changing that. It hadn't made him any younger.

The coast clear, the monk carried on, possibly none the wiser. Jacek followed him to the entrance of the old fortress and left him there.

"Well, Bandur, it was worth a try." He patted the dog's neck. Bandur leaned into him, soaking in the affection. "Let's head back."

They trudged back through the streets to the boarding house. The madam yelled at him for traipsing wet boots into the place, but he ignored her. Clomping up to their room, he opened the door.

The room was empty.

He gritted his teeth as pressure built up in his head and chest. Letting out a wordless yell, he thrust his fist into the nearest wall. The thin wood gave way beneath the force, caving into a splintery hole. Bandur gave a whine and stepped away from him.

Jacek pulled his fist back out, noting one knuckle had opened, leaving a trail of blood down his fingers. He watched the blood in silence, breathing slowly and deeply to calm himself. What was he going to do with Aleni? She was out of control. She no longer obeyed him and even gave him the sweet and innocent act with the braiding of her hair while plotting to run away.

An outcry from downstairs broke the spell of his reverie.

"What are you doing up there? Are you damaging my room? I'll have to charge you more now! Don't even think of running off without paying!" The woman raged on. Jacek stopped listening after a while. He had to think. Where would Aleni go? He had to look for her.

He trotted back down the stairs to the sound of the madam still yelling at him. She had a colorful vocabulary for a woman. Jacek retrieved olons from his coin purse and put them on the bench for her.

She shut her mouth finally and just gave him a hard stare. She certainly wasn't afraid of him.

"My apologies, madam, this is to pay for the damage. Did you see where my daughter went earlier?"

The madam gave a huff of air, obviously not pleased at him. But her face softened slightly at the mention of Aleni. "Ah yes, sweet girl. I saw her heading off toward the northern ward."

Jacek bobbed his head. "My thanks." He walked out, Bandur in tow.

North. It was a start. Could she have gone home? Or maybe back to the street kids? She was adamant yesterday that they were in trouble. Maybe she went back to help them. He would try with them first.

The snow had stopped now, and a few people had come out of their houses to clear the fresh dumping from their stoops. They had fashioned large shovels made from the curved bark of nearby trees. The richer people used metal shovels and servants, but here in the poorer wards, people made do with what they could.

As they saw Jacek with his dog, they scuttled back into their homes and closed the doors. He was determined to find Aleni, and his face must have shown it. It was also probably similar to his knife-in-your-gullet look as well. All the better. He didn't need anyone bothering him right now.

He set a quick pace through the streets, Bandur sometimes having to canter to catch up to him. The dog smelled around the ground, possibly looking for Aleni's scent, but there wouldn't be much after the fresh layer of snow. However, it didn't hurt to try.

"Bandur! Here boy." Jacek kneeled down to get to the dog's eye level. He grabbed the mutt by the sides of his head and looked him in the eye. "Where's Aleni? Can you find Aleni?"

The dog whined and Jacek let him go. Bandur took off at a run. Jacek wasn't sure if he'd actually smelled something, or if he just picked a direction to run in. Either way, he followed.

Through the streets they ran, Bandur barking from time to time, changing directions at intersections and even sometimes doubling back to sniff at the ground in places. Jacek was losing hope he had any scent at all. They were now certainly closer to the northern ward. They'd skirted around the center of town and the market square, and were now closing in on the Arena.

From the sounds of the crowd, there was a show on today. Could she have gone here to watch the fight? Bandur looked at the large stone amphitheater and barked. It was also entirely possible the dog had smelled the meat being cooked outside it for the patrons. What should he do?

Jacek stood in the street outside the Arena for a moment. Smoothing his graying beard, he looked around him. There was no sign of Aleni. People were milling around the various stalls set up outside the Arena to sell food and treats to the Arena patrons. Inside, the crowd roared with delight at the clashes of steel on steel. It was a bloodthirsty place, and Jacek had fought there himself many years ago in order to make money. He grew his name in the Arena.

He hadn't been back in a long time. He wasn't proud of what he'd done there. He'd told Aleni as much. Maybe it was the mystery of it that allured her to it. Maybe he should have told her more about it, so she wasn't curious. Either way, he'd better look for her in the stands.

After paying the price for admission to the burly guards at the gate, he walked in with Bandur and took his first look of the place.

The elves had originally built the Arena. They had probably used it for the Performing Arts or something similar. Tarken, Krodon's father, had turned it into a bloodthirsty sporting arena. People fought to the death here, and the slushy mix of snow and mud on the arena floor was permanently stained red now. It brought in a lot of money for the organizers in bets and entry fees. In this world, even the poor found a way to get in and get a piece of the action. Sadly, it was the only entertainment the city offered.

Jacek paid the entry fee and stepped through the gate. The crowd filled the Arena in rows of seating that slanted up from the edge of the fighting ring up to the stone walls all the way at the back. The best seats were closest to the ring, just behind a wooden wall erected to keep the crowd away from the fighters and the fighters in the ring until it was over. Not all fighters were there by choice.

Two swords clashed in the center of the ring, followed by grunts of effort. These two looked to be volunteers, based off their clothing, but Jacek could tell the slightly bigger one would have the upper hand soon. His footwork was good, and he swung the weapon with more proficiency than his opponent. It wouldn't be long now. Unless the smaller man was toying with him.

Jacek made his way up the nearest aisle to the back of the seating, watching carefully for Aleni in the crowd. People instinctively moved away from him and Bandur where they could.

He walked over close to the organizers' seating. It was a walled-in box just for the owners of the Arena. Tarken had had it built just for him and his servants so he could oversee the show. Right now it was filled with wealthy merchants. Jacek leaned up against the wooden wall, his arms crossed, the top of the wall ending just over his head. With his eyes he roamed the stands, watching for a small person with white hair. Although on second thoughts, she would probably wear her hood up, so it was entirely possible he would miss her.

He listened to the conversation of the merchants.

"Videer is going to win, Palim." The first man had a self-satisfied smirk to his tone.

"What? Balaac is clearly the better fighter! How could you know that?" The second voice, Palim, had a raspier quality to it.

"Because this is my Arena, and I call the shots here."

Palim's voice grew sulky. "Well, you could have told me that before I made a bet on Balaac."

"I stopped you from making too large a bet, didn't I? I can't give away all my secrets too soon."

"Surely to me you could, Vossler. How long have we worked together?"

"Probably too long, but never mind, what's done is done. Balaac will take a fall. He is being paid handsomely for it."

"If he survives."

Vossler made a non-committal noise.

Jacek watched as the bigger man appeared then to stumble on something and go down on his back. Videer pressed in quickly and jumped on him, sword pointed at Balaac's throat. The crowd roared in approval at the sudden change of events. Many leaped to their feet and leaned toward the ring to get closer to the action. People in front of Jacek blocked his view temporarily, but he heard the unmistakable sound of metal sliding through flesh and knew Balaac wouldn't be getting his payday.

Clapping came from the merchant's box.

Jacek closed his eyes at the sound, a bitter taste in his mouth. When did he get like this? He had been inured to violence for years. He had even killed people in the ring himself.

But this seemed senseless now. Especially after seeing it through Aleni's eyes the first time they had come through Amathnore together. She had been perplexed by the idea of people fighting and killing each other for sport. Now, after spending a year with her, perhaps her ideals had rubbed off on him. Now, he recoiled from the memories of his time in the ring.

Once the people in front sat down again, huddling together for warmth against the frigid open air, Jacek watched as two men carried Balaac's body away through a set of gates to a closed off area beyond. Jacek remembered the area well. There was a pen in the back for the dumping of bodies until after the spectacle. They were then carted off on a wagon and dumped out in the woods or in the harbor. It was a grim reminder after every fight for the next contestants up.

A tall, thin man walked out into the middle of the ring. He wore thick, expensive furs, showing he was well-paid and important. His voice was strong and carried clearly throughout the Arena.

"Wasn't that an incredible fight?" Although he was nearly standing in a fresh pool of Balaac's blood, he had a huge grin on his face. The crowd cheered at his words.

"Just when it looked like Balaac would prevail, the tables turned and he was overcome in the heat of glorious battle! What a tale of victory for Videer!" He held out one arm in the victor's direction. Videer raised both arms in triumph, turning in a circle to show himself to the audience. The crowd roared, standing to their feet again.

Jacek sighed, tired of the theatrics. Where was Aleni? He hadn't spotted her yet in the crowd. Perhaps he should move around further?

When the crowd seated themselves again, Videer walked out of the ring through the gates. The announcer remained.

"We have a special showcase for you today. The return of one of our newest and youngest fighters. This young one has been working her way through our ranks like a scythe through wheat." A few started cheering and clapping, the crowd growing with excitement. Jacek sat up straighter, his heart pounding against his ribs. It couldn't be, could it?

"You know her, you've seen her, she's the one and only Elyon!" The announcer, his voice risen to a fever pitch, turned with a flourish to face the gates that were opening again.

Jacek uncrossed his arms, his right hand going to his axe at his waist instinctively. He didn't remove it from its loop, however. He waited.

As the crowd cheered again, they stood, people directly in front of Jacek blocking his view briefly. He raised himself to his full height, moving to peer between heads. Bandur let out a bark, but Jacek barely noticed.

From out of the gates, Aleni walked into the ring, a sword in hand. Jacek's heart leaped into his throat.

⁓⁂⁓

Icas struggled with the little girl on his way to Sesk's chambers. She was bound at the hands and gagged, but her feet were free. He held her tightly by the arm and half-dragged her along.

At one point, she planted her feet and resisted him, her dark eyes burning with defiance.

Icas stopped, nearly letting her go. "If you don't walk, I'll have to carry you, and that won't be dignified."

The young dark-haired girl hardened her gaze, but she took another step. She had grit; he had to admit. Being a street kid though, that would harden her. But she looked to only be about eight years old. And her teeth looked too good to have been a street kid for long. How had she ended up there?

He'd grown up with parents, but they didn't care a whit about him. Never touched him, sometimes forgot to feed him, and he often wore tatters until he made enough noise for them to buy him something warmer. The streets had seemed like an attractive option at the time.

Once he was old enough to look after himself, he took off on his own. He'd been self-sufficient ever since. Selling his services as an information gatherer. Over the years, he'd grown a contact network all over Selendria. Now he was one of the most sought after spies.

He realized as he half-dragged her along, that he felt sorry for her. She had obviously done well to survive this long, only to be taken by the old man just because he wanted her power stone. Something about it didn't sit nicely with him. She was so young, after all.

But, a job was a job. Sesk paid, so he did it.

They reached Sesk's chambers, and he entered, pulling her behind him. When she saw the old man, she struggled again, but Icas threatened to slap her and she calmed.

"Ah, there you are. This is the girl with the power stone?" Sesk stood in front of his desk with his hands behind his back.

Icas retrieved the stone from his pocket and handed it over to Sesk. "It seems to give off warmth."

Sesk pawed over the stone, stroking it lovingly. It glowed with a reddish color, increasing the heat in the room. "Where did you get this, girl?"

Icas removed the gag. The girl shook her hair free and worked her mouth open and shut. She did not reply.

Sesk stepped closer. "I said, where did you get this?" He held out the stone in front of her face.

She just stared back at him in defiance.

Sesk swung a backhand at her face. Icas had to hold her arm to stop her from falling. He held her firmly, but gently. He didn't need to be cruel. Sesk brought enough of that.

She straightened herself, rubbing with her bound hands at her cheek. A red mark blossomed where Sesk's hand had connected. Finally, her eyes held fear. She obviously hadn't experienced much violence in her short life.

"Tell me!"

Tears formed in her angular eyes. "It was my mothers," she said between sobs. "It was just a normal stone until this girl came along and changed it."

"Changed it? How? Who was this girl?"

"Sh-she had white hair. And magic. She changed the picture on the stone and then cut her hand and touched it to it. It glowed real bright and then went red." She gulped down another sob and glanced up at Icas, her eyes pleading at him.

Oh gods, those eyes. Focus on the stones around the fireplace. Don't look at her. What was wrong with him? He'd never gotten soft on a mark before.

"Hmm, interesting." Sesk studied the stone in his hand. "Blood, you say. Were her ears pointed?"

"I-I don't know. She had them covered with a scarf."

"Ah. Of course. Deep blue eyes, pale skin? About this high?" He held his hand out.

The little girl nodded.

"Right. Thank you for the information." Sesk turned his head to Icas. "You can get rid of her now."

He jolted. "Get rid of her? As in, kill her?"

"Of course. She's a loose end."

"Right." Icas turned to the door and pulled her along with him.

"Wait! What are you going to do with me?" The little girl protested. He would have to gag her again. But he didn't want to kill her. He drew the line at killing kids. Killing anyone, really. He was a spy, not an assassin. Sesk had overestimated his ruthlessness.

Maybe Vossler would take her. Then at least she would be alive.

Chapter Thirteen

Aleni marched into the ring with determination. This was it. This was what she had been working toward. The big fight. She would finally prove, both to the crowd and to herself that she could win. That she could look after herself. That she could protect herself from anything.

Hiding it from Jacek had been difficult. She longed to tell him, but knew he would never approve. If he didn't let her along to the jobs he did, there was no way he would allow her to fight in the arena. He must never find out. This would be her last fight, then she would end it.

After the crowd settled back down, she stood a few feet from the announcer, waiting patiently for her opponent to enter. The leather grip of the sword in her hand was cold but reassuring. Somewhere, a dog barked. It reminded her of Bandur. She was glad he was with Jacek, but she missed him now. Even though this was her fight, she longed to have the dog by her side.

She was on her own today. Holding herself tall and straight, she tried to exude confidence and competence. She puffed her budding chest out to convince both the crowd and herself that she was ready.

But the truth was, it still scared her. Every time a fighter came out of those gates toward her, her heart leaped and her stomach curdled. Her body trembled with fear. Every fighter had been a man. Every one bigger than her, and every single one reminding her of Krodon. No matter how many she faced, her body reacted the same. She had thought that by facing them over and over again, she would become immune to it, but it almost seemed to increase. Her own dread each time just added to the fear. When would she be free of this?

Finally, her opponent sauntered out of the big iron gate. A mountain of a man, bristling with muscle and carrying a large two-handed sword and a shield. His name was Broggar the Fierce. The latter part obviously added by himself. However, this would be tough. At least he would be slow. That was her advantage. She was fast. But one hit from him, even with a fist, would be enough to take her down. She had to avoid that at all costs.

The arena went quiet as Broggar stepped further forward. An icy breeze whipped past Aleni's face. The dirty slush under her feet crunched. The announcer skittered out of the ring; the gates closing with a finality after him. Aleni gritted her teeth and focused in on the man in front of her. She paced slowly to the left, gripping her sword and watching his movements. She hadn't seen him fight yet. Having to be back in the woods with Jacek meant she wasn't around to see all the fights. Did he have a weakness? Was there a set of moves he stuck to, or was he a man of all disciplines?

Broggar didn't waste time parading around. He rushed in, swinging at her on a downward arc. Aleni dodged to the side, and the fight was on.

Jacek couldn't believe what he was seeing. How had he not known? She had deliberately hidden this from him. Why? Deep down he knew the answer. Because he would have forbidden her, of course. What was she thinking? She could be killed.

Bandur barked again, clearly agitated. Jacek put a calming hand on the dog's head, knowing how he felt. Conflicting emotions rang through him. Fury, frustration, fear, but then pride. Aleni would be the smallest and youngest fighter the Arena had ever seen. And she had obviously won every round she'd fought. And somehow they didn't know she was an elf. She had at least kept that a secret. A headscarf folded tightly into a wide band around her head covered her ears, letting her white braid flow out underneath it.

Then all the tension inside left him and he let out a huge breath as realization hit.

This meant she wasn't the killer.

If she had been here fighting all the times she'd been in town, she most likely didn't have time to stalk and kill monks. The time she had come home covered in blood would have been because of this, not because she was a serial killer. He wiped a trembling hand down his face and tried to breathe evenly.

Jacek pushed his way closer to the edge of the ring. He made sure there were a couple of people in front of him, so Aleni didn't notice him. The last thing she needed was to see him at a crucial moment and lose concentration. That would be a death sentence for her. Even gripping the top of his axe, he knew she was a capable fighter. She had made it this far. He owed it to her to at least see this out. If something bad happened, he was close enough to jump the fence and help. He kept a firm grip on Bandur's fur to make sure the dog didn't jump over ahead of him. Bandur knew she was there, letting out a little whine, his body poised to spring. Jacek held him tight on the ruff of his neck.

Broggar was taller even than Jacek. He dwarfed Aleni, whose mere five feet made her look tiny and easily crushable. Thankfully, Jacek knew better. She was stronger than she looked. And she possessed her elven speed.

He watched the large fighter carefully, assessing him. He was definitely strong, and it probably would only take one strike from him to kill Aleni, but his footwork wasn't the best. Jacek guessed he had trained to use his size as an advantage, leaving out movement as a priority. Footwork was incredibly important, especially for someone like Aleni. She needed to dodge out of the way of a strike more than she needed to block.

When Broggar made his first move at her, a gigantic downward blow that would have split her in half, he knew that even blocking was useless here. If she blocked a blow like that, it would shatter her arm, elf or not.

She easily dodged the blow, moving to the side to get out of the way. She wasn't moving at her full speed, possibly aware not to alert people to her preternatural abilities. Or maybe she wanted this to be a fair fight.

Broggar righted himself quickly from the miss, turning to face her again. She stood at the ready, her sword up in front. She held no shield, but Jacek knew that would be useless for her anyway. She smiled at Broggar. Not in a friendly way, but in the way a predator would look at prey. Jacek allowed a smile of his own.

The crowd shouted various encouragements at the two fighters as they circled each other. Broggar stepped in again and swung a right-to-left strike at her head. She ducked and moved toward him, under his sword arm. Broggar righted himself quickly and jumped back out of the way, avoiding her sword aimed at his groin. He was faster than he looked.

He pushed out with his shield at her in retaliation. She jumped back lithely.

Jacek could hear Broggar from the stands, as the fighter raised his voice for the benefit of the crowd.

"You're going to die here, little girl. I don't care if you're a child. Means nothing to me. I will crush you like a bug." He stamped his foot to drive home his words.

"Promises, promises," Aleni replied with a straight face.

Aleni feinted toward Broggar with a side strike that looked for all the world like she was committing to it. Broggar blocked it with his own large blade, but as he did, she spun around and slashed into his back from behind. It was an incredibly fast move bordering on being not humanly possible. Jacek looked around at the crowd to see if there was an unusual reaction. But the people only cheered.

Broggar arched his back in pain, grimacing. Aleni danced away as he stumbled slightly. This would have been a good moment to strike at him further, but she seemed content to stand back and see what he would do.

The crowd roared with approval, and it looked like Aleni was playing to them. She knew the game. Please the crowd and you were even more likely to win in the long run. Not all fights were won on ability alone. Jacek knew this. And from the conversation he'd overheard before, the last fight was testimony to this.

Aleni darted around her opponent, circling quickly to keep him from constantly looking out for her. She moved fast, but not inhumanly fast. Not enough to give herself away. Broggar was sliced a couple more times, on the leg and the upper arm, before he started roaring in pain and frustration. The crowd loved it.

Aleni smiled up at the crowd and lifted her sword up in the air to encourage them. They screamed their approval even more. She moved in once more for another strike, but Broggar was ready. He took the slice of her blade across his chest, cutting through thick leather, but probably barely cutting him underneath. Jacek watched with dismay as his shield came around and hit Aleni full on in the face.

Her small body went flying back with the force of the blow. A full second felt like an eternity before she hit the ground, landing hard on her back. The mud and snow thankfully softened her landing, but the strike to her face had clearly stunned her.

Jacek gripped the head of his axe with such force his knuckles popped. He leaned in, focused only on his daughter, willing her to get up. Blood poured down over her mouth and chin from her nose. It looked broken. She was trying to lift her head up, but he suspected her vision was swimming.

"Get up," he whispered. "Come on, girl, get up." He prepared himself to leap in if needed. Broggar was taking the moment to congratulate himself in front of the crowd. Blood poured from his wounds as well, so he was probably covering for a moment to rest.

Bandur barked a few times, as though he sensed Aleni's distress. Perhaps he did. The dog could not see over the wall into the Arena, but Jacek had long sensed there was a magical link between the two.

Aleni still hadn't gotten to her feet. "Get up!" Jacek yelled. The crowd drowned out his voice.

Broggar finished his parading and turned back to Aleni. He raised his sword and shield and stepped toward her.

Chapter Fourteen

The gray clouds, threatening to drop more snow – always more snow - blurred in the sky. Aleni blinked her eyes rapidly to clear her vision. Pain exploded out from her nose, and she could feel a warm wetness on her lips and chin. She tasted the iron tang of blood and from the crunch she felt on impact, knew the blow broke her nose. How did she not see that coming? She had got complacent and dropped her guard. The fear had gone and with it her instincts.

Now the fear returned. Maybe it wasn't such a bad thing. Maybe it kept her sharp. Shaking her head to clear it only increased the pain. Movement in front of her had her lifting her head to see what was happening. Broggar stood over her, his sword held aloft with both hands.

He brought the sword down, aiming for her chest. She rolled. The sword plunged deep into the ground.

Where was her own sword? She looked around for the weapon but couldn't see it. Broggar tried to pull his sword out of the Arena floor.

There. Her sword lay on the ground just past him. Great. Spitting blood out onto the ground, she took her knife from her belt, holding it point down in a fist.

Broggar finally ripped the enormous blade from the ground and brought it up in a firm grip. It shone wet from the slush of the arena floor. Comparatively, her knife looked ridiculous.

Broggar laughed, deep and throaty. "Are you planning to sting me, little bee?"

"I'm planning to kill you." As the words came out, the question rose in her mind, unbidden. Was she really? She had avoided killing so far. The only time she had before the Arena was in self-defense. There was also the slight matter of the organizer coming to her before the fight, asking her to take a fall and let Broggar win. She had scoffed at that, thinking they were joking at first. But they held their faces as straight as a measuring pole.

So while she was not willing to take a fall, was she willing to kill instead? She had no answer yet.

"You can try." Broggar laughed again.

Her vision finally clearing, Aleni sprinted toward him and leaped. Broggar swung his sword. She dropped just before reaching him. His sword missed the top of her head by inches. She let her feet give out under her so she could slide over the wet snow at his feet, light as a feather. Aleni sliced at his left boot. Made of a soft leather, it cut through easily. Blood gushed out, and he cried out in agony.

She let her body slide on past and sprang to her feet, grabbing her sword as she rose.

Broggar was screaming, trying to grab at his ruined leg. It hung uselessly, the foot flopping unnaturally on the end of the limb. His fighting days were over. He knew it too. He hopped on one leg to turn toward her, hate in his eyes.

He screamed at her. "You have to die now, little bee!"

The crowd roared at his words. There was a mixture of both their names being called out in support now.

Aleni watched him with pity. He would be a cripple for the rest of his miserable life now. And for what? Because he fought in a rigged competition for the entertainment of the masses and the rich? Aleni looked around at the Arena, seeing it now for what it really was. For how she'd seen it back in the beginning. Before she'd gotten fearful and angry and needed to prove herself. It was a pathetic spectacle. Her parents would not be proud of her. She had just ruined a man's life. And he was no Krodon. He had done nothing to her.

What had she done? Her face went numb as the blood drained out of it.

Broggar was trying to hop toward her. He had dropped the shield and the free arm waved up in the air to balance himself. He just looked ridiculous now. Aleni easily ducked and dodged the swings. As he got closer, she heard him whisper to her.

"Kill me. Please."

She raised her eyebrows at that. Did she hear correctly?

"Please. You've won. Finish the job. I can't live like this. It would be humiliating."

A mercy killing. Something she couldn't even do for Krodon after breaking nearly every bone in his body. And he had raped her and kept her captive. But Broggar was different. He was simply her opponent in a game.

He swung weakly again, an overhead chop she easily moved aside for. As she did, she decided. She jumped and tucked her feet up to land on his chest. Simultaneously, she drove her knife directly into his throat.

Broggar let out a gasp as he tried to breathe instinctively, but he closed his eyes. In relief? His sword dropped from his hand and he toppled backwards like a tree being felled.

Aleni rode his chest all the way down, her hand still on her knife.

Around them, the crowd jumped to their feet, screaming and roaring in glee at the bloodshed. The noise was cacophonous. But all Aleni could hear was the barely audible words only her elven hearing could have picked up in the clamor.

"Thank you."

She closed her eyes and hoped she wouldn't regret this.

***

Jacek sighed, his muscles finally relaxing. It was over. She was alright. They would have a long talk after this, but he was just relieved she had won at this point.

The announcer walked back into the ring. His face didn't look happy. What was this? She had won, hadn't she? The man looked up at the box where the organizers sat. Jacek followed his line of sight. He hadn't been able to see them before, but now from where he stood he could see three men sitting in the walled off area. Only two had spoken while he'd been listening, but he could guess which voice belonged to who.

On the right was a large man wrapped in expensive fur-lined clothing in green that had not even a speck of dirt on it. He was smiling, but not kindly. The one in the middle was a thin graying man with small eyes and a pinched look on his face. He was bald on top, but the back was grown out long and tied back at the nape of his neck. He didn't look happy. He gave a hand signal to the announcer that Jacek knew well. His blood ran cold, and he knew he had to hurry.

Pushing the people in front of him out of the way, he launched himself over the half wall to the Arena floor. Bandur scrabbled up after him. Weapons clanking, he moved directly for Aleni.

His daughter turned at the commotion, and her eyes widened.

"What are you doing here?" She looked horrified to see him. Bandur trotted up to her happily, jumping up to plant his front paws on her chest. She gave the dog a quick squeeze and a pat and pushed him down again.

"We are going to have a talk later, you and I, but for now, I'm getting you out of here." Jacek grabbed her by the arm and turned toward the gate.

"Stop! Why?" She didn't quite pull against him, but she wasn't aiding him either.

"Because things are about to turn to shit. Did you get asked to take a fall?" He turned his head to look at her.

She didn't reply straight away, instead looking back at the body of Broggar. When she spoke, it was quiet. "Yes."

"They don't like being defied."

They moved toward the open gates the announcer had come through, but before they could get there, the gates closed. Jacek heard the bar sliding across the other side. Trapped. He looked around the Arena and watched as armed men circled in to stand behind the wall of the ring. Blocking their escape. He finally let go of Aleni and drew his axe, advancing on the announcer who stood there looking nervous.

"You let us out of here, now!"

"It - it's you! You're..." he trailed off, pointing his finger at Jacek. "I-I'm sorry, I can't do that." The man glanced up at the organizer's box and back to Jacek, backing away slowly. Jacek advanced on him, but the man ran for the wall. With the help of one of the armed men, he scrambled over it.

Jacek bared his teeth at the soldiers, who held out pikes ready to strike if he got closer. He wasn't getting anywhere that way. He returned to Aleni and Bandur.

The crowd was now unsettled. Jacek felt a murmur run through the people, most of them unsure of what was going on. He had some idea, but they would have to wait and see.

"People of Amathnore!" The announcer now shouted from the organizer's box and the crowd quietened. "We have a special treat for you today! It looks like the Red Hunter has joined us once again for a special fight. Is Elyon your daughter?" The announcer had a smile on his face now, pointing to Aleni. However, the smile was not friendly.

Jacek didn't reply. He gripped the handle of his axe, savoring the comforting feel of the leather grip in his hand.

"Now we will all watch the fight of the century, as you both show us what you are really made of. The most legendary fighter of the Arena, the Red Hunter! And the newest and youngest champion of our day, against..." With a flourish he swung his arm toward the big iron gates. They slowly opened.

"Ready yourself," Jacek said in a low voice to Aleni. "Anything could come through those gates."

Aleni wiped her sleeve across her mouth to clear the blood. Her nose throbbed with pain. She nodded, gripping both her knife and her sword. Bandur stood between them, feet planted and eyes straight ahead at the gates.

There was a low growl and out from between the opening doors came a pack of goblins, pushed out by guards with pikes. There were five of them, and by the looks of the iron rings around their necks, they had been in captivity. The crowd let out a gasp of shock and then immediately turned into a frenzy of shouting and moving around to lay new bets.

Jacek let out a curse and backed up further to give them room, making sure Aleni followed his lead.

The goblins looked pleased to be let out of wherever they had been kept, moving around on the spot in a creepy dance. Their green skin glistened in the afternoon light. The biggest one saw the three of them in the middle of the Arena and snarled something at his pack mates. All five goblins narrowed in on them.

"Remember what I taught you about fighting a group. It applies here as well."

"I remember."

"Don't let them get you on the ground. You're dead then."

"I've got it." Aleni was sounding testy. Fair enough. His stress levels were certainly rising. If it was just him, it wouldn't be so bad, but with Aleni here too, there was more for him to worry about. He had to use all his wits if they were going to get through this alive. He didn't have his bow this time, to even the odds. Not even his usual bag of smoke bombs.

Goblins were fast, strong and vicious creatures. They had outlived the elves and were the dominant predators of humans in Selendria now. People in large groups hunted them, as fighting one on one with a goblin was usually a death sentence. Last time he had come up against them, after Aleni had run away from him early on, he had been lucky to fire at them from a distance, evening the numbers up quickly. Aleni had been extremely lucky they wanted to toy with her first.

Now they faced five goblins who were probably hungry, desperate and angry. Not a wonderful combination. Curse the organizers of this bloody Arena. Jacek glanced up at them, safe in their box. The fat man sat with a self-satisfied smirk. He would pay later for this.

The goblins moved as one toward them, all bunched in a group. Three went down on all fours to get their speed up. Jacek bent his knees and tensed his muscles in readiness. Based on their formation, Jacek positioned himself so only one could attack at a time. Bandur barked in warning at the goblins, then growled deep in his throat.

When they clashed, it was chaos. Jacek swung his axe at the first one's head. It whipped itself to the side to avoid the strike. A second one launched itself at him. It screeched with claws out to rake his face. A furry body slammed into the goblin from the side. Both goblin and dog went down hard to the ground.

But Jacek didn't have time to watch that fight, as he still had the first one on him. Swinging his axe, he was keeping him at bay. Where had the other three gone? No way could Aleni take on three adult goblins on her own.

Out of the corner of his eye, he spotted she was fighting with one in front of her, with another creeping up to the side.

Jacek pulled out his knife and threw it at its back. With a meaty thwack, it dug in deep. The goblin grunted and paused. It tried to reach for the knife, but it was lodged solidly between the bony shoulder blades. It couldn't reach it. However, it hadn't crippled the creature at all. Eventually it gave up and turned on Jacek instead.

Chapter Fifteen

Aleni focused on keeping the goblin in front of her at bay. It had two tiny horns protruding from its chin, which differed from the others. It was shorter, and its skin was a little more on the gray side.

She wondered if it was a female.

She didn't have time to wonder long, however, as the goblin was swinging at her with its claws outstretched, trying to maul her face.

It forced Aleni to move at full speed to get out of the way. She returned the attack between swings, trying to lop an arm or hand off if she could. The goblin was just as fast.

The last goblin was now advancing on her, looking like it was waiting for permission from the one in front of her to get in. It bounced from one foot to the other, snarling and growling impatiently.

It took all Aleni's concentration to fight this one goblin. She did not know how she could fight two. Jacek had done it in the past, but... well, he was Jacek.

The goblin in front swiped at her face again, forcing her to bend backwards. As she did, the goblin on the side reached in quick as lightning and grabbed at her head. She wasn't quick enough to get away. It was only the folds of the headscarf that protected her from getting gouged by the claws, but in doing so, it caught the headscarf and ripped it right off.

The frigid air hit her suddenly bare ears like an icy whisper to the heart. Her blood ran cold as she realized it exposed her. The goblins both paused, taking a second to realize what she was. There was a gasp throughout the crowd as the humans saw her ears. She backed away from the goblins; her hands going immediately to the sides of her head. She was still holding her knife and sword, however, so it was awkward and clumsy. She gave up and put them back down.

What would the humans think of her now? She wasn't one of them after all. Would she still be their hero? She looked around at the crowd, but there was a hush, then low voices muttering. They were all looking at her, some with eyes wide, some puzzled and some angry. The goblins seemed to know what was going on, and they were enjoying the moment too. Waiting to pounce on her when she was distracted?

Glancing over at Jacek, her only haven in this Arena, she watched as he landed a solid forward kick on the goblin in front of him, sending the creature flying back, giving him some room to look around. He caught her eye and her predicament registered in his gaze. All the goblins had paused now.

One was lying still on the ground, Bandur standing over him. The goblin's throat had been ripped out. At least one of them had prevailed. She focused on the dog and called to him in her mind. Bandur sprang over the body of the goblin and rushed over to stand by her side. She gave him a quick reassuring pat.

Jacek ran over to her. "What happened?" He had a couple of deep scratches across his left cheek that were oozing blood, but otherwise seemed unhurt.

"The goblin got my headscarf." She pointed to the one still holding the scarf in its meaty claws.

Jacek looked around at the crowd. "Well, it's out now. I guess you don't have to hold back anymore. Watch out!"

He spun to face the goblins rushing at them both.

Suddenly tired of the whole thing, tired of getting attacked, and angry that the organizers had put them in this position, she sheathed her weapons and put her hands out in front of her. Drawing on her power within, she let out a force blast that hit all four goblins and sent them flying back to hit the gate of the arena hard.

The crowd gasped and there was a stunned silence for a few seconds. Then a tremendous cheer erupted. Aleni dropped her hands slowly, gazing around at the people in the audience. They clapped and roared approval, throwing fists into the air and jumping up and down.

"They like me, Jacek!"

"Yes, I see that. But not everyone." Jacek pointed up to the organizer's box.

The man in the middle wore a frown. He sat still, his arms crossed. The two on each side of him looked more curious than anything. Trying to figure out what she was? No one had seen an elf before, although there were descriptions of them handed down. The ears were a giveaway for sure, but being supposedly extinct, some might not piece it together straight away and think she was some other sort of unknown creature.

"We have to get out of here." Jacek said.

"Leave it to me." Aleni stepped forward, focusing again on the goblins. They were pulling themselves up off the ground and moving toward them. The anger aroused in her again, fueling the power gathering inside her.

This time when she let loose at them, fire bellowed out from her hands. It flew out to engulf the creatures whole.

There was a roaring in her ears as the fire burned hotter and hotter as it drew from the surrounding air to grow and expand. What was happening? She hadn't expected this at all, and her own shock at the bright expulsion from within her made her falter, the source sputtering.

"Keep going, kiddo!" Jacek yelled.

She gritted her teeth and renewed her effort. The flames grew in intensity. Realizing it was her anger that fueled it, she fed it more. Bringing images to mind that she often pushed down. Images she hated. While her stomach twisted at the unwanted memories, the fire from her hands grew.

But she did not know how long she could keep this up. She could already feel a pulling from her chest, almost like she was out of breath. There was an awful smell of cooking flesh. She couldn't see the goblins through the flames, but she could hear the screeching.

Her chest tightened more as the seconds went on. Her head felt light and her vision swam. Tears ran down her cheeks as her eyes burned with pain. She was killing something with this. It felt... wrong somehow, like it wasn't meant for this.

Suddenly her energy gave out. The fire from her hands halted and her knees buckled. Her vision went black and she only just stayed conscious through sheer force of will. Putting her hands out, she caught herself on the ground, hanging her head. A large hand gripped her shoulder. There was a sizzling sound coming from the direction of the goblins. She was glad at this point she couldn't see. The thought of what the bodies would look like sent a shudder through her.

"Aleni? You alright?" Jacek's voice was gentle.

"Just give me a moment." She didn't want to alarm him by saying she couldn't see. The crowd was a mixture of cheers and horrified cries. What had she done now? Who was she, really? She didn't even know herself. Was she a monster? Just like the goblins?

As the blood rushed back into her head, she blinked a few times and light grew in her vision. Her eyesight was returning. Good. She waited a few moments more, and eventually the muddy snow underneath came back into focus. She still felt weak, but at least she could see.

She lifted her head and Jacek's firm hands helped her to her feet. He kept a grip on her arm as she wobbled slightly, still dizzy. Finally, she looked upon the charred remains of the pack of goblins. A lot of the flesh had burned away, leaving blackened bone and gristle. Steam rose from the bodies, arranged in a twisted display of terror. The goblins had died screaming in fear.

Bile rose in her throat, but she clamped her mouth shut to keep from throwing up entirely. She couldn't show any more weakness here. Not in front of all these people.

"Let's go, before they get any other ideas." Jacek gave the organizers' box an angry look and steered her toward the gate. He kept hold of her arm firmly, giving her support.

Aleni firmly kept her eyes on the gate as they walked past the bodies of the goblins. The smell made her almost gag, but Jacek's hand on her arm steadied her.

When they reached the gate, the soldiers flanking it moved their pikes out to cross in front of them. Jacek flicked his sword up to rest under the chin of the one closest to him on the left. Aleni put her hand out toward the one on the right menacingly. The two guards looked at one another for a second, then brought their weapons back to sit at rest beside their bodies.

Jacek nodded and tried the gate. Locked. He gave Aleni a look and stepped back.

Aleni closed her eyes and felt out with her power. She wrapped the bar on the other side in magic and with a great effort of will she lifted it from its cradle. There was a Tunk on the other side and the gate slowly eased open. Jacek gripped one door and swung it wide. Together with Bandur next to them, they walked through the competitors' area. Various people who helped behind the scenes stood there with their mouths open in astonishment as they passed through. Aleni ignored them, not wanting to see their judgment.

They hustled through the area, Aleni very aware that soldiers could come after them at any point. They could easily decide their numbers would eventually overpower them and then she and Jacek would be in trouble.

She glanced up at Jacek's face. A storm cloud had rested on it. She suspected the fire thing would be the least of her worries once they were safely out of harm's way.

⁓

The boarding house was far enough away from the Arena that Jacek decided it would be safe enough to lie low there. Better to hide out first until the heat died down before heading home. Less risk of being followed back to the cabin.

Once they got into their room, Jacek's heart pounded as he realized what he had to do now. He had to reprimand Aleni. He had never had to do this before. It would surely rip him apart. He cared about her more than anyone in the world and didn't want to lose her. Best to do it quickly. He rounded on her.

"What in the gods' names did you think you were doing?!" He kept his voice modulated to keep the volume down, but he couldn't keep the anger out of it. All his fears rose to the surface in his mind, threatening to burst out of his pores. What if she'd been killed? He was glad at this moment that he didn't have her powers.

Because of what she'd done, everyone had now seen her for who she really was. She was no longer safe because his worst fear had come true. What would they do with that information? They could hunt her down. She was a walking miracle, being the only elf alive, and that could be valuable to the wrong people.

Aleni removed her boots and crawled onto her bed, sitting with her knees up in front of her, her arms wrapped around them. She remained silent, sullenly staring into the middle distance. Bandur jumped up on the bed and curled up on her socked feet.

"They could have killed you, Aleni! How could you be so irresponsible? I have told you time and time again how dangerous it is out there for you, and you completely ignore me! Instead, you go looking for danger!" He paced back and forward inside the small room, wishing they were back at their cabin. "Why are you doing this to me? Do I mean nothing to you? Does my word mean nothing?" He hesitated, not sure what else to say. Frustration warred through his mind as she remained silent. How could he get through to her? Perhaps he hadn't warned her about the dangers of the Arena enough. He hadn't spoken of his time fighting there.

He sat down finally on his own bed, facing her. He tried to soften his voice a little and breathed in and out. "Many, many years ago, I fought in the Arena for money. It was before my name was out there as the Red Hunter. In fact, in the ring was where I eventually got the name. It was how I got so well known. They paid me to kill whoever they threw at me and make it look good. And I drew it out for the crowd's pleasure." He stared at his wet boots. "It's not something I'm proud of. Some people I killed were innocent."

A small noise came from Aleni, but she said nothing.

"It's not a good place, that Arena. The people who run it are corrupt and will do anything for money. Now you've just exposed yourself to them."

Silence.

"Are you trying to prove something? Surely, you know by now you can fight. I taught you."

She twisted her head toward him. "But when I'm fighting you, I know you're going easy on me. It's not a genuine test of my abilities!"

"You want me to go harder on you? Why didn't you just ask then?" Was she being serious right now? Was that all it was?

"It wouldn't be the same. Any way you did it, you would always stop yourself before going too far. You can't help yourself."

"So this is my fault?" Jacek fired her an incredulous look.

Aleni rolled her eyes. "No! Of course not!"

"So you take responsibility for this mess?" He pointed a finger at her.

"Yes, of course. I didn't expect it to go this way, though." She picked at her fingertips.

"No one ever does. Things have a way of getting out of hand, no matter the intention. That's life, Aleni." His voice softened slightly. The steam was running out of him. He studied her. Her face was a mess, with dried blood covering her mouth and chin. Her nose was still crooked.

"Here, let me set your nose before it heals wrong."

Aleni touched it gingerly, wincing slightly, then pulled her feet out from under Bandur to swing them around to the edge of the bed. The dog lifted his head, then went back to sleep. Jacek kneeled in front of her and raised his hands to her face. Gently he touched the nose, feeling for the break. She winced and jerked her head back.

"Sit still, I need to do this."

"I know you do, but it hurts. Do it quickly."

He placed both thumbs on either side of her nose, lining them up parallel with the bone. "Are you ready? I'll count to three."

Aleni gave a slight nod.

"One..." He jerked his thumbs down, pulling the broken piece back into place. Aleni let out a shriek and pulled back again, her eyes watering.

"You said you would count to three!"

He shrugged one shoulder. "I lied. See how it feels?"

She scowled at him.

Jacek sat back on his bed and watched her. She held her hands over her nose, breathing slowly out of her mouth. Jacek knew the pain of a broken nose and didn't envy her. But she would heal much faster than he would. He envied that. He just feared the day she received an injury too severe to heal from. They hadn't tested those limits yet.

"Why did you feel the need to try something so dangerous?" he said. "You could have died." He realized he was repeating himself, but he couldn't help it.

Aleni closed her eyes and took a deep breath. She spoke quietly. "And so what? Would that be so bad?"

Jacek's breath hitched. His face went numb. She couldn't mean that. He wouldn't stand for it. "Never say anything like that again! I don't want to hear that! Ever!"

"You don't want to hear a lot of things!" Aleni exploded. She jerked her face toward the wall, staring at it defiantly, her jaw set.

Jacek gave a wordless growl. "You're so stubborn!"

"And you're so pig-headed!"

Great. This wasn't what they needed. Why couldn't she just listen to him? Why did she have to always say things in order to shock him? He knew she didn't really want to die, otherwise she would have tried to kill herself by now. Wouldn't she? She was just trying to be obstinate now, which infuriated him.

He had never regretted taking her in as an orphan, but there were days he wished he didn't have to deal with her attitude. Which had gotten more and more acerbic over time. Sure, she was kind and helpful, but at times her mood would sour and she would stomp around the cabin or even spar with him more aggressively. He'd watched once or twice as she'd run out into the snow and plunged her hands deep into it. It seemed to be her way of cooling off.

He often felt ill-equipped to deal with her emotions. If someone needed killing or protecting from danger, then he was the man for the job. But sort out teenage moods? No sir. And he had little patience for it now.

"Stop pouting and sort yourself out. I don't want this happening again, Aleni. This was extremely dangerous. For crying out loud, I thought all the times you ran off, you were murdering monks!"

"What?!" She whipped her head around to face him. "You think I'm a murderer? And why monks?" Something seemed to snap in her and she swung her legs over the side of the bed, her movements jerky.

Shit. Maybe he shouldn't have said that. "I wondered for a bit. Someone was murdering these monks around town, torturing them and then cutting off their... uh, manhood."

"And you thought I was capable of that?" Her accusing tone cut through him, almost making him flinch. She grabbed her boots again and put them on. Jacek didn't know what to say. He just watched her silently.

With bitterness in her steps, she stormed to the door and flung it open, walking off down the hallway.

After taking a deep breath and letting it out, Jacek's gaze fell on Bandur. "How am I going to get out of this one, boy?"

The dog lifted his head and cocked an ear. Eventually he jumped off the bed and followed Aleni out the door.

Jacek sighed, grabbed their few belongings and followed them both out.

Chapter Sixteen

The woman who ran the boarding house was not happy. After the hole in the wall, they were no longer welcome.

"You must pay extra. For the hole. Ten olons."

"Ten! You must be joking. I paid you earlier." Jacek said.

She looked him dead in the eye. "I do not joke. I saw the hole. It will cost more to fix it."

He looked in his purse. He only had twelve olons left. The rest he had stashed at home in a hole in the frozen ground. Hopefully, they wouldn't need any more on their way out. Grudgingly, he passed over the money. He didn't want the trouble or attention of not paying.

The woman counted the coins and gave him a wintry smile. "Now get out of my house."

Jacek glanced at her sideways and opened the door for Aleni. They both stepped out into the glacial air, their breath immediately fogging. The night was quiet, with the crescent moon allowing a little light to see by. The sound of a door closing came from the next street over.

"Let's get our horse and get out of here." Jacek said, pulling his gloves on tighter.

"Whatever." Aleni wasn't letting him off easily. "You get him, I'll wait here."

Jacek turned toward the back of the boarding house to find his horse.

At the gate, something landed at his feet, hissing and smoking.

Jacek glanced down and tensed his muscles as realization kicked in. "Aleni, run!" He turned and launched off in her direction.

The grenade exploded.

A wave of kinetic force hit his back and threw him into the air. His head snapped forward as the blast wave threw pieces of ceramic in his direction. Something sharp sliced across the back of his head.

He landed heavily in the snow, his head swimming. He fought to stay awake, although the pain fought back. He looked around groggily for Aleni.

She stood a few feet away, her hands up and on fire. The flames pushed back at the darkness, lighting up the area. Men stood further down the street, swords in hand and intent on their faces.

As the men came at her, she threw fireballs at them. They seemed to come from all angles. Too many for Jacek to fight, even if he was on his feet. He put his hand out in front of him to grip the snow to crawl to Aleni, but a booted foot lashed out and kicked him in the ribs. He curled into a ball, gasping for breath.

Around him, it sounded like chaos. Bandur barked and growled. Men shouted and screamed, there were crashes as some went flying and hit nearby buildings. It sounded like Aleni was holding her own for now.

Jacek moved his head back out to watch her. A man tried to come up behind her, but she spun and kicked him square in the chest, sending him flying back.

They underestimated her abilities, even though they had probably come from the Arena. The organizers. They now knew who she was. They wanted her. For what, though?

Through a haze of blurriness, he tried to move, but again the booted foot attacked. He turned toward his attacker, grabbing at the leg. He got a grip with two hands and twisted them sideways. If the man attached to the leg wanted it not broken, he would have to twist with it.

The man apparently didn't want it broken. Once he was on the ground, Jacek whipped out his knife and plunged it into his neck. The man let out a gurgled gasp, trying to grab at Jacek's hand holding the knife.

But he had exactly no time to grapple with him, so he pulled down, slicing the knife through the throat until it was free. Hot blood spurted out onto the snow. The man died quickly, his eyes staring right at his killer until his last gasping breath.

Jacek tried again to get up. The world spun. He crawled toward the boarding house, hoping to use the wall to get to his feet. Then he could at least get his axe out.

Another strike came at his face, this time from a piece of wood. He moved just in time to make the cudgel glance across his cheek. Warm liquid spilled down into his beard.

He rolled onto his back so he could at least see his attacker. Knife still in his hand, he swung out wide with it.

The man danced out of the way. He swung again with his cudgel. This time going for the knife hand. With his senses slowed, Jacek saw the swing too late. The knife went flying.

There was a scream from further down the street. Aleni was doing her thing. But she would tire soon. Then what? Even she, with her elven speed and magic, couldn't fight that many men.

Jacek tilted his head up to watch her, even knowing that there were men surrounding him. At least if he was going to die, he could see her take out as many men as possible.

Blows rained down on him, and he covered his head with his arm to protect it. He tensed all his muscles to protect his body for as long as possible. His vision swam and threatened to black out as kicks and blows assaulted him.

Aleni looked tired, her face drawn and paler than usual. She slumped a little as she pushed out with force magic. Another man flew to crash into a wooden barrel.

A movement behind her alerted Jacek to another man creeping up. With all her energies focused on the many men in front of her, she didn't notice him. Jacek reached out to her, trying to call out, but just then a sharp pain in his side silenced him.

He looked down to see the hilt of a dagger sticking out of his side, just under his ribcage. Not an ideal place for it. A hand still gripped the hilt, the man attached to the hand grinning down at him.

"We're taking her, and there's nothing you can do about it," the man said.

Jacek whipped his head back up to look at Aleni. At the same time, she turned her head to him, probably hearing the man speak. She saw the other man approaching her from behind and flicked her sword out of its scabbard to slice across his belly in one lightning quick move. The man screamed and clutched at the wound, his knees crumpling. Aleni rushed toward Jacek.

"No! Jacek!"

But a burly form appeared behind her and raised his sword. Jacek tried to call out again, but his voice failed him. Only a whisper came out. Not even loud enough for Aleni to hear. The large fighter behind her brought his sword down and the hilt hit her squarely on the back of the head.

Her eyes rolled up in her head, and she crumpled to the ground.

"No..." he groaned.

He watched with growing powerlessness as the man flung her lightly over his shoulder. Bandur barked furiously at him, leaping for the man's arm. But he danced out of the way and swung his fist at the dogs head. It made direct contact, and Bandur flew to the side, landing heavily on his side in the snow.

Jacek's vision blurred again, and the blackness swarmed in. The surrounding snow grew unusually warm as he heard the large footsteps of her abductor stalk away.

* * *

There was a buzzing sound when Aleni woke. It seemed to come from inside her head. Pain radiated out from the back of it, but that wasn't what alarmed her most.

It was the fact she was lying on a bed. With her hands bound behind her back and a rag tied to fit in her mouth. Her heartbeat rose and her breaths came rasping out of her throat. Her body shook at the thought of what might have happened to her while she was unconscious. However, she noted she still had her clothes on, and she felt no pain anywhere else in her body. That was a good sign, at least.

But something was wrong with her mind. It wouldn't focus. It felt foggy and her thoughts raced. They flitted so fast she couldn't grab them to slow them down. What was wrong with her? A strange smell lingered in her nostrils. A sweet smoky smell. She couldn't identify it.

Aleni tried to wriggle her hands free, but the bindings were too tight. The fibers of the rope cut into her wrists. Even with her strength, they held fast. It was useless.

Sagging against the bare mattress, Aleni tried to summon her magic. But her thoughts couldn't coalesce long enough to grip it. She tried again and again, with all her strength to focus, but it was no use. They must have given her something to make her mind so muddled. And without the use of her hands, she wouldn't be able to focus it outside of her, anyway. Whoever they were, they were prepared, and they knew of her capabilities.

Turning her muddled attention to the surrounding room, she looked for a way out. The only light emanated from a single candle that burned on a little table next to the door across from the bed. There were no windows here, and the floor was made of well-hewn planks fitted closely together. The only other adornment in the room was a bucket in one corner, ostensibly as a privy. It was a slightly better cell than the last one she had been locked in. At least there was light.

She lay there for a long time, trying with everything she had to get her mind to settle, but it raced on and on.

Eventually she heard footsteps approaching from the other side of the door. A key clicked in the lock and turned with a scrape of metal against metal. More light entered the room ahead of four men. Two looked to be burly and strong, dressed like ordinary mercenaries, while the other two looked different. One was a little smaller, dressed in well-tailored warm clothes with a fur-lined hood hanging down his back. He had small eyes set deep in his face, and a dark demeanor. He did not look friendly.

The last man wore a black robe with the hood up and his faced obscured in shadow. He walked with the gait of an older man. His hands were scarred, as if from burns long ago. The skin stretched tight across his bones, but it did not sit smoothly. Something about him gave Aleni a bad feeling.

"Ah, here she is," the man in the robe uttered. His voice was breathy but strong. "Yes, I think she is the right one. But, we will have to prove it." He took a step toward her.

Aleni wriggled further back on the bed.

The smaller man whipped a hand out and gripped the older man's upper arm. "What are you doing? She's not yours yet."

The two mercenaries, who Aleni figured worked for the smaller man, stepped in between her and the robed man.

"No, and she won't be until I can prove she has what I want."

The little man didn't let go.

"Meaning, you won't get your money. Don't worry, it's a simple test." The robed man shrugged the hand off him. "Never touch me again. Or you will live to regret it."

The mercenary boss nodded to his two men, and they stood aside.

The older man stepped toward her again, pulling a knife out from some pocket in his robe. Aleni pushed her back up hard against the wall. As he got closer, she lashed out with a foot to kick him. He showed surprising speed and stepped back out of the way.

"Hold her down for me, will you two?" he said, looking at the two burly men.

She kicked out rapidly at the men as they approached, but her reflexes were too slow. They grabbed her legs and held them down hard. She cried out in frustration, wriggling in a vain effort to free herself. But they were too strong.

"Flip her over."

They manhandled her onto her stomach. Her heart rammed against her ribcage and pounded in her ears. What was he going to do to her? Was he going to rape her right here in front of the others?

But a sudden nick of pain in the middle of her palm ripped her away from her catastrophizing and back into the present. A warm trickle of wetness gathered in the centre. The robed man fiddled with something and then she felt something smooth, round and cold across her skin being dragged through the blood.

The robed man stepped back and the two burly men let her go. She flipped back over and curled up against the wall to protect her body from any further harm.

"There, that wasn't so bad, was it?" The robed man held up a small white power stone. A crimson stain marred its surface. It suddenly flared white light, and the room lit up for a brief second. When it waned, the stone settled down into a light glow.

The robed man pulled his cowl back to reveal his face. Aleni now saw further scarring on his neck, similar to that on his hands. The lines around his eyes showed his age, although Aleni was not good at gauging it; elves did not age like this. But he was at least older than Jacek.

"What just happened?" the smaller man asked, his mouth hanging open.

"I believe the stone is now activated with elven magic."

"She has elven magic?" The man looked incredulously at Aleni.

"She's an elf, you idiot. Look at the ears."

The man stared at her. "But I thought they were all dead."

The old man's tone was dry. "One has apparently survived." He eyed her shrewdly.

Aleni shrank back further from him, frantically trying to draw on her magic again, but it was no good. Whatever they had given her was blocking her access.

The robed man produced a leather satchel that jangled with olons. "Your payment." He handed the satchel to the smaller man.

The mercenary hefted the purse in his hand, a gleam in his eye. "The price just went up. My boss will want double."

"What?! We agreed on a price."

"That was before I found out who she was." He pointed at Aleni. "You tricked us. You told me she was just some insignificant orphan. Many of my men have been injured and even died trying to catch her. You also didn't tell me she would be accompanied by the Red Hunter."

"What did you do with him?"

"He's dead. Left him bleeding out in the street."

"No!" A sudden coldness fell over Aleni as she cried out. Her heart stuttered in her chest, causing a tight ache. No, it couldn't be true. Jacek couldn't be dead. He was as strong as a bear. He couldn't die. She drew in a shaky breath.

"I believe you've upset the girl now," the old man said. "Shall we discuss this elsewhere? I'm sure we can come to an agreement."

"Fine. She stays here under guard." The boss motioned to his two men, who nodded and followed them out of the room. The lock turned in the door and Aleni was alone again.

Silent tears tracked over the bridge of her nose as she tried to tell herself again that Jacek was not dead.

Chapter Seventeen

It was the barking that awoke him. His chest flooded with warmth at the sound. Bandur was close by, probably guarding him. He didn't deserve the loyalty that dog gave him, he was sure.

The wet coldness of snow seeped into his feet. It was still dark, so he reached out with his hand, trying to find his dog. Only bare snow greeted him.

Sharp pain radiated out from his left side as he moved. Warm wetness trickled down his side to his back, soaking his leather armor. Noting the location of the wound, it was likely the blade had missed any major organs, but he couldn't be sure. If nothing else, he would die from blood loss if he didn't get out of here soon.

"Bandur!" The air in his chest felt constricted. His voice came out weak and hoarse.

The barking stopped abruptly and suddenly a warm body pressed up against his right glove. Why was it still so dark? Where had the moon gone? He blinked rapidly. No, it was his eyes, not the lack of moon. He felt around and discovered his knife, holding it in a fist up against his chest. At least he would be ready if anyone came. Thankfully, the darkness was silent for now, except for Bandur's shuffling in the snow.

A high-pitched whine came from just above his face. Ripping off his gloves, he gripped the animal's fur, trying to ground himself somehow. His head was splitting apart. Had someone hit him with the sharp side of an axe? It sure felt like it. However, after a quick investigation of the back of his head with his fingers, there seemed to be too little blood for that. And a lack of a gaping wound. There was a knot at the base of his skull, though. Explained the blackness. It would pass. He'd seen it before.

He dug the back of his head deeper into the snow, allowing the icy cold to ease his headache and work on the swelling bump. He would have to be patient. But something niggled in the back of his mind. He couldn't figure out what it was. Something urgent, that couldn't wait. Something he had to act on. What was it?

After what seemed an eternity but was probably more like ten minutes, he saw a pinprick of light piercing the darkness. He blinked, trying furiously to focus on the moon above him. But it refused to coalesce.

Suddenly, heavy steps rushed toward him. He raised his knife in front of his face, his other hand out in front to block whatever was coming. His heartbeat quickened, unsure of himself without his sight. He caught the outline of a person standing over him. Lashing out with his knife, he missed as the person danced away. Bandur barked furiously at the person, but stayed close to his master's side.

"Stop! I am here to help." The voice was a man's. A Lontar accent.

"Why would you help me?" His voice came out in gasps. It was getting harder to breathe. He tried to keep it even and controlled. This had to be a trick.

"Because you are my only hope."

The words stopped him. Who was this? How could he possibly help this man in his condition? He was dying. He could feel it. He'd lost too much blood. But something still bothered him. Something he'd forgotten. Something very important.

"Explain," Jacek said. He had nothing to lose at this point.

"My daughter is missing. Now they have yours. We can work together."

With lightning shooting through his muddled brain, his thoughts cleared. Aleni.

"Aleni! Aleni!" He yelled. He tried to get up. They'd taken her. That was what he'd forgotten. But his body failed him. He had no energy to move.

"Stop!" The man crouched at his side, putting his hands on Jacek's shoulders, holding him down. "You are in no condition to help her now. I will help you."

Jacek gripped the man's arm tightly. He still couldn't see him properly. "I have to save her!" He coughed and pain from his side lanced through him.

"We will. Together. But first I need to look at your wound."

Help? What sort of madness was this? People didn't offer help in Amathnore. In all of Selendria. Who would help?

"No, I can find her on my own." He tried again to get up. But his body just wouldn't obey. His breaths came in gasps. He'd failed her. She would be trapped again, like in Krodon's fortress. She would be terrified. She needed him.

His thoughts were a jumbled mess, but still his body wouldn't work. Pain channeled out from his side, slamming into his head in waves. The darkness encroached again, and soon he knew no more.

—⁂—

Time lost its meaning. The pain was Jacek's only anchor in a sea of swirling memories and sensations. He got some sense that someone had moved him at some point, but he did not understand where he lay, just that it was indoors. He had the sense that someone was there from time to time, but he couldn't figure out who it was. Aleni? Where was she?

After some time, he realized someone was tending to his wound, poking and prodding it, which woke him from his troubled sleep. Agony shot through him from his side.

His vision blurred still, but he could see more light, the source of which seemed to be a lantern near the bed where he lay drenched in sweat. A fever burned in his body, creating confusion in his mind. Who was this person tending to him? Where was he? Was he safe? What had happened to him? Where was Bandur? And Aleni?

That last question troubled him the most. He couldn't quite remember when he had last seen her. He only knew she should be here somewhere, with him. Did she know where he was? Had he possibly been kidnapped? He had to get out of here. But alas, the fever soon pulled him back down into the abyss of darkness and he questioned no more.

The next time he became aware, his head felt clearer. His body no longer felt so hot. However, the blanket covering him and the mattress underneath were both drenched with sweat. It left him feeling chafed and uncomfortable.

He waited for the next time his carer came near, feigning unconsciousness. Someone soon entered the room, their footsteps creaking the floorboards. When he felt a hand fiddle with his wound, he grabbed the hand in as strong a grip as he could. Nowhere near his usual strength, he knew, but he had to try.

The person pried themselves loose carefully. Jacek lashed out with his other hand, trying to strike at their head. But they stepped back out of the way. In short time, his vision dimmed, and he fell exhausted into another deep slumber.

When he woke, they had tied his hands to the sides of the bed with hemp rope. Throat closing up, he jerked against the bonds, but it was useless. They held him fast. Cursing, he let out a wordless roar, sitting up in the bed.

His vision was better this time, the room only slightly blurry. It was small, with one window, likely on the second floor of a building, by the view of the morning sky outside. The walls were basic wooden planks, nothing fancy. The floor was equally plain and dirt strewn. However, the bed had a mattress now stuffed with clean straw, which was not cheap, so it was not a complete hovel. It must have been changed sometime while he was unconscious.

Bandur lay curled up near the foot of his bed, on a blanket on the floor. At his outburst, the dog had lifted his head. With a small whine, Bandur got to his feet and came closer to lick Jacek's face.

"Hey boy, I'm glad to see you. Could you help me with these?" He pointedly looked at his wrists, straining them against the ropes, but Bandur didn't pay any attention to them, preferring to lick him instead. Jacek pulled his head back. "Alright, alright. That's enough. I'm clean. Thank you."

He had been lying bare-chested with just a blanket over him to ward off the chill, but as he sat up the blanket had fallen to his waist. Inspecting his side, he found the wound stitched expertly and remnants of a poultice lined the outer edge of it. The smell was not pleasant. It still hurt, but he sensed the danger had passed. His head felt clearer now, and fever no longer wracked his body.

A wave of exhaustion fell over him. He lay back down carefully, trying to protect his side as much as he could. He was very weak.

Boot steps sounded on a stairwell outside the door to the room. His carer was returning.

The door opened to reveal a dark-haired Lontar man. Jacek hadn't had a lot to do with the Lontars over the years, but he held nothing against them. They stuck to themselves and were fair traders to the general populace.

Jacek narrowed his eyes at him. He looked familiar. It was the man who had ambushed them on the road to Resahil. The one he left in a ditch on the side of the road.

Was he truly an ally now, or was he playing some strange game to punish Jacek? People and their intentions had always perplexed Jacek. It made it hard to trust. The fact his hands were tied did not bode well.

"Good, you are awake. Your eyes look clearer too." The man held a pitcher of water and a wooden cup. He took a few steps and reached the side of the bed. Crouching on one knee, he filled the cup and put the pitcher on the floor. "You must drink."

Jacek kept his mouth firmly closed and his head flat on the bed as the man offered the cup to his lips.

The Lontar man stared at him for a few seconds. "If I was going to poison you, I would have done that already."

Still Jacek didn't move, staring him down.

With a sigh, the man took a sip from the cup and pointedly returned the stare.

After another few tense seconds, Jacek gave in. He was extremely thirsty, and he knew he needed to regain his strength if he was to get out of here. He would play along for now. He lifted his head to receive the cup.

Once he had had his fill, he lay back and rested. Just holding his head up for that long had drained him. He drew in deep gasps of breath.

"You are still very weak. The fever has taken a lot from you. I was not sure you would live." The Lontarian way of speaking was very formal. Born from a language made up of mostly vowels and only a few consonants, it made it very hard to decipher and even harder to speak.

Jacek said nothing. He was perplexed by Bandur being very silent around the man. He wasn't attacking or barking at his captor. Had the man drugged him? But the dog didn't look drugged. He looked fully alert and sat quietly on his haunches at the foot of the bed.

"I am sorry about the ties, but they are for my safety. You... well, you tried to attack me once before. I could not be sure you would not try again. I am sure you were just feverish and confused."

"What makes you say that?"

"Well, I am trying to help you. My name is Thu. I have nursed you back to health in my home. I tried taking you to the hostel you were lying outside of, but the woman there does not like you for some reason."

Jacek grunted at that.

Thu sighed. "So I had to drag you several blocks to my house. Your dog followed us."

"Yes, why is it you're not ripped to shreds by his teeth?"

Thu gave him a strange look. "I think he knows I have been helping you. He is not a stupid animal."

Jacek had to give him that, even begrudgingly. Maybe he could trust him. Maybe. "Fine, then untie me. I'm no longer feverish."

"First, tell me your name. I only know you as the Red Hunter. Surely that is not your name."

Jacek took a deep breath and let it out. There was no use keeping his name a secret. "Jacek. And this is Bandur."

Finally, the Lontar man nodded and untied his hands, letting the rope fall to the floor. Jacek knew he had little strength, so he lay still. For now.

"My daughter," Jacek croaked out. "Where is she?"

"Do you not remember?"

Jacek wracked his brain, trying to recall. Something about her fighting in the street, throwing fireballs at men coming at them. But what happened after that? It was blank. He shook his head gently.

"They took her. I think by the same people who have my daughter. They have been taking children all over the city. For what purpose, I am not sure. But I believe it is the Brotherhood of the Creed of Redemption." Thu's dark eyes burned with fervor.

"Why do you think that?"

"I have been following them for some time now. I have... questioned some of their monks." He fell silent after this admission.

Jacek jerked his head back in Thu's direction, his heart speeding up. "Wait, that was you? The men in the alleyways, with their dicks cut off?"

Thu looked down, pulling his arms across his torso to grip each elbow. "It is not something I have done before. But I was desperate to find my daughter."

Jacek couldn't fault him for that. He remembered the state of the bodies. "You were angry as well." He couldn't quite keep the accusing tone out of his voice. Emotions had no place in an interrogation.

"Would you not be?"

"I have spent years training myself to not have emotions in those situations. So as not to compromise myself." The last two words came out as a growl.

Thu was silent for a bit. Then, "I am not the master assassin you are, I will readily admit that. Nor do I want to be. The men died too quickly. Yes, I was angry. And I suspected they were doing something sexual with the children, which is why I left the bodies in that state. I wanted to scare the Brotherhood." Thu sat back nearly on his rump, crouched with his knees up and his arms around his ankles.

Jacek let out a sigh. He could identify with the fear of having his daughter missing. But Aleni could look after herself. She had means other children didn't. Maybe he just had to wait and listen for the fallout to find her?

But what if she was wounded or hampered in some way? They knew of her power, surely they had a plan to damper it? If it was him, he wouldn't take her without one.

Frustration rose again in his mind. He needed to get out of this bed and look for her. But he was still too weak.

"What do you know so far?" he asked.

Thu looked back up at Jacek. "I know the Brotherhood has been taking the street children exclusively."

"I thought you said they took your daughter?"

"They did." Thu went quiet for a second, letting out a breath. "She was... running with the street children."

Jacek didn't reply to that. It wasn't any of his business. Nor did he care, really.

But Thu explained. "Things haven't been easy since my wife died."

Jacek let out a sigh. He was going to tell him a sob story. He glanced at the open doorway. He couldn't exactly get up and walk out.

"I was so distraught over her death that I forgot about my daughter. She was only six. Instead of looking after her, she looked after me. I stayed in bed most days, not talking or doing much of anything. Her mother had taught her well. She cooked and cleaned our house just like Eka did. But I did not notice." He hung his head. "I was a terrible father."

Jacek closed his eyes in the hope Thu would think he was asleep and stop talking. But the Lontar man seemed as oblivious to Jacek as he had been to his daughter. Maybe Thu should have used this technique on the monks. He might have got more out of them.

"I was a terrible husband too. It is all my fault. I know that now. Eventually I got out of bed more. I took to drinking to forget my troubles, but my daughter had had enough. She ran away. I have only seen her once since. She was running with some street kids. When I called to her, she looked at me, then ran away. She wanted nothing to do with me."

The story didn't inspire Jacek toward the man any further. Thu seemed to be a failure at whatever he set his hand to. Ambushes, torture and even fatherhood. However for now, Jacek needed him. But was he really the right person to ally with in the search for Aleni?

Chapter Eighteen

It took two more days before Jacek had enough energy to get out of bed. His eyesight had returned, although his head still throbbed. The pain in his side wasn't as bad as it had been. Thu had done his job well. The Lontarians were known for their knowledge in healing. As he clambered out of the bed, Thu tried to stop him, claiming he needed to heal more, but Jacek wouldn't hear him.

"Get off me." Jacek pushed Thu back, but it didn't have his usual strength to it.

"You need to rest more. If you are not careful, you will rip your stitches." Thu waved at Jacek's side.

"I'm well aware. I need to find Aleni." He reached for his leather jerkin. Pain shot through his torso, and he halted for a second until it waned. Breathing shallowly was probably best right now. Maybe not too much twisting, either. He moved carefully and purposefully as he re-donned his armor.

Bandur got to his feet, his tail wagging as he stared at Jacek lovingly. Jacek would need him for the next steps.

"What do you know of these people who took my daughter?" Jacek asked.

Thu cleared his throat nervously. "Ah, not a lot. I cannot even be sure it is the same people. What did they look like?"

"Well-armed, wearing armor, organized, but not as much as Tarken's men were."

"That does not sound like the Brotherhood. Maybe they hired a mercenary outfit."

That could make it more difficult. "What about people connected to the Arena? She'd just fought there and angered them by not losing a fight they'd arranged. Two fights, actually."

Thu looked out the window, thinking. "It is possible. The merchants who run it have a lot of money, they have connections and power." He looked back at Jacek. "If you take these people on, both the merchants and the Brotherhood, it may be more than even you can handle. Especially in your current condition." He waved at Jacek's injury.

"I don't have a choice."

"What about your friends?"

Jacek stared at him.

Thu shuffled his feet. "Uh, the ones from the road to Resahil. The ones that adeptly killed the people I hired."

"Do I look like I have friends? I hired them too."

Thu opened his mouth in a big 'O', then shut it.

After Jacek struggled to put his leather armor on over the top of his fur-lined jerkin, Thu stepped in to help. With a sigh, Jacek allowed him. If it helped him get out there quicker to find Aleni, then he had to suck it up.

Once he was ready and had his weapons strapped on, Thu ran off to get his own warm coat and boots on.

"Come on Bandur, let's go find our girl."

Together, man and dog stepped out into the snow. Along with a thick layer on the ground, there was a fresh light falling of snow. It seemed to capture any slight sound and smother it in silence. Jacek hoped Bandur could find a scent in this. Once Thu joined them, they set off for the boarding house a few blocks away. It was impressive Thu had carried him this far the other night. He knew he wasn't light.

It took ten minutes to get to the spot outside the boarding house; longer than Jacek would have liked. His injury was slowing him down. Bandur had to stop and wait for him. It grated on him, but there was nothing he could do about it.

Finally, the boarding house came into sight and Jacek picked up the pace, despite a complaint from his side. Ignoring it, he pushed on. Inspecting the ground on the surrounding street, he found no footprints. It was a long shot, anyway.

"Bandur, find Aleni."

The dog looked at him, then put his nose to the ground, sniffing around the street. Jacek tapped his finger on the top of his axe at his side, drumming out a pattern, waiting. Eventually, Bandur moved off in a definite direction. Jacek moved after him, ignoring the groans from his body.

"Come on," he called out to Thu, who was inspecting a spot on the ground.

The two moved off down the street, following the dog. They turned left down the next street, where an armorer's workshop sat among a bunch of houses. The banging of a hammer on metal carried through the falling snow. Only the most wealthy could afford to have metal attached to their armor. Jacek only wore hardened leather, having to rely on his quick reflexes to avoid getting sliced by a sword.

Unfortunately, that hadn't helped in the ambush. Although, he knew that the thick layers of leather had stopped the knife going in any further, which accounted for him being on his feet now. He briefly wondered if it would be worth getting metal put on his armor, but dismissed the thought, knowing it would slow him down and make a noise at the wrong time.

Bandur sniffed around the ground outside one house, going back and forward in front of it. Looking up from the ground, he looked around, as if to find Aleni.

"What is it, boy?" Jacek kneeled at the dog's side, placing one hand on his back. Bandur panted and whined. He sniffed at the ground again, but didn't move. Finally, he sat. This was a sign to Jacek that he'd lost the scent. Where he was sitting was the last spot he could smell Aleni.

Jacek looked up at the house, then got to his feet. It was two stories, constructed of well-cut planks of wood and sealed with mud and straw to keep the wind out. But it was in a bad state of repair. It looked abandoned. All the shutters were closed, but some hung dangerously off one hinge. The front door looked heavy and impenetrable.

"Do you think they took her in there?" Thu asked.

"It's possible. Bandur's lost the scent here."

Thu stepped onto the front stoop and knocked.

"What are you doing?" Jacek moved toward him with an angry step.

Thu took an unsure step back. "Um, seeing if anyone is home."

"It's unlikely, and even if they were, you've just alerted them to our presence." Jacek's tone came out annoyed. Was Thu going to be like this the whole way?

He sized up the large door. It looked too heavy to kick down. He would have to go for the quieter approach. Pulling out his lock tools from his pouch, he crouched in front of the handle. Below it was a small keyhole. As he worked on the lock, he looked back at Thu.

"Go around the back. Make sure no one's escaping."

Thu nodded and headed off around the side of the house. Jacek doubted the man could handle anyone who could come out of the house, but Thu was all he had. He wished he had someone like Solel or Mular with him instead. It was the first time in his life he wanted competent backup. Had his time with Aleni changed him that much? He had grown accustomed to knowing someone was there to have his back in a fight?

Shaking his head to dismiss the thought, he focused on his work with the lock. After another few seconds, he slid the bolt back with a twist of his tools. Quickly he put the tools away and stood, pulling out his knife. He turned the handle and pushed the door open.

With the loss of her magic, Aleni was lost in her mind. Her head wouldn't stop swimming, and her body shook uncontrollably. What were their plans for her? How could she escape? With Jacek possibly dead, how could she go on? She cried for a long time, leaving the mattress around her head damp with tears.

Her parents were in her thoughts a lot. Again and again she wished for them to come back to life and rescue her, obliterating all the evil men who would do her harm. They were the most powerful elves of all, being the king and queen. They fought hard in the war over the land. Until the humans had wiped them out with a cowardly illness that halted the elves' ability to heal themselves. They were no longer impervious to disease and minor injury. Aleni was the only one who hadn't contracted it, since her parents had hidden her away by then.

She wept for them; she wept for her people. She wept for Bandur, even though she had no idea of his fate.

A guard stood outside her door. Once a day, he would enter the room with a plate of food. He untied her hands and stood with his knife out, ready to strike if she tried anything. There were no utensils; she had to eat with her hands. He would wait until she had eaten all of it, and drunk all the water from a cup, then tie her hands back up again and take the plate and leave.

Whenever he entered, she would plead for him to let her go. That there was some mistake, and she wasn't the one they were looking for. He never replied.

It was her only human interaction for two days.

The bare light from the lone candle in a sconce next to the door was the only physical thing she could focus on. Aleni stared at the flame all day, trying to organize her thoughts into something cohesive. But it was no use. What was wrong with her? She couldn't get her mind to think clearly enough to work it out.

Spent of energy from the weeping, she sank down into sleep when she could. But even then, there was no peace. Her sleep had been restless a lot lately and now was no exception. Nightmares plagued her unconscious mind, filling her with fear and making her heart race. She would wake with a gasp, sweating and panting as if she had just run from one side of the forest to the other. While the horrible feelings would linger, the memory of the dream itself would fade away, just out of reach.

Chapter Nineteen

The door swung open and Jacek rushed in. His senses sharpened for any movement. He spun, checking all around. There was nothing. The house was silent.

"Bandur, hunt." The dog ran off to search the house ahead of him.

The building wasn't much warmer than outside. Holes in the floor revealed the dirt beneath. High up, patches of walls were missing, letting in the wind and snow. A pile of white had gathered in one spot on the floor below a rotten break in the upper part of the eastern wall. Snow fluttered in to gently drop on the growing mound.

Jacek made his way to the back of the house, checking in each room as he went. Bandur had already cleared them, but old habits forced him to check. He found a door at the back locked with a wooden bar. Sliding the bar out of the bracket and placing it quietly on the floor, he opened the door to find Thu on the other side.

"Bandur's checking upstairs," Jacek said. He turned and moved toward the staircase in the middle of the building. Thu's heavy soled walk was far from quiet. Just as well there was little point in being silent now.

Up the stairs, Jacek spotted Bandur's back legs and tail sticking out of a doorway off the hall. He was growling. Jacek rushed to him, his knife up and ready. What he found was unexpected.

Aleni was not there. Instead, an older man wrapped in rags in a futile effort to ward off the cold crouched in the corner of the room, cowering from Bandur. He had one hand out, palm up, as if that would ward the animal off. Jacek checked all corners in case someone was hiding. They were empty. He focused on the man.

"Who are you?" Jacek said.

He spoke quickly. "My name is Fromir. I mean you no harm. I'm just sheltering here from the cold. Please don't kill me. I'm sorry I stayed here, I'll leave straight away!"

Jacek sheathed his knife and stormed across the room. Grabbing Fromir by the ragged shirt, he pushed him up against the wall, getting in his face. "Where is she? Where is my daughter?"

Fromir, eyes wide and mouth dropped open, struggled to speak. "I - I don't know!"

"My dog traced her scent here, to this house! You must have seen something! In the last two days, was a young girl brought here?"

"I'm sorry, sir. I saw nothing!"

"How long have you been here?"

"A-about a week, sir."

"And you saw nothing? Heard nothing? I find that hard to believe."

"M-my hearing isn't so good. I didn't even hear you entering!"

"Isn't that convenient?" Jacek's blood rushed through his veins, making his head pound. Pain stabbed in his side, now spreading out to his lower back. His patience was running thin. He released the man, who crumpled to the ground, his arms over his head protectively.

Jacek paced the room. This man had to know something. Had to have seen something. He just had to get it out of him. He was probably scared of the mercenaries. Well, Jacek would just have to make him more scared of him instead.

He looked to Thu, who stood in the door behind Bandur. He shrugged. No help there. Bandur had stopped growling, but was still on guard, staring at the older man.

Jacek rounded on Fromir, racing at him and leveling a fist at the man's head. He pulled his punch at the last second so as not to do too much damage from this angle. He just wanted to scare him, not kill him.

Fromir fell onto his side under the blow. The skin on his face was still intact, but a red mark showed where Jacek's fist had connected. He covered his head again with his hands.

"Tell me what you saw!" Jacek yelled in his face.

"I told you! I saw nothing! I swear!" Fromir's voice went up an octave as he spoke.

Jacek aimed a kick at his side. "Every time you tell me that, I will hurt you!"

Fromir wheezed. "I promise you, sir, I'm telling the truth! I wouldn't lie to you, I wouldn't."

"Why don't I believe you?"

"I couldn't answer that." He coughed and sat back up with a wince.

Jacek went to punch him again. A hand caught his arm. Jacek turned on Thu with red in his brain. How dare he?

"Stop. The man clearly knows nothing." His voice was quiet.

"And what would you know about this sort of thing?"

Thu looked away and cleared his throat. "I know that most men, when faced with a choice of pain or no pain, will usually choose no pain."

"Some are conditioned to take it."

"I do not believe this man is one of them." Thu's quiet tone somehow cut through the rage inside Jacek and calmed him somewhat. He looked down at Fromir cowering on the floor. He was right. This was just a desperate, ignorant old man.

Jacek let out a huff of air and stepped back. It would not get him any closer to Aleni. He cursed under his breath. Still feeling the need to punch something, he swung his right fist at the wall next to the door. With a loud splintering of wood, his hand went through the thin wall, right out the other side.

Not bothering to pull his hand back through, he rested his forehead against the wall, his eyes closed. Breathed in and out. This had been a waste of time. Aleni probably hadn't ever been here. Maybe outside was where they loaded her on to a horse or covered her in a thick horse blanket.

He had to stay positive. He would find her. He would free her. Even if it meant ripping the town apart.

He kept seeing her in his mind's eye as he'd last seen her. The hilt of the sword hitting her in the head and her crumpling to the ground. Then that bastard throwing her over his shoulder like a dead boar, completely helpless.

Jacek hadn't felt that powerless since his parents died. He had survived this far without getting close to anyone. Now that he'd made a connection, she had been whisked away. His heart ached at the thought of her being hurt again. His only hope was that she was more valuable alive than dead.

With that thought, he straightened and pulled his hand back through the hole in the wall. His glove had protected his knuckles. Luckily, this house didn't have a bossy woman in charge of it. He couldn't afford another payment for a broken wall.

"Let's go." He stalked out of the room. Bandur's nails clicked on the wooden floor behind him.

Thu's noisy footsteps followed them down to the ground floor.

"Now what?" Tu said.

Just before opening the door, Jacek turned to face Tu and sighed. "We need to go to the Arena. There must be a connection to there. It's not a coincidence that we were ambushed not long after Aleni revealed herself in the ring."

"Revealed herself?"

Jacek hesitated. How much should he tell him? The secret was out now. He studied the Lontarian. His face looked earnest. He had lost his daughter as well, although not quite in the same circumstances. He was probably not going to capitalize on the knowledge himself. He wasn't enterprising enough for that.

"She's an elf."

Thu's mouth went slack. Then he smiled and shook his head gently. "I am sorry. For a second I thought you said she was an elf."

"I did." Jacek put on his best 'believe me' look. Aleni called it his 'believe me or else' look. His stomach hardened at the thought of her, but he pushed it aside. It wasn't useful to think about her too much right now.

"You are not joking?"

"Do I look like someone who jokes?"

"But - but how? The elves are all dead."

"One survived. She was in a bad situation and I helped her out of it. In return, she helped me. She's tagged along ever since. Don't ask any more than that." He held up a palm to stress it as Thu opened his mouth.

He was suddenly uncomfortable explaining their relationship any further. He wasn't even sure why. There was nothing untoward about it. She was his daughter now. He cared for her. And he was proud of her. But somehow, having to explain it all in words to this man was... difficult.

"Oh. That... is unexpected. And explains a lot. The way she chased me down that day on the road..."

"She can get a little carried away." He cleared his throat. "The point is, she has magic. And magic she barely understands. It seems it's evolving. Or at least new skills are emerging. She ended up showcasing it in the ring when they threw a pack of goblins at us."

"They what?" Thu's angular eyes opened wider.

"You know what? This is all their fault. I'm going to go down there and give them a piece of my mind. Let's see how chatty they get after I'm through with them." He swung around and opened the door with more force than he intended. A wave of dizziness suddenly hit him, and he had to grab the door frame with one hand to steady himself.

"Are you alright?" Thu put a hand on his shoulder.

Shrugging him off, Jacek blinked a few times to clear his vision. After a couple of seconds, he pushed on down the two steps out into the street. It was still snowing. The day had moved on into late afternoon, but there was no sun. Blotted out by the ever-falling snow.

He needed to get his horse. The Arena was a fair walk away, and in his condition it would be arduous and not efficient. Everything he did had to get him closer to Aleni as quick as possible. That was all that mattered. His pride be damned.

He started off in the direction of the boarding house. His horse was still in the stables behind it.

"Hey, where are you going?"

Oh, right. Thu was still here. Jacek stopped and turned. "I'm going to get my horse. Do you have one?"

"Yes, I have one." Thu ran to catch up. "I will retrieve it and meet you at the boarding house." He ran off in the other direction.

Jacek trudged through the snow back to the stables. He used one of his last two olons to pay the ostler, then bridled the stallion and threw a riding blanket over his back. Jacek had to admit, but only to himself, that it was harder than usual to mount up. He almost couldn't stifle a grunt as he got his leg over his mount's back.

When he rode out into the open air of the street, Thu was coming up toward him on an old bay gelding. The horse looked ragged and tired. Hopefully, there wouldn't be a need for hard and fast riding. The horse would never keep up. He simply gave Thu a nod and moved his horse onward toward the Arena.

As they got closer to the huge amphitheater, the snow finally abated. It was getting later in the day and he was feeling hungry. And sore. But mostly hungry. But he still had to find whoever ran this Arena and question them.

Dismounting outside the huge main gates, Jacek tried them but found them barred from the other side. There was a side entrance he knew of, so he headed there. Thu and Bandur followed close behind. The side gate was shut but not locked. Someone must still be here.

Five minutes later, he found a small, shaven-haired man sweeping the back training area. His clothing was not well-tailored or that warm, but it wasn't rags either.

"Hey! You!" Jacek called out to him.

The man startled and turned to face them as they approached.

"Yes, sir?" His hands gripped his broom tightly as he shuffled on the spot. He didn't quite meet Jacek's eyes.

"Who runs this place?"

"That would be Vossler. He is my boss's boss. He is in charge of everything." There was a strange lilt to the man's words that Jacek couldn't place.

"Is he here?"

The man shuffled from side to side. His tone was flat, with only a few inflections. "Oh, no. He would have gone home by now. He doesn't like to stay late. He leaves all the hard work to others and doesn't even thank them for it. My mother always taught me to thank people, but no one else ever does it. She says it can make people like you. I don't like Vossler. Not just because he doesn't say thank you, but also because he's mean. But I always get paid, so that's good." The man nodded in satisfaction and went back to his sweeping.

What an odd man. But he was correct. And honest. Which was more than he could say of many others. Which made him alright in Jacek's opinion. There was a refreshing simplicity to him that was appealing.

"Where does he live?"

"Oh, I don't know, sir. But Helam will know. She's in the next barn, feeding the wolves. Did you know wolves run in packs of up to thirty?" He pointed to a large door that led to a staging area for animals. "Thank you." He said it in a sing-song way, then turned from them and continued with his work.

Jacek couldn't help but smile a little at the man. He hoped no one was mistreating him, as often happened around here. Especially for people who were considered 'different' or didn't function the same way as most. Jacek had always been aware of such people, but he had had little to do with them.

There was a kid who lived on the streets at the same time as him back in Omel Ortheiad who was like that. The other kids wouldn't let him run with them because he was different. Jacek was ashamed to recall that he had done nothing to help the boy. Eventually the kid had died from starvation and the cold.

"What's your name?" Jacek said.

"Neran, sir." The man didn't look up from his meticulous sweeping. There was a certain order to his movements, as though he was moving through an invisible grid.

"Neran, you're doing a good job. You should be proud. Thank you for your help."

The man lifted his head and beamed at Jacek. "It worked! You like me!"

Jacek gave a small smile. "Yes, I do Neran. Good day."

As they walked away from Neran toward the next barn, Thu moved quickly to match strides with Jacek. "That was uncharacteristically kind of you."

"Shut up."

They found Helam in front of a set of three cages, throwing meat through the bars. Jacek glanced in and saw a wolf in each one. They used them in the ring sometimes to make it interesting. He would feel sorry for the wolves, but they often got the better of their opponent. Which was justice enough for them being caged.

The woman feeding them was tall and well-built. She looked like she had fought in the Arena herself once upon a time. A red scar ran from above one eye vertically down her face all the way to the edge of her mouth. It was not a fresh scar, but it had a while to go before it would turn white. Jacek knew from experience. He could still feel the pull of the scar that bisected his own face.

"Are you Helam?" He kept his voice flat.

The woman did not turn to look at them. Bandur growled at the wolves, who froze and stared him down. The biggest one growled in return.

Jacek ignored them. "I need to know where Vossler lives."

"And why would you need to know that?" She continued to throw meat through the bars, but the wolves ignored it, still staring at Bandur.

"I owe him money and want to pay up." He'd learnt long ago not to telegraph his moves.

The woman grunted. It was probably a likely story. Surely there were many people who owed the man money. She turned to him finally with a bored look. But once her eyes had taken his face in, her visage changed. "Wait, I know you. You're the Red Hunter. You were in here a few days ago. It was all anyone could talk about."

Jacek resisted rolling his eyes. Being so recognizable did not always have its perks. But perhaps he could still turn this around to his advantage. "I owe him for the fight we were supposed to lose." He wouldn't specify exactly what he owed Vossler.

"Oh, right. Yeah, I heard about that." She looked down. "Is it true your daughter is some sort of witch?"

Jacek froze. The cold suddenly seeped into his core and expanded through his body. Is that what the people believed? Could that be what Vossler and his goons thought? Mostly, witches were seen as crazy women who cast 'spells' on people, but in reality it was all just words. Aleni had displayed her power in the open for everyone to see. Surely they would realize with her ears uncovered what she really was. But he'd underestimated their stupidity. A witch. Jacek sighed and let his muscles relax. He wasn't sure if that made her more or less in danger.

"I don't know what you're talking about. Are you going to tell me where Vossler lives, or not?"

"He's over in the West quarter. Third street south of the tower. Big place that takes up a lot of the street. You can't miss it." She put her finger up in warning. "But don't try anything, he's well guarded."

"Of course." He turned back to his dog, who was still eyeing up the wolves with a stiff body. "Bandur, leave." The dog obeyed immediately and followed him as he strode out.

Back outside, they retrieved the horses and headed toward the west quarter.

"So they don't even realize she's an elf?" Thu wondered out loud. "Is it not obvious?"

"Of course it's obvious. She usually wears a headscarf to cover her ears, but it came off in the fight. And surely you noticed her eyes."

Thu nodded. "Bright blue. Unnaturally so. But I was a little distracted by her knife in my groin."

Jacek had to grit his teeth to stop the grin. "You deserved it."

Thu sighed. "Yes, I probably did. It was a stupid thing to do."

"Indeed, it was. You didn't do your research very well, did you? You didn't know it would be me guarding the bastard. And the best mercenaries I could find. Where did you get your men from?"

Thu winced. "The coal mine," he mumbled.

Jacek couldn't help it, he laughed. "Those underfed and overworked skeletons? No wonder we took them out so easily."

"There were a couple of ex-guards in there I convinced to join me. They hated Sesk as well." His tone sounded injured.

"Well, look where that got them. Although if Sesk is behind this, I will be a little sorry for that. But only a little." Jacek suddenly caught himself. He was talking a lot. This wasn't like him. He hadn't spoken so many words to someone apart from Aleni in years. Not since his days with the grey bandits. He didn't even like Thu. Why was he babbling so much with this man? The answer disturbed him, so he kicked his horse into a trot and moved on.

Chapter Twenty

The trot didn't last long before his side was screaming at him to stop. Pulling back on the reins, he looked back to see where Thu was. The Lontar man was not as proficient a rider, but he wasn't too far behind.

Bandur ran along between them, his tongue lolling out the side of his mouth despite the cold. He always looked like he was smiling when he was running like that. But somehow today it didn't look like a smile. The dog's eyes contained a seriousness to them that made Jacek wonder if he missed Aleni.

Once Thu had caught up, Jacek kicked his horse back into a walk. "You're slowing me down," he grumbled.

"*I* am slowing you down? I think that wound is slowing you down." Thu looked at him sideways. "I am not fooled, friend."

Jacek had no reply for him. He was right, but Jacek wasn't about to admit that.

As the sun set and the day darkened into night, they arrived on Vossler's street. Helam was right, it was easy to spot the house. It dwarfed all other houses. The sprawling manor sat back from the street, with a perimeter wall around the grounds to ward people out. Two men, one quite tall and the other average height, stood at the gap in the front, armed with swords and wooden shields.

Jacek and Thu dismounted and tied their horses up to a hitching post on one side of the street. Jacek then moved to the shadows of a house further down the street, grabbing Thu as he went. Bandur knew the drill and stuck close.

Peering out from behind the house, the assassin scoped out what he could from his position. The guards didn't look too alert. Even bored. Although they were wrapped in fur-lined clothing and leather armor, they were probably still cold. That can make a man less alert. But after some consideration, he decided he wouldn't go through the front.

Without saying a word, he turned and moved past Thu toward the back of the house. He stalked silently through the gaps between the houses that backed on to each other, making his way toward the northern wall of Vossler's house.

The shadows were lengthening, which was exactly how Jacek liked it. Finally reaching the wall, he stood underneath and surveyed it. Seven feet high and made of large stones molded together with mud and straw, it would have deterred most people. But at six and a half feet himself, it was no problem.

This could be easy to get in. But first he had to scope out the perimeter. Motioning for Thu and Bandur to wait there, he followed the wall all the way around to the other side. In a couple of spots, there were barrels to stand on that enabled him to see over the wall and into the grounds. A lone guard walked around inside the perimeter, moving from the front to the backyard in a loop. The house itself had a soft glow coming from almost all windows.

There were two floors, with wings bordering the main house to create a sprawling, stretched out building. Hopefully Vossler had a large family to house in it. Although, knowing his type, he probably lived alone and just had servants. What a waste.

He returned to Thu and Bandur and gave them a simple nod.

Jacek took a few steps back and ran toward the wall. Catching his leading foot on a protruding stone, he leveraged himself up and twisted to sit on the top. His side grumbled at the movement, but he ignored it.

Bandur stood silently in the snow at the base of the wall, staring up at him. Should he take him or not? Considering his current condition, it might be useful to have backup. He glanced at Thu. Not well built, and a poor fighter, he didn't hold out much hope of usefulness from him.

He clicked his fingers and bowed low with his arms out. Bandur stepped back a little and then jumped, scrabbling his back paws up the stones into Jacek's arms. He gave the dog a quick squeeze then released him. Bandur licked up the side of his face as he positioned himself on the foot-wide wall.

Then it was Thu's turn. Jacek sighed and leaned down to put his arm out. The Lontarian did a run up and stepped up the stones to grip Jacek's hand. With a pained grunt, the assassin pulled until Thu could grab the top and pull himself up.

"Now remember," Jacek whispered, "silence is the key word here." He pointed to Thu's feet. "No clomping around. Step lightly and follow my every move."

"Well, of course. What are you trying to say?" His face had a completely puzzled look.

Jacek narrowed his eyes, but didn't reply. The man couldn't be that dense, could he? Surely he knew how loud he was? Shaking his head, he jumped down the other side of the wall and hastened to place his back against the side of the manor. Bandur landed lightly in the snow and stayed close to his side. Thu followed with a less graceful landing, almost falling on his side.

Together they walked around to the back of the manor. The guard was standing with his back to them, staring up at the clouds hiding the moon. Jacek dispatched him silently, lowering the body to the snow gently and silently.

The back door leading into the kitchens was unlocked, so they slipped inside with little fuss.

However, there was a cook in the kitchen preparing food for the evening meal. He was bent over a bench and didn't notice them enter. Jacek rushed up behind him and hit him on the back of the head with the handle of his knife. The large man dropped like a stone. Jacek caught him and looked around for somewhere to stash him.

"You did not kill him?" Thu whispered.

"He was unarmed. I don't kill unarmed people."

"I suppose I have that rule to thank for my life."

"Correct."

"Are you glad you have that rule now?" Thu gave him a cheeky smile.

Jacek stared at him. What was he getting at? Shaking his head in dismissal, he spotted a pantry door on the other side of the kitchen. "Help me with him, will you?"

Thu dropped his smile and sighed. Together they dragged the heavy cook into the pantry and shut the door on him. Jacek found a kitchen utensil and jammed it in the latch so the door wouldn't open.

Now where? He had to find Vossler. Normally he would have done his research and got a layout of the manor. He would have a basic schedule for Vossler and any movements of staff. But not tonight. There was no time for any of that. Aleni's life was in the balance.

He led the others to a winding stairway in one corner leading up to the second floor. At the top they came out into a hallway stretching the length of the house. As Jacek stuck his head out of the stairwell to look down one end, a man called out from the other direction.

"Hey! Who are you?"

Shit. Time to go loud.

Jumping immediately into the offensive, Jacek's axe was in his hand before he'd topped the stairs. The guard drew his sword and yelled out for others to back him up. Jacek had no idea where anyone else was hiding, but he had to move quickly.

The guard got within strike range and slashed his sword down at an angle. Jacek caught the sword in the crook of his axe and twisted. The sword flipped out of the guard's hand and clattered to the floor. With a quick thrust back up with his axe, he sliced across the man's chest. It cut through leather to flesh underneath and blood flowed.

The man screamed, staring down at his bloody chest. Jacek finished him with a chop to the crook of his neck. The guard's head nearly came off with the blow. The body crumpled to the floor, spitting blood across it.

With his own blood pounding in his ears, Jacek looked up to see another two guards run out into the hall and give a shout. He moved forward to meet them. A growl from behind him announced Bandur jumping into the fray.

The dog bounded ahead and leaped at the guard on the right. His jaws closed around the man's throat and hung on. With a garbled cry, the man fell to the floor, weakly trying to wrestle Bandur off him.

The guard on the left stared at his mate in horror, almost missing Jacek's overhand chop toward his head. Just in time, he lifted his sword to block the axe. Once again, Jacek used the crook to hook the sword away. But the guard twisted and held tight to his weapon. This man appeared at least moderately skilled.

The guard stabbed out with his sword at Jacek's belly. With his left wrist guard, Jacek swatted the weapon to the side and stepped in to push the man into the wall with the head of the axe. Once he'd pinned the man, Jacek drew his knife and buried it in the man's neck. Blood flowed out of the guard's mouth and his eyes stared at the assassin as he breathed his last.

Breathing heavily, Jacek held on to his knife and let him fall as he stepped back. On the floor, Bandur was still shaking the guard in his jaws, but the fight was over. The man was dead.

"Bandur, drop." The dog released the guard, his mouth dripping with blood, and met his partner's eyes. "Good boy."

Jacek glanced back to check on Thu, only to find the man wrestling with another guard at the top of the stairs. Thu had grabbed his sword hand and was trying to get the weapon off him. The guard was only slightly bigger than Thu, but he was on a lower step, so he didn't have a good vantage. However, Thu wasn't getting very far.

Jacek flipped his knife around to hold the bloody blade. Gripping it tight so as not to let it slip, he threw the knife at the guard. The handle hit the man cleanly in the temple with a dull thud. A killing blow. Thu was almost pulled down the stairwell as the guard dropped. Once he realized what was happening, he let go, holding his hands up on either side of his head. He looked back at Jacek, wide-eyed and breathing heavily.

"Thank you!"

"Grab my knife." Thu could use it for a weapon. He obviously needed it.

The Lontarian rushed back down the steps to retrieve the knife. Jacek turned back to the hallway where the guards had appeared from. Chances were Vossler was close.

The first door on the left led into a large bedroom. Empty. Across the hall, another bedroom was also empty. He moved on. The next room on the right led down another shorter but wider hallway. A glow came from a room on the left. Jacek headed for that.

Before he reached it, another guard stepped out, sword in hand. He was almost as tall as Jacek. He gave a smirk at the assassin and positioned himself into a fight stance.

"The infamous Red Hunter. I've waited a long time to fight you. Finally, I get my chance." The man grinned. He waved a hand dramatically. "The Great Rhazien versus the Red Hunter in a fight to the death!"

Jacek rolled his eyes and placed his axe back in the loop at his waist. He drew his sword from his back. It would give him a longer reach and a bit more swiftness. The hallway was wide enough for it. Time to teach Rhazien a lesson about pride.

The two swords clashed with a ringing of steel. A spark briefly lit up the dark.

Pushing against the other blade with his, Jacek pushed Rhazien away with the bottom of his boot. The guard stumbled back until he got his footing under him. But he didn't have time to do much else. Jacek was on him in a second.

He barely got his blade up between them to parry Jacek's blow. The two traded strikes and parries, moving back and forward in the hallway. Neither one gained any ground.

Rhazien advanced forward to strike out at Jacek with his sword. As he did, he flicked a foot out to hook Jacek's ankle. The Red Hunter stumbled and nearly went down. His sword fell from his hand.

He was tiring quickly. Too quickly.

He maintained his footing only by hitting the wall. Instinct had him immediately drop until he hit the floor. As he did, Rhazien's blade stabbed into the wall just above his head.

Jacek reached up and smashed his arm against the flat of the blade. The weapon flew out of the guard's hand and clattered a few feet away on the floor. Rhazien stared down at his empty hand, shocked.

Jacek pushed up from the floor and tackled him around the waist. Air whooshed out of the man's lungs as they both toppled to the ground. With brute strength alone, the two wrestled for dominance, rolling around with punches and elbows.

Rhazien tried to hook his leg around Jacek's to roll him onto his back. Jacek countered with his own move. He quickly got him pinned with an elbow to the throat.

But Rhazien was strong and rested, and Jacek was injured and weakening. With his throat being choked, Rhazien bared his teeth at the assassin. He flung out a fist at his face.

Jacek couldn't move in time and took the blow just above the eye. His eyebrow split open and blood flowed freely down his face. The force rolled him to the side.

Covering his eye with one hand, he kept the other eye on his opponent. Rhazien rolled up onto his knees, clutching his throat and wheezing for breath. He reached for his sword which sat a few feet to the side, against the far wall.

Jacek's heart pounded harder, making his chest hurt. Exhausted and out of options, he frantically wracked his brain. Could this be his end? Images of the sword slicing through his chest ran through his mind. He reached for his axe, still in its loop at his waist. But it was twisted from all the rolling around. It wouldn't pull free.

The guard had his sword in his hand. He raised it up over his head and focused in on Jacek.

With one eye still squeezed shut to ward against the blood, Jacek took a deep breath and swallowed. Fastening a picture of Aleni in his mind, he sent a silent apology to her.

With a snarl, Bandur ran up behind Rhazien and leaped on his back. The dog latched his massively powerful jaw down on his shoulder.

Rhazien screamed.

Seizing the brief reprieve, Jacek got to his feet. Dodging the flailing sword of the guard he finally freed his axe from the twisted loop. He raised the weapon.

"No!" Rhazien cried out. He tried to raise an arm to block. But it was no use.

With a mighty overhead chop, Jacek buried the axe-head in Rhazien's skull. The guard's eyes went dull and unseeing just before he fell forward, Bandur still riding his back.

Jacek pulled the axe out of the bloody mess and let out an enormous sigh. He stumbled back to lean on the wall. His muscles felt spent and weak. Something he hadn't experienced in a long time. He just needed to stand still for a moment. Chest heaving from his exertions, he gave a relieved smile to Bandur, who now sat on the guard's back as if to own the body as a trophy.

He wiped at his eye with the fur lining sticking out of his sleeve to clear the blood off. His eyebrow stung, and he touched it gingerly to check it for severity. It didn't seem too bad. But he'd have a black eye tomorrow.

After resting for a minute, it took him a moment to realize that someone was missing. Where was Thu?

Chapter Twenty One

The glow emanated from a large sitting room with an enormous fireplace. Candles dotted the room, but the flickering light of the fire created a sense of comfort that seemed out of place in this house.

After wiping the blood clear of his eye, Jacek found Thu with the knife to Vossler's throat.

"I got him for you. He is not going anywhere." Thu emphasized it with a pull on the knife against the skin.

Vossler, a man with nearly forty years on him, had long gray hair tied back at the nape of his neck. His receding hairline, however, made the ponytail look like it had pulled all his hair back from his head. His small eyes were deep set and angry.

"I'll have your head for this! Both of you! My men will kill you!"

Jacek glanced back out the doorway into the hall where the Great Rhazien lay in a pool of blood. "They tried."

Exhausted beyond measure, he surveyed the room. Vossler was sitting on one of two expensive armchairs by the fire. Between the two chairs stood a small table with a tray of food on it.

Jacek took the seat facing Vossler, being careful not to look too relieved to be sitting down. But he did make sure to look comfortable. Removing his gloves slowly, he selected a choice piece of meat from the tray. He sat back and ate it slowly, savoring the beautiful flavor and making noises of enjoyment and satisfaction. He took a few more pieces until he gauged the silence had gone on long enough.

"So tell me, what did you do with the girl?"

Vossler's eyes flicked down to the knife at his throat, then back up to Jacek. "What girl?"

"The girl who fought in the Arena today. My daughter. I'm sure you remember."

"How could I not? We've never seen such a fight in the Arena."

Jacek leaned forward, his leather armor creaking. "So you decided you wanted her for yourself? She would make you a lot of money, no?"

Vossler wet his lips with his tongue. "It was tempting. But I would have no way of controlling her, would I? Unless there is some limit to her power?"

Jacek didn't reply to that. Instead, he took another piece of meat, licking his fingers afterwards. All the time he stared at the captive man.

"So why did you take her?"

"I didn't!"

"Maybe your men did?"

"No!"

Jacek stood, towering over the man. He bent over, getting in Vossler's face, ignoring the pain stabbing his side. "I. Don't. Believe. You. You had better start telling me the truth, or I might let this man loose on you." Jacek gestured toward Thu.

Vossler looked a little puzzled at that. Like he had been expecting something else.

"This is the man who's been turning monks into eunuchs."

Vossler's eyes widened, and he took a large breath in, swallowing hard. Thu gave Jacek an annoyed look but said nothing.

Jacek sat back down and took a piece of bread from the tray. The food was helping. He was getting some energy back.

"So what will it be? Do you ever want to bed a woman again?"

Thu moved the knife down toward Vossler's groin. Vossler sat up straighter. "Um, I, er..."

"Come on, Vossler. Don't try my patience. I'm normally a very patient man, but when it comes to my daughter's safety, I lose it quickly." He lowered his voice a little more on the last point.

Vossler started to shake. "Alright! When I saw what she could do, I ordered my men to take the witch."

Jacek didn't correct him. The less they knew about her true origins, the better.

"And where did they take her?" He grabbed another piece of bread along with a cup of spiced wine. It wasn't what he usually drank, but it was liquid at least.

"To the Restless Hands."

Jacek frowned. He wasn't familiar with it.

Thu spoke up then. "It's a gambling den near here."

"Do you own it?" he asked their prisoner.

Vossler nodded, swallowing hard. He kept glancing down at the knife pointed at his groin.

"How do you know it?" Jacek asked Thu.

"I, uh, may have visited once or twice." Thu stood up straighter, the knife finally leaving the vicinity of Vossler's crown jewels.

"Of course you did." Jacek stood.

Vossler moved quickly then, making a grab for Thu's knife hand. Thu, taken by surprise, struggled to keep the weapon. Vossler stood, turning to face the Lontar, wrestling the man for the knife.

Jacek took a step toward them and grabbed Vossler's head. With a twist, he snapped the man's neck. The body flopped to the ground like a fish, Vossler's eyes wide open in shock and death.

Thu stood there with his mouth open, hands wide, staring at the body. He still held the knife. There was silence for a second, then Thu spoke. "You know, he was technically unarmed."

Jacek shrugged. "Close enough. I was waiting for him to make the move."

Thu's eyes opened even wider. "You knew he was going to do that? You could have warned me! What if he got the knife off me and stabbed me?"

Jacek gave another shrug and reached for some more food. "This food is good. You should try some."

Thu stared at him. Then, letting out a large sigh, he stepped toward Jacek. "What I should do is look at that cut on your eyebrow."

* * *

Icas hurried through the corridors of the huge castle. Sesk wanted to see him. He hadn't moved straight away, wanting to finish the task he was doing first, and now he'd kept Sesk waiting too long. The old man would be grumpy about it. Which would make him even more annoying.

He found Sesk's office and knocked on the door. A voice called out to enter, so he opened the door and stepped in. Sesk was standing next to the fireplace, staring into the flames. His fire put out much more heat than Icas's own. What wood did he use?

"What do you have for me, Icas?" Sesk interlocked his fingers tightly, his tone petulant. Yes, he was grumpy.

"Regarding what, exactly?" Icas was investigating several things for Sesk.

"The girl. Can we get her out of there?"

Right, the elf. "We don't have a hope of grabbing her."

"What?"

Icas shrugged. "They have more men than us. And better trained. Vossler is powerful. I warned you going up against him was foolish."

Sesk gritted his teeth. "And I warned you not to talk to me like that."

"You pay me to get information, not to be polite." Icas sat down on a soft armchair, his legs dangling over one arm. He enjoyed poking the beast when he could. It was a fine line to walk, but it made life interesting.

Sesk took a deep breath and let it out slowly through his nose. "I haven't gone up against him. Yet."

"And I don't suggest you do. The man has many resources."

"Not as many as I do."

Icas held out his palm face down and waggled it. "Different sort of resources. The ones that count in a physical fight."

"And if I can get the girl off him, I can change that."

Icas frowned. "You can?"

"I can."

"Why not just pay him then? You have the money."

"It's the principal of the matter. We agreed on a price. Then he changed it once he knew how valuable she was. I should never have done the test in front of him."

"You couldn't do the test anywhere else. He wouldn't have let you. And you had to verify he got the right girl."

"The ears might have been enough."

Icas sat up. "Does she really have pointed ears?"

"Of course she does, you idiot."

The spy stared off into the middle distance, unperturbed by Sesk's name-calling. "So it's true. The elves are back. They're not all dead." This was incredible. He pulled his gaze back to Sesk. "There is a slim chance we could grab her if we create a diversion."

"What? Why didn't you mention this before?" Sesk rounded on the spy.

"Because of the aforementioned word 'slim'. It would be risky. And of course then you would have Vossler on your back."

"Let me deal with Vossler. How many men would you need to pull it off?"

"Just me. Any more than that and the 'slim' goes down to none."

Sesk pulled his desk chair out to face the armchair Icas sat in. "Tell me the details."

Icas swiveled around on the armchair to face the old Deacon. He gestured to the fireplace. "First, you must tell me what wood you use."

Chapter Twenty Two

The sky was darkening and houses were shut up and barred by the time Jacek, Thu and Bandur approached the Restless Hands, pulling up half a block away from the entrance. Jacek's stallion stomped impatiently in the snow, snorting out clouds of warm breath.

"I know, you want to go to bed." Jacek patted the animal on the neck. "But we have to find Aleni first. Then you can rest all you want." He turned to Thu. "What do you know about this place?"

Thu looked thoughtfully at the squat wooden building. "Well, it's a gambling den." He went silent, just staring at the building.

Jacek's patience was running thin. His voice came out with a hint of danger. "And?"

Thu put his hands up. "Alright, alright. It is primarily a cards and dice place. No game boards or betting on roosters like some other places where anything goes. There are guards on the door, monitoring everyone. If you are caught cheating, they kill you. Or beat you and leave you for dead if you are lucky."

"How charitable of them."

"Yes, indeed." Thu didn't catch the sarcasm.

"How many?"

"How many what?"

Jacek sighed, holding himself back from strangling the man. "Guards."

"Oh. Ah, four, I think."

"You think?"

"It has been a while since I was there. I was not scoping the place out to raid it last time I was there."

He had a point.

"Entries and exits?"

"Main entrance is the front door. There is another door in the back of the common area, but I don't know where it leads. I have only ever seen the owners use that door."

"Alright. We'll have to wing it. Follow my lead." Jacek kicked his horse and moved forward.

"Jacek." Thu kicked his own horse to catch up. "Do you think they have my daughter?"

"I don't know." He looked back. "But we'll find her."

They left the horses tied up out the front of the building and entered through the front door. Inside, the room was warm and well-lit. Men crowded the tables, yelling and laughing around various games of cards and dice. Drink flowed freely.

A large man with a shaved head and one eye approached them. He was expressionless, but his one eye didn't miss much. It roamed over Jacek in particular.

"Weapons must be given up at the door." He crossed his arms as if to say it was non-negotiable.

Jacek placed a protective hand on the axe head at his hip. "And who will look after them? You?"

The one-eyed man motioned to a large chest by the door. Another man, this one much smaller and beholding of two eyes, unlocked the chest and opened it to show various weapons inside. Jacek weighed up his options, eyeing up the various security men in the room. He would have to play along for now. There were too many of them.

Clenching his jaw, he handed over his axe, sword and knife to the smaller man with the key to the chest.

Both the one-eyed man and the holder of the chest key looked expectantly at Thu. He stared back at them, oblivious.

"Weapons?" Said the one-eyed man.

"Oh!" Thu held up his open palms. "I have no weapons."

The one-eyed man looked him up and down and then nodded, satisfied. Thu was no threat. But he gave Jacek another suspicion-laden look before motioning with his head for them to move on into the gambling den.

Jacek surveyed the room. Lanterns hung low on the walls in order to light up the cards in people's hands. Ten circular tables filled the room, surrounded by men who were at least as well dressed as he and Thu were. He wrinkled his nose at the smell of cheap beer and old sweat. The air hung thick with pipe smoke. He had never been a gambler, or a cards player. He knew the basics of dice, but he wouldn't have called himself an adept. This was not a scenario he was comfortable in. He did not know where to start.

"Want me to pick a table?" Thu whispered in his ear.

With an annoyed jerk of his head away from Thu, Jacek gave a reluctant nod. Telling Bandur to stay by the door, he followed Thu toward a table off to the side. It was a good pick, offering a view of the entire room. From there, Jacek could keep an eye on everyone and have his back to a wall. With a nod to Thu, Jacek indicated he should sit at the table and play. Thu patted down his pockets and produced only a half-olon. He gave Jacek a forlorn look.

Sighing, Jacek reached into his coin pouch and produced his last olon. Handing it to Thu, he said, "That's all I have left with me. Make it count."

Thu nodded readily and sat down.

Jacek observed the room. In the wall on the far side was a door with a man standing next to it. He had the look of a guard to make sure no unauthorized person could get through. Heavyset and muscular, he didn't look easy to get past.

Two men stood against the wall to Jacek's left, hands clasped together in front of them, staring out over the crowd, watching. Jacek caught one of their gazes, took the man's measure, then looked back to the table where Thu was engaging in the game of dice.

The crowd was noisy. Gambling men readily laughed and joked with each other at the tables. Two strikingly beautiful women walked among them, serving drinks. They were an easy distraction for several players. Jacek was willing to bet the house won a lot of games because of those two.

A noise of disappointment erupted from Thu and he sat back on his chair.

"What happened?" Jacek asked.

"I lost that round."

Jacek clipped him lightly on the back of the head with his hand.

"Ow!" The Lontar man held his hand to the spot on his head.

"I better get some money back out of this!" Jacek muttered to him.

"Do not worry. I know what I am doing."

Jacek doubted that, but kept his mouth shut. They didn't need others at the table suspecting they were up to something.

Over on another table, there was a sudden shuffle of movement. Shouts of dismay and annoyance rang out. Two men stood, shouting and pointing at each other. The two guards standing against the wall moved over to the commotion.

One of the men shouting grabbed at the other, trying to get at the other's sleeve. He eventually produced a card, holding it up triumphantly. The cheater tried to deny it, but it wasn't his lucky day. The two guards grabbed him between them and marched him toward the front door.

The cheater cried out, trying to maintain his innocence, but no one would listen. Everyone in the room sat and watched as they dragged him out. They could still hear his cries even after he was outside. After a few seconds, the cries were cut violently short. Not long after that, the guards re-entered the den and took their places against the wall as if nothing had happened.

Jacek glanced over at the guard standing by the door at the back of the large room. He hadn't moved an inch. How could he get through that door faster and more efficiently? He needed to keep moving. It was killing him to just stand here and watch. Anything could be happening to Aleni, and he had to put a stop to it.

He thought back to when he found her in Krodon's dungeon. She looked so tiny back then, in a dirty, thin dress. Chained to the wall, completely helpless. She had been terrified, thinking he was there to do something horrible to her.

His chest ached at the thought. Stop. He had to focus on the now. Getting through that door needed to be his main priority. He leaned down to Thu and whispered.

"Ask them if they have any women available."

Thu frowned and looked back at him. "Do you not think you are getting a little sidetracked?"

Jacek threw him an annoyed look. "Dealer," he called out to the house man at the table.

The man was gathering up the dice, but he looked up at Jacek.

"Do you have any women available?"

The man frowned, looking like he didn't know how to answer. He eventually shook his head.

"What about younger girls? Got any of those?" That sort of thing wasn't completely unheard of in Selendria, but it wasn't ever advertised.

The dealer visibly startled, then looked uncomfortable. He glanced over at the two guards and caught one of their gazes. The one on the left pushed away from the wall and walked toward them.

Jacek bristled, straightening. He clenched his fists in preparation for a fight. With the back of his hand, he tapped Thu on the shoulder. "Back me up." Whatever use that would be.

⁓

With a start, Aleni woke from her restless slumber. Drenched in sweat and panting, she realized she must have been having a nightmare. As she tried to remember what it was about, the images bounded away from her conscious mind like a rabbit caught in a hunt. She was left with only the feeling of distress.

Then she remembered where she was, and her heartbeat increased again. She looked around the little room, but the candle in the sconce next to the door was the only decoration apart from the bed she lay on.

There was a sound outside the door. Was that what had woken her? Was someone coming?

The handle turned and the door opened quietly. Too quietly. This didn't feel like her guard bringing her dinner. He was loud and brash and didn't care to be quiet. Who was this?

A slim man entered the room. He walked with a slumped posture and had a mole under one eye. Stringy brown hair flopped un-cared for on his head. He walked on the balls of his feet, moving like someone who wasn't supposed to be there. He glanced behind him, back out the door, but after a second turned back to Aleni.

"Who are you?" Aleni moved further back on the bed, up against the wall.

"My name is Icas. I'm here to take you out of here." The man pulled out a dagger from his belt and moved toward her.

Heat pulsed through her body and her heartbeat sped up. She panted. "What are you doing?"

The man straightened and waved his knife in her direction. "Well, I have to cut your bonds, don't I?"

"Did Jacek send you?"

He narrowed his eyes. "I don't know who that is."

"The Red Hunter."

His eyebrows lifted briefly, as though he had just received some important information. Had she said too much?

"I believe the Red Hunter is dead."

Tears sprang to Aleni's eyes. Her throat ached. "No. No, it can't be true!"

"Oh, settle down," he said impatiently. "I don't have time for tears." He reached down behind her and cut through the ropes around her wrists. She had to admit, the feeling of release was palpable.

He cut through the ropes around her ankles as well. She swung her legs around to place her feet on the floor. She felt weak and dizzy all of a sudden.

"Can you walk?" The man re-sheathed his knife.

Aleni pushed off from the bed to stand. But her knees suddenly gave out and she would have fallen if not for the man grabbing her under one arm. She hung there, only upright because of his strength.

"Fine, we'll do this the hard way." The man bent down and scooped her up over one shoulder. Her legs now dangled down in front of him, her bottom up in the air. "If you make a noise, I will knock you out."

The sudden feeling of terrified helplessness washed over her. What was this man going to do with her? Take her off to have for himself? Would she be a slave to him now? She thought briefly about crying out, but the thought of him taking her while she was unconscious terrified her even more. At least she was awake to fight if he tried something.

She was being taken out of here. And here was not where she wanted to be. That she knew for certain. Maybe this man meant to free her afterwards? He didn't seem malevolent. Just impatient.

She would just have to wait and see.

Chapter Twenty Three

The guard reached Jacek and Thu and openly looked them up and down. "You causing trouble?"

"I simply asked if there were any girls available. If that's causing trouble, then I'm guilty." He raised his hands.

The guard looked down at the dealer with a pointed look. They knew something, Jacek was sure of it.

Pointing to the door on the far side with the other guard, Jacek said, "Where does that door go? Have you got girls behind there?" Being so close to where Aleni could be eroded his ability to keep his emotions in check. His breathing grew heavier and louder.

The guard's eyes moved over to the door, then back again furtively. "I think it's time for you to go." He reached up to grab Jacek by the open seam of his leather armor at his neckline.

In a flash, Jacek gripped the hand and twisted it the wrong way. Bone cracked. To his credit, the man didn't scream. He groaned through gritted teeth instead.

Thu got to his feet, the chair scraping out behind him. The dealer also stood. He looked like he didn't know what to do.

Thu punched him in the face.

The next thing, chaos erupted in the room. Men all over the tables started brawling, going for their dealers. Some men went for the other players at their tables. The room was all movement and noise.

Jacek punched his man in the face as hard as he could. The wound in his side griped at the movement and something tore loose. Jacek pushed on. He shoved the man toward another table. The guard lost his balance and his full weight fell on it. It collapsed and the surrounding players jumped on the guard.

Jacek made a beeline for the door on the far side, using the chaos as cover. He grabbed men along the way, pretending to get involved in a fight with them. With a head butt to one guy and a punch to another, they went down. Jacek did not know where Thu was. He lost him in the surging crowd.

A crash of glass came from somewhere. The room lit up in an orange glow, coming from a corner to Jacek's right. He turned his gaze to it and saw a table alight with flame. One of the lanterns had been knocked off the wall. The wood and spilled alcohol mixed to spread the fire quickly. Men screamed and ran in all directions away from it, adding to the tumult.

The man at the door stayed where he was, but he now crouched in a ready stance and flicked his gaze all over the room, looking uncertain. He had a sword in his hand. Jacek kept his eyes on him as he pushed his way through the men trying to scramble clear of obstacles to get out.

Suddenly he felt a heavy hand on his left shoulder. "Stop!"

Spinning, he launched a fist at whoever it was. It turned out to be the second guard from the side of the room. The man, who was a lot shorter than Jacek, ducked.

The firelight caught the glint of a knife in the guards hand.

The weapon came straight at Jacek, aiming for his gut. With his palm, he pushed the hand to the side and stepped in. Lightning quick, he jabbed two fingers into the guards left eye.

The guard dropped his knife with a screech, and both hands went to his eye. Jacek retrieved the knife from the floor before anyone else did. Abiding by his rule, he threw a fist at the man's jaw.

The guard dropped like a rock; out cold. Jacek took an extra second to grab the man's money pouch at his belt. Payment for being an asshole.

Jacek turned back to his goal, knife in hand.

The fire had grown, spreading up the wall and licking at the beams on the ceiling. The room grew stifling. Wood crackled. Men clamored to get out the front door, trampling others. He heard a bark. Bandur. Hadn't he got out?

Jacek paused in his advance on the back door. He had to get his dog. Shoving through the frantic men who were no longer fighting, he made his way toward the front door. The bark came again.

"Bandur!" he called out. "Come here, boy!"

As he got closer, he spotted Thu. He was at the chest where the weapons were kept. He was bent over, fiddling with the lock.

"Thu!"

The Lontar man looked up and spotted him. Jacek shoved someone aside and closed the gap between them. Bandur bounded up beside Jacek. He let out a breath of relief at seeing his dog safe.

"What are you doing?" Jacek asked Thu.

"You will need your weapons." He held up the key in his hand, then motioned with his head to the guard unconscious on the floor. "He did not object."

Smoke was filling the room, making it harder to see, and even harder to breathe. Jacek coughed and bent over, covering his mouth with the crook of his elbow. "Well hurry, we're running out of time!" If Aleni was beyond that door, she was in even more danger with this fire spreading.

Quickly, Thu bent over the chest again. In another few seconds, he had the lock open and lifted the lid. Jacek reached in and grabbed his sword and axe. Thu took Jacek's knife.

After slinging his baldric over his torso, he fitted his axe into the loop at his belt. "Come on." Bent over to avoid the smoke gathering on the ceiling, Jacek pushed against the flow of the crowd to the back of the room. Like a large rock in a stream, people moved around him, despite the panic.

Heat rolled across the room from Jacek's left. Sweat trickled down his skin under his armor, making it chafe in places. The fire now blazed across two walls of the large gambling den and was making its way rapidly across the ceiling. He pushed on.

The guard at the far door came into view. The door was open, and another man was shouting at the guard, pointing frantically at the ground. The guard didn't like what he was hearing. The door slammed in his face and the guard turned back to the burning room with a stricken look. He still held his sword, but his face was dripping with sweat and he did not look confident.

Jacek gripped the stolen knife, his own hands sweating under the gloves. The heat was stifling.

As they approached the guard, he saw them. Swinging wildly with his sword, he attempted to keep them away.

"Back! I'll cut you in half!" The man yelled over the din.

"You'll try," Jacek mumbled. His axe was in his right hand in a second.

As the longer blade swept across the gap between them, Jacek caught it with the axe. Sliding the blade into the crook, he caught it in a locked position and pushed down. The sword flicked out of the man's sweat-slicked hand and flew toward them. With his left hand, Jacek caught the blade carefully alongside the stolen knife.

The man's eyes widened. He turned and tried to open the door. But it was locked.

Jacek stepped forward and rapped the man across the back of the head with the pommel of the sword. He dropped to the floor.

Wasting no time, Jacek dropped the sword and lashed out at the door with his boot, just under the handle. The door burst open with a splintering of wood. The latch broke right off, falling to the floor.

With Bandur and Thu behind him, Jacek led the way down darkened steps to a floor below.

Chapter Twenty Four

Underneath the Restless Hands was cooler than up above. The fire's heat had yet to reach the area. However, smoke poured down after the trio, gathering around them like a malignant mist. Jacek coughed again, covering his mouth with the crook of his elbow.

"Aleni!" His voice rang out down a darkened corridor. The glow from the flames upstairs only faintly catching the edges of doorways. "Call out!"

He tried the first door on his left. Inside, a small room contained only a rough bed. On it lay a small body. Blood pooled underneath it, dripping down onto the floor. Dark hair cut close to the scalp told him it wasn't Aleni, but his heart clenched anyway. The child had only just been slain. It looked like someone had gone through and 'cleaned house'.

He stepped out of the room, but Thu pushed in after him. He rushed to the bed to inspect the young girl's face.

"It is not my daughter." Thu let out a heavy gasp.

"Then let's keep looking." Jacek moved over to the door on the right. Empty. Then on down the hallway. The next two were also empty.

The third held another young girl, about fifteen years old. She was alive. Blonde hair cropped to the shoulder and matted into a nest of knots. Her hands and feet were bound with rope. Quickly, Jacek cut through them.

"Have you seen another young girl, with white hair and deep blue eyes?" Jacek asked the girl, his heartbeat quickening.

She was shaking by now. She rubbed her wrists and shook her head. "I - I've only seen other men." She broke down in tears.

Jacek's tone was gentle. "I'm sorry. Most of the people holding you are now dead. We'll get you out of here." He put a hand under her elbow as she stood carefully.

Back out in the hall, Thu pointed to the stairs that led back up into the Restless Hands. "The fire is consuming everything up there! We cannot go back that way!"

"The man who locked the door would have another way to escape. We'll find it."

Thu nodded and led the way on.

They found another young broken body, then in the next room another live girl. Tu cut her bonds and let her free. She followed them readily. Jacek was puzzled by the reasoning of killing some girls and not others.

Only two rooms to go. One on the right and one at the end of the hallway. Off to the left at the end of the hall, Jacek spotted a door at the top of some steps. He hoped that led to the outside. But first he had to get Aleni.

The smoke was filling the hallway, making it harder to see. Both he and Thu bent over further to keep their heads out of the smoke. Thu opened the door on the right and entered.

On the bed, a small form lay face down. Black hair fell around the little head in a fan. Thu reached out a tentative hand to the shoulder. He turned the body and let out a gasp.

"No," he groaned, his voice breaking. "My little Thiri."

Jacek stared at the body of the little girl. She couldn't be more than eight years old. They had cut her throat. As he watched Thu crumple over her, sobbing, he realized how easily that could be Aleni. And that would be himself.

The thought galvanized him into action. He swept out of the room and went to the last door at the end of the hall.

A single candle lit this room. There were no windows, but he could see enough to a bed on one side. It was empty, but something caught his eye.

Crossing to the bed, he found a small beaded bracelet that had been cut through. Some beads had come off the string.

It was Aleni's. The one he had given her after Resahil.

Enclosing it in his fist, he held it close to his chest. She had been here. Pulling his glove off with his teeth, he laid his other palm down on the thin mattress. Still warm. She had been here recently.

Bandur padded up to the bed and sniffed at it. He let out a bark then a whine, looking at Jacek. He sat, as if to say, I found her.

"Yes boy, she was here." The smoke from the fire must have confused Bandur's sense of smell to only find her scent up close.

As he lifted his hand, he spotted a long white hair caught on it. She had definitely been held here.

"Aleni," he whispered. A ball of pain grew in the back of his throat and one eye watered. A single tear tracked over the bump of his facial scar and dripped onto the floor.

He sniffed suddenly and slapped at his face to wipe away the emotion. There was no time for that now. It was useless to him. It was useless to Aleni as well. Emotion would cloud his judgment and cause him to make mistakes.

Also, the building was burning down around him.

He replaced his glove and stuffed the bracelet in his coin pouch on his belt. He returned to Thu, who was still sobbing over the body of his daughter. Jacek couldn't blame him, but they had to go.

He grabbed the man under one arm as if to lift him. "Come on. We need to go."

Thu looked up at him, his face wet with tears, his angular eyes puffy. "I cannot. I have to stay here with her. I have nothing left. I may as well die here."

Irritation warred with compassion in him. He didn't have time for this. He reached down, scooped Thiri's small body into his arms and walked back out the door.

"Hey!" Thu scrambled to his feet and stumbled after Jacek. The two young girls followed closely.

Up the steps on the left, Jacek repositioned his light burden so he could turn the handle on the door. Thankfully, the door opened. The freezing night air blew in.

Behind them, the roar of the fire rushed down the passageway toward them.

"Run!" Jacek yelled, waiting for the three others to get past him before leaping out through the door and launching himself away from the building. A massive fireball burst out of the door. Heat singed the back of his head.

He twisted and landed on his back in the snow, Thiri's limp body on top of him.

The fireball hit the night air and collapsed into nothing.

Jacek let out a held breath and let his head fall back into the snow. It felt good on the back of his singed head.

He turned his head to see Thu lying next to him. Bandur stood a little further off, watching the smoke pour out of the open doorway. The two girls scrambled up from the ground and ran off down the darkened street.

The Lontar man was lying on his stomach, but he was staring at Thiri in Jacek's arms. Jacek sat up, gathering her into a more dignified position.

"Thu, I'm sorry," was all he could think of to say.

Thu reached out to take Thiri from him. Jacek carefully passed her over. The tears flowed freely down Thu's face.

"Why didn't you just let me die with her?" Thu's voice broke. "I deserve a death like that."

The idea baffled Jacek. "Because you still have a life to live. You have things to offer." A thought came to him, but he hesitated to say it out loud. He warred with his better judgment for a second before giving in. "I need you."

Thu looked up then, finally looking at Jacek. "You do?"

Jacek didn't quite meet his eyes, looking into the distance just over Thu's head. "My daughter is still missing. I... need your help." He then met the Lontar's eyes. Desperation drove him now. "She. Needs your help." He did not know how he was going to find her now. He needed all the help he could get.

Chapter Twenty Five

Aleni struggled for a short while, but soon found her energy lagging. Besides, it was useless. The man who carried her was light on his feet and crafty. He held her in such a way that made fighting him almost impossible. And in her current weakened state, it made it even harder.

They moved through the darkened city at a considered pace. The man stuck to the shadows, staying unseen by anyone. He was good at it. Aleni observed his tactics as if it were not her he was carrying like a sack of tubers. He moved like a thief. Not so different from Jacek. Melding into the nooks and crannies of the buildings around, becoming the shadows.

Finally, they crossed a bridge that spanned a frozen moat and approached the old fortress that used to belong to Traslek. Jacek told her the Brotherhood had taken it over after all Traslek's men had disbanded. A bold move, as that sent a message to the people of Amathnore. Someone new would take over.

But so far, all they had done was sell their rocks and preach their message about the god Ixtar. Aleni didn't understand the appeal of praying to and worshiping a god. Her people called the world Cithrel, the 'All-Mother', but they didn't worship her. She was simply the mechanism that gave life, and in return they gave back. A cyclical process. A mutually beneficial relationship.

It seemed the humans of Selendria needed a higher power to believe in. To worship and ask for miracles from. She had to admit, their plight was a dire one. Living in the world as it currently was, always winter, made it extremely difficult to live long in it. Society was bereft of empathy and compassion. And as a result, general wellbeing did not flourish.

Her people had prospered in the way they lived. Everyone helped and valued each other. Even her parents, as the leaders of the elves, did not place themselves above anyone else. They had protected her from the war, and the sickness that followed, but that was because they loved her and had the ability to do it.

At the thought of her parents, she teared up again. Oh, how she longed for them to come back from the dead and rescue her.

The gigantic fortress loomed above them as they got closer. Her captor approached two men guarding the main gate.

"Halt." One of the guards said. "Identify yourself."

"It's me, Icas." Aleni's captor sounded bored.

"Oh, it is you. Didn't recognize you in the dark. Who have you got there?"

"If it was any of your business, I would have told you already. Now stand aside."

The guard nodded and waved him on. Icas was obviously some-one high ranking. Aleni must be a high value target. What did that mean for her future? Was she to be someone's exotic concubine, like

Krodon? Or did they have some other purpose in mind? She recoiled internally at the possibilities.

Inside, it instantly reminded Aleni of Krodon's own fortress in the south. Images flashed through her mind, accompanied by the ever-familiar fear. Her breathing came harder and faster, and she squeezed her eyes shut to block it out. If only she were outside, she would plunge her hands deep into the snow, letting the pain from the cold block out all thought.

But whatever was wrong with her mind, the reason she couldn't focus, actually helped. As soon as the thoughts started, they were whisked away again, making her mind race into blankness. She embraced the sensation, using it to slow her breathing and calm down.

They moved silently through the stone fortress.

On the second floor, Icas opened a heavy door and stepped inside a large room. In the middle sat a table with three wooden chairs around it. The outside of the room was lined with bench tops with various strange paraphernalia on them. Icas dumped Aleni in a chair and reached for some rope on a bench.

Now that she was back upright again, the room spun as she got her bearings and the blood rushed back into her extremities, causing painful pins and needles. She still felt weak, but tried again to reach for her magic.

For a second, her hopes rose as she touched the edge of it. But it was just out of reach. Her mind couldn't get a hold of it. Whatever they'd been dosing her with, it was still working.

Frustrated, she gritted her teeth as he tied her to the chair. Once he finished, he left the room without a word.

She waited.

The room was lit by sconces in measured intervals around the walls. Aleni studied the gear on top of the benches, hoping for something to help her get loose. No knives or anything obvious lay about. Jars of liquids and herbs sat in rows. Cuttings of plants and hides of small animals sat in seemingly unorganized piles. What was this room? Some sort of place to concoct experiments? Was there a herbalist or a chirurgeon here somewhere? Could she appeal to them for help?

The door opened. Snapping her gaze from the benches, she saw a man in a robe silhouetted in the doorway. Squinting, she tried to look into the folds of the cowl. With her elven eyes, she could make out an older man. It was the same man who had been at the last place, trying to buy her. This was not good.

The man stepped into the room and removed his cowl. Creases formed in hills and valleys over his face, puckering together to form the strange scar tissue on the left side of his face. Bloodshot eyes peered out under folds of skin. His posture was stooped, his hands dangling at his side.

His face fascinated her. She had not seen many older humans, and the way their skin aged was so different to what she was used to. Elves did not age in the same way. Their skin remained smooth and youthful for their entire lives. The only sign of the very old was an inability to use magic anymore.

"Who are you?" Her voice croaked as it came out. She hadn't used it in some time.

"I am High Deacon Sesk." The old man ambled around, studying her. He smelled like old wine and wood smoke.

Then she realized where she had seen him before. On the road to Resahil. Jacek's employer. She had actually protected him a few weeks back. The thought galled her. "What do you want from me?"

"I want to know about you. How old are you, my dear?"

Aleni kept her mouth shut. He wouldn't get anything out of her. She tried to focus on the feel of the wooden chair beneath her. The grains stood out roughly under her touch, the wood not sanded smooth.

He shook his head. "Never mind. Your power, it is obviously innate in you. Can you draw on it now?"

Aleni couldn't help herself. "If I could, you'd be in flames." She bared her teeth, straining against her bonds. Fibers of rope cut into her wrist. The pain kept her in the moment when her mind wanted so badly to leave this place.

Sesk jerked his head back, the only physical sign her words had affected him. "I've already been burned." He gestured to his face. "And I lost everything because of it. My wife, my livelihood." His voice caught as the words tumbled out. "But I rebuilt. Stronger and with power. You couldn't possibly understand what I've been through, my dear."

"I'm not your dear!"

"Yes, yes. You're The Red Hunter's daughter, right?" He clicked his tongue. "But really you're not, of course. You couldn't be. You're not even human."

"He adopted me. My parents are dead."

"And now he's dead too."

Aleni glared at him. She wouldn't give him the satisfaction of seeing her grieve. No weakness.

"Are you the last of your kind?"

She sat silent, staring at the scars on his face.

"Very well. It seems the drug they've given you is working to keep you powerless. The little man told me what he was using. I will continue with it. And when I'm finished with you, you will give me all you have."

Sesk turned suddenly and walked out of the room, closing and locking the door behind him with a loud click.

Aleni was left alone to wonder what he meant.

Chapter Twenty Six

Jacek shivered as he rode behind Thu back to his house. The cold reached peak unpleasantness after midnight, and the moon was just over its zenith. The Lontar rode with a heavy head and slumped shoulders as he carried his daughter in his arms.

Jacek's chest tightened as he watched him. He would feel much the same if that was Aleni. She was his whole world now. If she died, there would be nothing left for him.

Before he met her, he was content to be alone. But since she had entered his life, he now couldn't imagine it without her. The thought of what she could be going through turned his stomach.

If these people would easily slit a little girl's throat, what would they do with Aleni?

At Thu's house, Jacek and Bandur took the horses around the back, allowing Thu to go inside with Thiri. An open shed provided a space for the horses to shelter. He took his time rubbing the animals down and giving them grain and water.

With heavy feet, he and Bandur finally made their way inside the house. He found Thu sitting on the floor next to a low cot. Thiri was lying with cloth wrapped around her throat to cover the gaping wound. Thu stared at her, his face blank, not moving.

With no words to comfort him, Jacek set about making some hot tea. They both needed fluid and heat. He built up a fire in the fireplace and hung a pot to boil over it. Searching through some cupboards, he found two cups, some tea and bread.

Bone weary and sore, Jacek brought the small meal to Thu and sat down near him. For Bandur, he produced a package of half-dried meat from his saddlebags. The three sat in silence while sipping their tea and eating.

After a long while, Thu spoke, turning his head to look at Jacek finally. "Thank you, my friend."

On account of the man's grief, Jacek let the designation pass. He shrugged, not used to reacting to gratitude.

Thu turned back to his daughter. "She was so bright, my little girl. You only had to show her something once and she could do it. Even though she was young, she understood more about the world around her than she should at her age."

Jacek nodded, listening.

He spoke softly now. "She understood more about what my wife suffered than even I did." His face hardened. "It was that Creed of Redemption that did it. She believed so much in the power of the stones, that... well, it killed our son. Those people poisoned her mind!" He turned back to Jacek, the anger burning in his eyes.

Jacek remained silent.

"Instead of blaming them, as she should have, she blamed herself. She thought she did not have enough faith. And that was the reason the stone did not work."

Despite having warmed up by the fire, Jacek felt a coldness fall over him. He was starting to get the picture. "Did she -?"

Thu nodded, tears dripping down his face. "She hung herself two weeks later. She could not live with the guilt."

Jacek turned his gaze away, staring at his boots. "I'm sorry."

"So am I, my friend. So am I."

Jacek left him to his grief, knowing he could do no more. It made more sense now, knowing the full tragic story. He didn't mind hearing it this time. There was a strange, unknown feeling in his mind now when he thought of Thu. When before he was an annoyance, there was now something else. Some sort of connection.

Shared pain.

He took Bandur upstairs to the little room he had woken up in that same morning. There was nothing else he could do tonight. He did not know where Aleni was now. It pained him to have to stop and rest while she was still out there, but he would be no use to her dead on his feet.

A sharp pain in his side reminded him of his injury. He stripped off his leather armor and checked the bandage. Thu had done his work well. The stitches had held, even through all the fighting. He'd heard of the Lontarian skill with medicine, but this was his first experience with it. Perhaps the stories were true.

He lay down and made room for Bandur to lie next to him. The dog curled himself up next to his friend. Jacek stroked his soft velvety ears, drawing comfort from the animal.

He hoped wherever Aleni was, she was safe enough. His mind churned over with worry, and he lay there for a long time until exhaustion pushed him into a fitful slumber.

Morning light coming through the window woke him. His body ached all over. Remnants of the night before. He would have bruises on bruises before this was all over. However, since he'd been healed from the Wasting Sickness a year ago by the Elven healing stone, he had been fitter and healthier than he'd ever been.

He also seemed to heal faster than usual. Nowhere near as quick as Aleni, but faster than a normal human. He didn't question it, just accepted it.

He pushed Bandur off the bed and got to his feet. Stretching, he worked out the kinks in his muscles. He donned his armor again and strapped on his weapons. Checking the money pouch he'd taken from the guard, he found eleven and two half olons inside. Good enough.

He made his way down the stairs, but stopped halfway. Something was different down there. He sensed lots of people. Even Bandur's ears perked forward. He drew his knife, held it behind his back and continued down.

In the main room where he'd left Thu, he found him surrounded by many people. They all looked similar in different ways. Some were young, a couple were older, others nearer Jacek's age. Fourteen pairs of dark eyes turned to Jacek and stared. Some had fear in their eyes and looked ready to bolt, others held mere curiosity.

One smiled at him. It was a child. Jacek couldn't figure out the gender, but it didn't matter. He allowed himself to relax a little. These people didn't look like a threat.

Thu jumped up suddenly. "Oh, I am sorry, this is my extended family. When someone in our bloodline dies, it is tradition for everyone to come and spend time with the... deceased." He looked down at Thiri still lying on the cot.

Jacek stared at all the people. They stared back. The weight of his armor and weapons hanging off him was a reminder he was heavily equipped for battle. But not equipped for this. This was completely alien to him. The fact that this group of people would support each other in their grief and even have a sense of community... this was strange.

He had to get out of here. Before he did something stupid. Or someone got hurt. Or both.

The people packed the room, making leaving out the back door difficult. So he turned for the front door.

"Wait!" Thu picked his way through the people and reached Jacek's side. "Where are you going?"

"I need to leave. I still need to find my daughter."

"Well, please, take some food with you. My family has brought much with them."

This too surprised Jacek. What was with these people? Did they actually care about each other?

Thu spoke in his native language to another woman. She nodded readily and got up and went to a food preparation area. After several seconds of waiting, she was back. She passed a cloth-wrapped bundle to Thu, who passed it on to Jacek.

"I wish you well in your search, Jacek. Please, come back when you have found your daughter. I would go with you, but I must deal with funeral rites here."

Jacek nodded soberly. "I understand. Do you have any ideas where I should start looking?"

Thu's eyes hardened. "The old fortress. The Brotherhood. I am sure of it."

Jacek wasn't. Knowing Thu's story, the man had a bone to pick with the brotherhood. Jacek had found no hard evidence they were involved.

"Perhaps you should search out your friends who were with you on the road to Resahil? They could help, no?"

The mercenaries? They were competent, yes, but they weren't his friends. Not that he needed them to be. He had some money now from the guard at the Restless Hands. He could pay them to help him. Although it wouldn't be much.

He would have to try.

He nodded and left out the front door, Bandur following at his side. Around the back, he tucked the food bundle into the satchels still slung over his horse's back.

Riding out into the town, he headed for a tavern that mercenaries frequented. It was a common place for people like them to find work. Called the Lethal Mercenary, subtlety was not its strong suit.

The day was cold, but it wasn't snowing, and the sun was out. Jacek almost resented the presence of the sun, but decided it was more helpful than hindering. Having some warmth while out looking for Aleni would be one less thing to worry about.

A street away, a woman wailed in mourning. Someone else had probably died. All other nearby talk and laughter died with the sound. It left a grievous pall hanging in the air, and Jacek hurried on to get past it.

It took him ten minutes to get to the Lethal Mercenary at a mounted walk. It was situated near the docks, not far from the one the sailors frequented. Run by a man named Baden, an old retired mercenary, he had purposefully made it a hub for people of his ilk to find work. He made sure he was always neutral in his dealings. He didn't care who was looking for what work, as long as they paid fairly.

Spotting the sign with the crossed swords hanging over the entrance, Jacek pulled his horse up outside the tavern and dismounted. He tied the stallion to a railing and reached in his bags for some food for Bandur. He chucked a bone with some dried meat still on it onto the decking. Bandur jumped on it and settled down to chew on it.

"Stay there, boy. Guard the horse." Bandur cocked an ear in his direction, but continued to chew. Trusting the dog, Jacek went inside.

The immediate warmth of the big open room greeted Jacek like a comfortable blanket. The smell of roasting boar over the large fireplace and the hiss of fat dripping into the fire set his stomach to grumbling. He should eat while it was available. Save the food bundle he had for later.

The tavern was only a quarter full. The people who frequented this place were more sedate than the sailors, so it was quieter. Wooden benches scraped on the floor as men moved around. Jacek spotted Baden serving a pitcher of drink to a group of well-armed men at one table. The tavern owner caught Jacek's eye and walked up to join him.

"Didn't think I'd see you here so soon. Something go wrong with the mercs you hired a while back?" Baden narrowed his eyes.

"No. They were fine. Actually, I'd like to talk to them again."

"Well, one of them's here." He gestured with his head to a back corner.

Jacek nodded. "Thanks. Can I get some food and my usual to drink?"

"Sure. I always keep that swill in stock. Mostly for you."

Jacek ignored the jab and

crossed the room to the table in the corner.

"Solel." Jacek nodded to the woman.

She sat back and nodded in reply, motioning for him to join her.

"What brings you back here, Jacek?"

He sighed. "My daughter."

Solel leaned forward. "The one who came out of nowhere on that last job and kicked ass?"

He couldn't help it, he gave a small smile. "That's her. Her name is Aleni."

"I liked her. Even though we never spoke. She has good potential. Of course, trained by you is a big advantage." She sat back again and sipped at her drink.

Jacek grunted in reply. "Well, she's missing. She was kidnapped a few days ago."

Solel sat forward again, leaning her elbows on the table. "What? Why would someone kidnap her? Surely they would know you would come after her? Do they not know who you are?"

Jacek ignored the first question. "Oh, they know who I am. They left me for dead."

Solel nodded slowly, her green eyes distant. "So who would want her?"

Jacek let out a deep breath again. "Half the town now. Aleni had been sneaking behind my back and fighting in the Arena. She'd made a name for herself, winning every fight she was in. Including the ones she wasn't supposed to win." He looked pointedly at Solel.

"Ah. I see. So... Vossler?"

"Dead."

"Before or after you found him?"

"What do you think?"

Solel gave an understanding smile and took another swig of her ale.

"He'd had her taken to a gambling den on the other side of town."

"The Restless Hands? I think that's one of his."

Jacek nodded. "It's now a smoldering ruin. But Aleni had been taken just before it burned down."

Solel raised her eyebrows. "You don't muck around, do you?"

"Not when my daughter is in danger."

She nodded. "Fair enough. I would probably do the same. So do you know where she is now?"

"I'm not sure entirely, but one source thinks she's in the hands of the Brotherhood."

"Deacon Sesk's Brotherhood?"

Jacek nodded. "The same."

Solel made a noise in her throat. "That's ironic. After all we did to protect him. Including all she did."

"True. I hate to admit it, but..." He cleared his throat. "I need help, Solel." He looked her straight in the eyes.

"I can see that. If the Brotherhood does have her, you'll have a hard time getting her out of that old fortress. They have many people now. And the funds to have it guarded well. With their reputation, the guards will be sycophantic too. More dangerous."

Jacek nodded, shifting his weight on the chair.

"I can help. And don't worry about payment. This I'll do for free."

"You'll get paid." He didn't want to owe anyone. "But we'll need more than you and I."

Solel looked worried. "You'll need an army to get into that fortress."

Chapter Twenty Seven

The world was upside down. Aleni's view of the dimly lit room swung backward and forward, making her even more dizzy. Her head, full of pressure, felt like it was about to burst.

She was hanging from a rope around her ankles from a beam on the ceiling of the room. It did not give her a sense of wellbeing for her future. Two guards had come in and untied her from the chair. She tried to fight them, but one clubbed her over the head with the handle of his knife, leaving her reeling and senseless. She remained conscious, but not able to move.

Between them, the two guards tied her ankles and raised her up to hang from the beam. The other end of the rope was tied to a bench on the side of the room. The bench was attached to the wall, so it wasn't going anywhere.

Then they had left her alone.

In pain from the blow, and the blood now rushing to her head, she struggled to stay conscious. Her arms hung limply, making her shoulders ache. She had lost sense of the time of day. Maybe it was nighttime, because her body felt like it needed to sleep. There was a musty smell in the air, mixed with something acidic.

Tears of exhaustion blurred her vision. She just wanted to sleep and never wake up. When would it all be over?

Just then, the lock turned, and the door opened. Deacon Sesk stepped into the room, closing the door behind him.

"There you are, my dear." His voice sounded slithery and slimy to Aleni. Her stomach turned.

"What are you doing to me?" Aleni croaked out. She really needed water.

"I have an idea. Some way I can get your power." He crossed the room and retrieved an earthenware jar with a wide opening. Positioning it underneath her, Sesk pulled out a knife.

Aleni's heartbeat rose, thudding in her head. Was he going to kill her now? Was this it?

Now that the time was here, Aleni wasn't sure she wanted to die. She wanted to see Jacek and Bandur again. Even if they were dead. She wanted to see her horse, Beinn. She wanted to see the foal being born. Then to see it grow and become strong.

She couldn't die now. She realized she had too much to live for. Even if it meant she carried on without Jacek. Maybe Bandur was alive. Maybe she could carry on Jacek's work in his name. Perhaps she could run away up north into the mountains and live there on her own, away from everyone.

"What are you doing?" she said, her voice trembling. She tried to move her arms, but they were sluggish and her fingers wouldn't move.

Sesk batted away her attempts to reach for him. He cut into the seam at her shoulder and ripped the sleeve of her leather jerkin off. He then grabbed her right wrist and gripped it away from her body. Aleni watched helplessly as he took the knife and sliced down her forearm, opening a vein along the way.

Blood squirted out in a fountain and fell to the floor. Sesk re-positioned the jug and held her arm in one spot.

Aleni felt faint as she watched her lifeblood flow out of her, pulsing in time to the rhythm of her heart. It was like a morbid song playing her death knell. Why did it have to be so slow? She wept, waiting for her death.

But then she felt a tingling in her arm, different to the throbbing pain of the cut. She looked down to see the flow ebbing. Her vein was closing, healing on its own. She watched, fascinated, as the blood-flow lessened, eventually stopping altogether. Her healing power was working hard to keep her alive.

Dizzy but elated, it was short-lived as Sesk realized what was happening.

"No you won't. Your healing ability is impressive, my dear, but there is an easy fix to that." He brought the knife up again and sliced down to reopen the wound.

"No!" Aleni cried out in pain and desperation.

"I will have this!" Sesk declared. The jar was filling up as the blood pulsed out again. Much of it was getting on the floor as well.

The room began to get darker. Were the candles running out? Aleni stared at one of the open flames, sitting in a holder on one of the benches. But the flame still burned strong. It was her vision that was blacking out. She blinked and let out a sob, trying to fight it, but it was no use. The pain and sorrow accompanied her as she felt life ebb away.

Chapter Twenty Eight

"Are you saying just the five of us are going to storm that fortress?" Dunvern pointed back over his shoulder in the general direction of the Brotherhood's headquarters. "Are you mad?"

Jacek still had trouble with Dunvern's accent, so he wasn't entirely sure he understood every word, but he got the gist from his tone. Solel had helped him get in contact with the three others of his original crew, and they all sat around a table at the Lethal Mercenary.

Baden wandered over with a tray of drinks and handed them out. Only Jacek didn't have an ale. No one commented on it. They knew better.

"He's not mad," Rilaiz said, grinning, "he's desperate."

"If they have my daughter, I will go in there, with or without you."

Rilaiz waved his hand in the air. "And I'm sure you could do it. But you may not come out in one piece. There are a lot of very loyal warriors and monks in there. And these monks can fight, you know that."

"So, help me."

"I'm all for daring plans, but I prefer the ones where I come out alive." The blonde Rilaiz took a swig of his drink.

"The odds were against us on the road to Resahil."

Rilaiz scoffed. "Those were pathetic miners. Skinny and not well trained. It was hardly a challenge."

"You're better than the guards in there. And the monks. They're trained, but most don't have a lot of experience," Jacek said. "Besides, we're not attacking it openly. We'll go in using stealth. It's the only way in." He drank his Dire Sip, trying not to make a face as he realized it was a stronger brew than he was used to.

"So you have a plan?" Mular spoke for the first time. The large black man said little, but when he did, it was usually worth listening to.

Jacek leaned forward, propping his elbows on the table. "I do. We need to visit a temple of Ixtar."

⁓

The midday sun hid behind cold gray clouds when they approached the stone temple of Ixtar. There was a smell of humidity in the air. Jacek inspected the sky from the east to the west. A storm was coming. Soon.

The temple was an old elven building, one of only a few still intact after the war. The stones sat together with such skill that it required no mortar to keep it all together. One could not even fit a knife blade in the cracks between the stones.

It rose fifty feet up from the ground, roofed with carved stone slates that curved and fitted into each other as smoothly as the stone. Snow gathered in spots on the slates, breaking up the monotony of the gray stone. It was a marvel of engineering to the humans, but Jacek suspected it was something rather ordinary to the elves. He'd seen much more impressive buildings in the ancient elven city under the mountain in the north.

People milled about outside the temple, some sitting on the grand steps leading up to the entrance in the hope they could talk to one of the monks. They were thin and had few layers of clothing. Certainly no furs. Only a couple of monks came and went, rushing past the people in a show of importance. The poorest reached out to them as they passed, wanting handouts of money.

To get into the temple, one had to pay a coin in tribute, but Jacek refused to give money to the corrupt religion. He led his team around the side of the vast building, looking for a side entrance. On the western side, he spotted what he was looking for. Hidden behind some high shrubbery was a locked door. The mess of footsteps in the snow told him they used it frequently. He ordered the others and Bandur to move out of sight on the other side of the shrubs and waited to the side of the door.

He didn't have to wait long. Within five minutes, the lock clicked, and the door opened. As a monk stepped out, Jacek grabbed him and swung him around to push his face against the wall.

The force of the contact with the wall knocked the breath out of the monk, and he gasped in shock, trying to breathe. Jacek's cohorts stepped around the bushes and joined them. Mular closed the door quietly and leaned on it.

Jacek gave the monk a moment to catch his breath, then flipped him around and covered his mouth. "Let's go take a walk."

The group moved away from the temple and found a quiet gap between two buildings that was closed off at one end by a wooden wall. Mular took up a position at the entrance, facing out with his arms crossed. He was a formidable sight that would discourage investigation by any passersby.

Jacek half-dragged the monk to the end of the lane, which was only about ten paces long. He got in close to the man's face, taking in the fear and surprise. He still had his hand over the man's mouth.

"I'm going to take my hand off, and you're not going to scream or make any noise I don't approve of. If you do," he glanced up at Solel, "she will run you through so quickly, you will not have time to regret your actions before you die. Do you understand?"

Solel drew her sword slowly and silently from its leather scabbard, her face hard and cold.

The monk's head bobbed up and down readily.

Jacek slowly removed his hand, waiting to see if the man did anything. But the monk's lips, thin and pale, stayed firmly shut. The man had a long thin face dotted with moles. His dull brown eyes darted back and forth between Solel and Jacek.

"I'm looking for information. Do you know anything about a girl being taken and held at your headquarters in the fortress?"

The monk shook his head violently. "I don't, no."

Jacek narrowed his eyes. Could he be covering for his beloved leader? "If you lie to me, I will order my dog to rip you apart piece by piece. You will not enjoy it." He pointed to Bandur standing quietly behind him. He seemed to know he was being talked about and opened his mouth as if to smile, his sharp teeth showing clearly.

"I swear! I'm not lying to you!" The man's eyes widened, and a sweat broke out on his forehead despite the cold.

Jacek looked up at Solel. She nodded. He agreed with the assessment. The monk wasn't lying.

"Alright then, have you noticed anything different lately about Sesk? Any changes at the fortress, or even at your temple?"

The monk thought for a second, then his eyes brightened. "Yes! We've had a few new stones arrive in the last day."

"What's so different about that?"

"They're real! They actually work, they have magic. Almost all the stones we sell are just ordinary polished stones. But these we were told were real, and we tested them. One gives off a warmth like a fire, another acted as a shield, and yet another knocked one of my brothers off his feet with some sort of force!" He spoke rapidly.

Jacek sat back on his heels. This definitely meant they had Aleni. She was the only one who could activate those stones. "Do you know where they might hold someone captive?"

"I don't know, but one of my brothers went to the fortress last night. And he said he saw High Deacon Sesk going into a room on the second floor that was guarded by a warrior. My brother didn't know what was in there, and when he asked the guard, he was told to move along. Perhaps this person is being held there?"

"Perhaps." Jacek stood finally and stepped back. To his group, he said, "get rid of him and take his robe. Make it quick. He didn't lie to us."

The monk's eyes widened, and he struggled to get his feet under him as if to run. Solel moved in quickly and Jacek turned away, no longer interested. There was a crunch of bone and then silence.

Jacek had no sympathy for a man who would knowingly con people into parting with their hard-earned olons for nothing. Even though Jacek had no faith of his own, he found it despicable people would use others faith against them. Even if that faith was unwarranted. He had never believed in the gods. To him, they were simply man-made constructs that gave people hope in a hopeless world. It was the nature of man to strive to find something more powerful than themselves to appeal to for help.

The creation of the gods was also a great way to control people. And that was what Jacek despised the most.

"We need more robes." He pointed to Rilaiz and Dunvern. "You two, get us four more."

"What do you want us to do with the monks inside them?" Dunvern asked.

Jacek shrugged. "I don't care. Use your own discretion. Just make sure there's two big enough for Mular and I." He caught the tall man's eyes as he stood side on at the entrance to the alley. Mular gave him a barely perceptible nod.

Jacek stared up at the darkening afternoon sky. Gray clouds gathered in from the east and were making their way toward the city, obscuring the blue like a disease. He sniffed the air. That all too familiar sweet pungent smell hit his senses. The storm was close.

Chapter Twenty Nine

The first thing Aleni wondered as she awoke was if it was all a nightmare. Surely, everything that had happened was another one of her terrifying dreams? But then the ache in her shoulders hit her. The pain of the rope wrapped around her ankles, and the continued pressure in her head.

She blinked her eyes open.

The light from the candles in the room pierced at her vision. She squeezed them shut again to ward off the pain. After a few seconds, she tried again. It was getting better.

The first thing she saw was a pool of her blood on the stone floor below her. It really had happened. She was lucky to be alive. With that thought, she realized it was true. She was lucky. And she was glad. She wanted to live.

With renewed hope, she raised her arms, trying to get some movement in her shoulder joints. The pain sharpened, but then receded as she moved them around. Her ankles burned where they were tied together, holding her entire weight. The fibers from the rope cut into her skin.

The room was empty. Sesk had gone. But something else was different.

Her head was clearer. It wasn't completely normal, but she felt she could focus more. The fog had gone. Had the drug gone out of her system with most of her blood? She checked her arm. Her skin felt cool and moist to the touch. The wound had closed over, but there was still a mark there. In time that would disappear too. How long had she been out?

She was still weak and tired. But with her head clearer, maybe she could escape? Twisting her body up a little, she tried to reach for the rope around her ankles. But the weakness in her muscles caused her to collapse back into just hanging.

Could she try magic now? With the fog gone, maybe she could get to it. Taking a deep breath, she reached inside for the white ball of power. It was there, but tiny. Hard to reach. Her inner self couldn't quite go that far. She let out the breath and hung there for a little while longer, gathering strength.

Then she tried again. This time she got a little closer to reaching it. But it was still not enough.

So close, yet so far. Normally she could grasp it with ease at a single thought. But now, she would need to rest more. Licking her lips and trying to swallow, her mouth felt like it was full of sand. Dry as a bone. Hopefully, there was some water in here somewhere.

After closing her eyes for five minutes, she drew on what energy she had, taking in deep breaths. Turning inside herself, she reached again for her magic.

The glowing ball sat deep in her core, tiny and weakened. With tentative hope, she grasped for it.

And touched it.

The white glow surged outward, moving into her being. Aleni spread out her left hand and pointed at the rope around her ankles. The strands sparked and smoldered. A wisp of smoke curled up from the bindings. Not wanting to burn herself, she left it at that and waited for the rope to burn through.

Letting out a held breath, she relaxed a little and let go of the magic. But she kept an eye on the rope, not wanting to be caught unaware when it broke. She dropped her arms and held her palms flat in preparation.

Hours passed, or so it felt like before the rope gave a creak and then the strands snapped. Down she fell but her arms were not strong enough to hold her weight. They collapsed instantly, and she fell onto her right shoulder, her body crumpling after it. There was a wet splat as she landed in the pool of her own blood, spattering through one side of her white hair.

Pain shot through her body, aching in places she had been unaware of. Aleni lay there for some time, allowing herself to rest. She knew she didn't yet have the strength to stand.

After waiting and breathing carefully for some time, she attempted to get up. At first it was just to her hands and knees. But that was better than lying down. She could still move. So she looked around for water. By one of the benches, she spotted a wooden bucket. Crawling to it, she found it half full of water. She dipped a hand in and brought it to her lips.

It was brackish, and not fresh, but it was wet. Not caring at the taste, she took a few mouthfuls. Her stomach rumbled and she realized it had probably been some time since she'd eaten. Could she find some food in this place somewhere?

Just then, the sound of footsteps carried through the wooden door from the hall outside. They stopped outside the door. With considerable effort, she pushed herself to her feet and rushed to the hinge side of the door.

Her muscles ached and weariness still plagued her body, but if she was to get out of here, she would have to pull on reserves. She was determined to live and get out. She hadn't survived everything in Krodon's dungeon just to die here at the hands of some old man.

The lock turned, and the door latch opened. The door itself swung inward, concealing Aleni behind it. In walked a robed monk with the cowl down. It was not Sesk.

There was a gasp as the man saw Aleni was not where they had left her. The singed ends of the rope still glowed.

Seizing the moment, Aleni leaped on the monk's back. He immediately struggled with her, trying to throw her off. But she clung on tightly, her legs wrapped around his torso. She gripped his head in both hands and twisted it in a move she'd seen Jacek do before.

It didn't quite work. There was a grunt from the monk as his neck was twisted. But she didn't have the strength to break it.

He bent over and flicked his butt up while pulling on her arm. She flew over his head and landed on her back on the cold stone floor. The breath whooshed out of her lungs. Gasping, she tried to drag in more air.

The monk grabbed at her leather jerkin, dragging her back toward the pool of blood. All she could do was try to gasp for air. Finally, after a terrifying moment where she thought she would pass out, air rushed back into her starved lungs.

With the monk bent over her, this was the perfect time to execute a move Jacek had taught her. She wrapped her arms around his neck and pulled his head in close. Still lying on her back, she lifted her head and clamped down with her teeth as hard as she could onto his ear.

He screamed, trying to pull away. She let him, but didn't let go of his ear. The appendage ripped off, flooding her mouth with blood. The monk let go of her, his hands going to the bloody spot on the side of his head. His eyes bugged when he saw the ear in her teeth.

Spitting the ear out to the side, Aleni gathered her feet up close to her body and pushed out to land them flat on his chest. He went flying back to hit his head on the corner of a bench. Dazed and probably in incredible pain, the monk sat on the ground clutching his head and moaning.

Spotting a long metal tool on a bench, Aleni grabbed it and swung it at the man's head. He finally rolled to his side, out cold. Blood pooled under his head from the missing ear.

"Serves you right, asshole," Aleni said. She dropped the tool and went back to the bucket to wash her mouth out from the blood.

Breathing heavily from her exertions, Aleni moved to the door to see if anyone was coming. It seemed this room was in an isolated part of the castle, for the hallway was empty. No one must have heard the screams either. She'd got lucky.

She had to find somewhere safe to hide. And food. She must get her strength back if she was to get out of here.

Perhaps a nearby room had somewhere to hide? She set off, moving on silent feet to investigate.

Chapter Thirty

"Hey, there's one there." Dunvern pointed toward the gate of the castle where two warriors stood guard. A robed monk approached, spoke to the guards for a few seconds, then passed on through to the keep behind. "Now, what did he say to get in?"

Jacek and his team were all gathered close together behind a stone wall across from the bridge outside the castle. It was getting harder to see, as the darkening clouds gathered overhead, ready to drop their load. Jacek squinted up at them. Any minute now.

"Maybe it's just the fashion. Perhaps the guards have a thing for robes?" Rilaiz grinned.

Jacek frowned at him and turned back to watching the gate.

"I have to admit," Rilaiz went on, "these are comfortable. And warm." He picked at the black material now covering his leather armor and weapons.

"Don't tell me you're thinking of defecting?" Dunvern teased him.

"A man will do a lot for warm comfortable clothes."

"You two are ridiculous," Solel scolded them. "How can I take you seriously?"

"Oh, don't worry, love. My sword will prove itself all on its own." Rilaiz gave her a sideways glance.

"Call me love again and you won't have a sword." Solel said matter-of-factly.

"Shut up, all of you." Jacek spoke up. "Pay attention. What are we going to say to the guards? I don't want a fight."

"We could tell 'em we're there to clean the floors?" Rilaiz rubbed his hands together for warmth.

Jacek ignored that.

"Wasn't there a new chapter set up in Resahil?" Mular asked.

They all turned to look at Mular. He had been silent until now. The big man looked down at the snow and shifted his feet.

"What I mean is, we could claim to be from there." He motioned toward the guards. "They might know a lot of them on sight. Having five strangers suddenly turn up will cause questions. This is an explanation as to why they won't know us."

They were all silent for a second, then Jacek nodded. It was a solid idea. "Alright, let's go with that."

Lightning flashed overhead, lighting up the surrounding area. They all stared at the sky. Thunder soon followed, booming across the vista. Drops of fat rain fell, making little divots in the snow. It would turn to slush soon. It was going to get more and more miserable.

Perhaps they could use the urgency of the storm to convince the guards to let them in. Jacek just hoped there wasn't any secret word they had to know to get in. If he was in charge of security, that's what he would implement. Actually, he would put more guards on the gate. And have some up on the battlements. But the parapets were empty of people. The Brotherhood were not warmongers. They simply won control with people's minds and hearts.

Very different from Krodon and Tarken. Possibly even more dangerous. But from all accounts, there were still plenty of armed men inside the fortress. And they still had to find Aleni.

The rain poured down, soaking through their robes and threatening to give away the presence of their weapons underneath. Jacek had had to leave his sword behind as he couldn't conceal it under the robe. But his axe and dagger still sat in their customary places. He had a pouch full of his usual tools and smoke bombs. Bandur was in the care of Tu. The Lontar man was going through the preparations to cremate his daughter. He had appreciated having Bandur there to comfort him.

He stared at the castle. Aleni was in there somewhere. Hopefully not being tortured or abused. When this was all over, he would have to take her far away from here, where no one could get to her.

He thought again about her words just before they took her. Did she really want to die? If so, no matter where he took her, she would never be safe. Not if she meant harm to herself. He did not know how to protect her from that. Tying her to a tree for the rest of her life wasn't exactly feasible.

Her actions at the Arena spoke of her need to be free to do what she wanted to do. Each time he sought to keep her protected at home, she simply took off on her own. That wasn't working. He had to figure out another way to keep her safe.

Another pair of monks walked through the rain to the guards. After a quick exchange, they passed through. Jacek turned to his group and spoke.

"Alright, let's go."

Together, they got to their feet and straightened their robes. Jacek pushed Dunvern in the front and pulled his own cowl low over his face. He was too recognizable to be the spokesperson. "You speak for us," he whispered.

Dunvern gave a nod in acceptance and started out at a steady walk. Even though it was raining, all the other monks had approached at the same measured walk. Maybe it was something to do with their vows. Jacek's muscles tensed up at the slow pace and proximity to their goal. He made an effort to relax. It didn't work.

They got to within ten feet of the guards when the two warriors held out their pikes and crossed them over each other in a large 'x'. One was older, perhaps four decades, while the other was younger, only in his twenties. They wore leather armor with certain patches covered in metal.

"Halt. Identify yourselves," the older one spoke in a commanding tone.

"Kind sir," Dunvern's accent suddenly thickened. "We are simple Brothers from the newly established chapter in Resahil. We have journeyed long and are very tired from our exertions. Please may we take our ease in your grand domicile and have an opportunity to serve the esteemed High Deacon while we visit the city?"

Jacek was impressed with the eloquent speech, but he didn't think the guards would go for it. Inside his robe, he clenched the head of his axe, but kept his face lowered.

The older guard stared at Dunvern for a few seconds with a puzzled look on his face. He then shared the look with his comrade who shrugged. They most likely didn't understand every word. Maybe they should have made Mular be the spokesperson? This wasn't going to work. Jacek mentally readied himself for action.

"Go on through."

Jacek almost jerked in surprise. That was it? No searching them for weapons or at least checking all their faces? What sort of guards were these? Just for show? If he had been their boss, they would be fired by now. Or dead.

But it was in their favor, so he made no movement except to follow Dunvern into the courtyard beyond.

It was a large area, perhaps fifty feet across, where the ground was a mix of mud and slushy snow. The late afternoon was pouring into evening as the light grew to dark. Several monks crossed the courtyard from one end to another, entering a door into a side building. The main entrance, with its tall double wooden doors, loomed ahead of Jacek's group. One of the doors sat ajar, open to mendicants, but warded against the weather.

Jacek gave Dunvern a gentle push toward the door. Somehow they would have to find their way around inside without being found out. Jacek didn't know the first thing about the Brotherhood's behavior to each other inside these walls. He just remembered they were quiet on the road to Resahil. Even Deacon Sesk spoke rarely. Reticent he could certainly be, but it was Dunvern and Rilaiz he worried about.

Dunvern pulled the door open and stepped inside. One-by-one, Jacek, Rilaiz, Solel and Mular followed. Water streamed down Jacek's beard, dripping onto the front of the thick material of the robe. The group made quite the puddle on the floor of the entryway, all tensed and waiting for any signs of attack. But the high-roofed room was quiet. Outside, the rain beat down on the steps and door. Despite being in the enemy's den, Jacek was glad to be out of the storm.

Rushing footsteps reached Jacek's ear. He turned toward the sound, coming from the other side of the doorway leading out into the depths of the castle. Shortly, a small robed man appeared, his cowl down to reveal a naturally bald pate and a pallid, round face.

"Evening sirs. My name is Rhikhad. Can I help you?" The man lifted his nose to look down on them, even though half the group towered over him.

Dunvern spoke slowly, so as to be understood. "Ah yes, kind sir, we are postulates from the new chapter of the Brotherhood in Resahil. We have journeyed here to visit with your esteemed headquarters and perhaps learn from you in the way of the Creed." He gave his head a little bow to finish.

"Right. Of course. Well, come with me then. And wipe your feet." The little man swept his robe around dramatically to return the way he had come.

A large mat covered the spot in front of the doorway, and the group dutifully wiped their feet clean of mud and water. With Jacek and Solel keeping their cowls up and heads down, they moved after the little monk.

He walked swiftly, only pausing to point out objects or places of interest. There was a painting of the Deacon himself, resplendent in crisp robes and displaying the puckered scars on his face like a badge of honor. And over there was the very first stone the God Ixtar blessed with power and gave to the Deacon. It was encased in a wooden box with a glass lid. Jacek doubted very much it was activated. Otherwise, it wouldn't be in the box.

Dunvern, as the spokesperson for the group, pretended to be fascinated by the tour, engaging their guide with careful questions that reinforced their seeming interest.

Rhikhad took them to a large eating hall with tables and benches. A couple of monks sat together at one of the tables with bowls of steaming stew in front of them. The ceiling rose high overhead and a huge fire pit sat in the middle of the room, a large blackened log flickering on it. For the first time in a while, Jacek felt warmth push through the damp of his leather and ease into his bones. It was a discordant sensation in this place of unease.

"You can dry yourselves by the fire and our cook will provide you with food at the far end there." The pale man gave a short bow of his head. "Blessings of Ixtar to you all. I will come and find you later to show you to your lodgings." He then turned and left the room in a hurry.

Rilaiz gave a low whistle once he was gone. "If I'd known it was this easy to get food and a bed, I would have joined long ago."

"The downside being you would have to listen to that old crone con people out of their money every day," Solel crossed her arms and rolled her eyes.

Rilaiz shrugged. "Might be worth it."

"You're disgusting." She shook her head.

"Why do you care if people are being conned or not?" Rilaiz shook out the front of his robe in front of the fire. The others gathered around the fire pit as well.

"Because it doesn't help society at all. And I have to live in the society."

"How so?"

"Well, for example, say the local baker gets sucked into it. He spends what little money he has on useless rocks. Or paying tribute to a god that doesn't exist. Then he doesn't have enough money to buy flour or other ingredients he needs to make bread. Then his business suffers. Other people in the community have nowhere to buy bread, they go hungry and die. Some of those people are providers of goods and services themselves. It's all compounded when the majority of the community are sucked into it. They waste the few olons they have on the hope of a dubious salvation instead of buying food for their families or goods for their businesses. The problems are worse and more people are affected. Eventually, society will break down when there aren't enough people to keep it afloat." Solel's eyes sparkled with passionate fervor. This was obviously something she felt strongly about.

Rilaiz's eyes had shot up almost to his hairline. He didn't speak for a few seconds, his eyes thoughtful. "I had never thought of it that way. I always thought it was just best to mind my business and only do anything good if I was being paid."

"It's always better to be good no matter what. It's what will save us in the end. I believe everything will work better if we work together and look after each other. I know that's a strange concept, but I've seen it work on a small scale."

"Where?" Jacek asked. He thought of his own parents. They had had the same thinking. But it was what had got them killed.

"Down south, on the lower continent where I come from. There is a little village there called Riveracre. My father is the Chief councilman there. He showed people there how to look after each other and make sure everyone had food and shelter. The village thrives. There are no deaths from the elements or hunger. We all help with protection of the settlement from goblins and there is even public entertainment for everyone to enjoy."

"Public entertainment?" Dunvern echoed. "What is that?"

Solel shook her head. "Barbarians, you lot. It's where a group of people play music together and everyone dances and has fun."

They all looked at each other in mute consternation. Except for Jacek. Aleni had talked about such things. Her people loved music and dancing. Aleni herself was an extremely graceful dancer, with an ethereal voice. He often played his wooden pipe and she would sing and dance. The memories of those times pulled at his heart. He longed to be home with her again, doing exactly that.

With his thoughts now back on Aleni, he gazed around the hall, wondering where he should start looking for her.

Chapter Thirty One

The food from the kitchen at the far end of the eating hall was serviceable and hot, but not extremely tasty. For Jacek, it was fine. They only ate to keep up appearances as hungry travelers. After drying off in front of the fire, they sat down and ate.

Every minute they weren't moving around looking for Aleni was torture for Jacek, whose muscles sat tensed the whole time, waiting for action. The two monks in the hall gave them curious looks, but did not speak. The kitchen hands did not speak to them either. Jacek wondered if there was some sort of vow of silence, or if they simply did not like strangers.

After half an hour, Rhikhad returned. He informed them he had prepared rooms and they were to follow him.

Outside the large hall in the wide passageway, six guards stood off to the side. They stood in a small circle, trying to look casual and whispering amongst themselves.

Jacek wasn't fooled. He gave Solel a meaningful look, but shook his head. He wanted to see first where Rhikhad was taking them.

Rhikhad ignored the guards and moved on ahead at a hurried pace, as though he had important things to do and no time to waste. In Jacek's mind, he was just hastening his death.

The guards walked casually at a distance. They weren't fooling anyone.

As they walked, Jacek glanced through any door that was open, hoping to see Aleni, although he knew it was a long shot.

Rhikhad led them up a flight of stone stairs to the second floor. The hallways here seemed to run off in all directions. Closed doors sat along the halls at various intervals, but none gave any indication of what sat on the other side.

Finally, the little monk stopped outside a single door and opened it.

It opened outwards.

In Jacek's experience, doors that opened outward were not designed to be opened from the inside. In addition, there was a lock on the door.

He stood behind Dunvern, who faced Rhikhad. Jacek turned slightly, trying to see around the cowl covering a lot of his face. He caught a glimpse of the guards behind them, waiting. Reaching through a slit in the side of his robe, he furrowed in his pouch. He looked at Solel and Rilaiz next to him and nodded. He then prodded Dunvern in the back and sprang into action.

A ceramic smoke bomb thrown behind him broke open and white smoke poured out, blocking the view of the guards. Mular, Solel and Rilaiz launched themselves through the growing smoke and attacked.

Dunvern went for Rhikhad. The monk blocked a blow aimed for his head with an arm and immediately went on the defensive. Dunvern then pulled out his knife, and the monk was dead in a few seconds.

Jacek stripped off his robe and dumped it on the ground. As soon as his axe was in his hand, his muscles relaxed. He went into battle mode. His mind quietened, focusing only on obstacles and enemies and how to overcome them. He moved through the smoke and joined the fray.

Identifying his allies first, he swung and blocked with his axe. His body went into an automatic way of moving that required little thinking. Years of experience woke his muscles and let them take over. He allowed no emotion in this space, and all his rage subdued.

The guards fell before him like chaff. Mular, Solel and Rilaiz each had a guard to contend with, but Jacek took out three warriors in an economy of movement and skill. He left them where they fell and ran down the hallway, calling Aleni's name. If she was conscious, she should hear him and try to let him know where she was. Hopefully, even if they gagged her, she could make a sound some other way.

He strained his ears to hear over the clashing sound of fighting behind him.

Aleni jerked awake. Something had woken her, but she couldn't figure out what it was. Where was she? This room didn't look familiar, and she couldn't remember how she'd got here.

An ornate bed with four posts and draped in gold and blue was the most prominent piece of furniture in the room. With a flash of unwanted memory, Aleni remembered now how she had got here.

She'd snuck around after escaping the room with the rope and horror and had found some food and water in a small kitchen nearby. She'd then found this room tucked away around a dead-end corner.

She had avoided the bed and tucked herself in behind an upholstered armchair near the far wall to eat and drink. The food made her feel much better, and the water restored her dry mouth. She didn't even remember falling asleep.

Aleni listened for a second to figure out what had woken her. Faintly, she heard the clashing of metal nearby. Had they found her missing and sent out soldiers to search the castle? She had to hide better than this.

She checked in a cupboard. It was full of linens and bedding supplies. She wouldn't fit in there. Running her eye over the room, she spotted a tapestry next to the bed. Did it just move?

Aleni crossed to the woven picture hanging on the wall and pulled it to the side. In behind was an opening, just big enough for an adult to step into, although it would be cramped. Plenty big enough for her. It led into pitch darkness. Cobwebs covered the entrance, but she swiped them aside.

Her stomach clenched. She had no idea where this led. And even with her elven sight, she couldn't penetrate the darkness. There was simply no light to amplify.

The clashes of metal continued in the distance. It almost sounded like fighting, but that didn't make any sense. Either way, she didn't want to be found, so this was her only chance to get away.

Taking a deep breath, she stepped into the unknown, letting the tapestry drop into place behind her. The darkness was absolute.

With her hands outstretched in front, she felt her way along the passage. The stone was cool and dry to the touch, covered in decades of dust and cobwebs. The musty smell spoke of disuse and age. This passage was obviously long forgotten. But where did it lead? Hopefully not a dead end.

She had to keep reminding herself that at least it was away from the oncoming soldiers.

—⁂—

Most of the rooms were empty. Jacek checked every one. Each door he opened, he called out Aleni's name. Nothing. Where would they be holding her? Was there a dungeon below the fortress, like in Krodon's? Jacek's stomach turned at the thought. Aleni did not need more of that trauma on top of what she had.

He opened a door that had a lock on the outside, similar to the one they were being led to. Inside, he stopped cold. A frayed and burned rope end hung from the ceiling. Below it, blood pooled on the floor. A lot of blood. He kneeled down next to it and tapped a finger in it. Fresh. And still slightly warm. His heart clenched. Was this Aleni's blood? He couldn't know for sure, but the length of the rope left hanging above indicated the person who had hung there was not very tall.

Had they killed her and already taken her out to be dumped in the snow?

He stood and gripped his axe tighter. He couldn't jump to conclusions yet. He would search this place from top to bottom first before looking outside for a body.

Out in the hall, he moved on, searching through every room. A lot were empty. No one came across his path.

Finally, Jacek's luck ran out. He opened a door into an occupied room. A very occupied room. As in military occupation. It was a large dormitory. Over thirty pairs of eyes scattered all over the room in various states of dress, turned to stare at him.

Those odds were not conducive to living. Time to run.

He sped back down the hallway in the direction he'd come. There was silence now where before there was fighting. Behind him, he heard many heavy footsteps following. A glance back confirmed the men in the room now carried swords and were pursuing. Some were dragging on armor as they moved.

He rounded a corner and came upon his team. They had all removed their robes and looked far more formidable in their armor.

"Move it," Jacek said. "Incoming." He jerked his thumb back over his shoulder.

Without hesitation, the four mercenaries fell into a running step behind Jacek.

After another couple of turns, they came upon the stairs. A large group of monks marched in their direction, blocking off the other side of the hallway. Jacek turned and led them down the stairs.

He raced through his options. He wasn't leaving without Aleni, so the only other thing to do was continue the search. But with the rabble behind them, their odds had diminished on surviving a direct fight. He had to narrow down the playing field so only a few soldiers could engage at once. It might buy them time.

Turning down another hallway, he spotted a set of double doors, with one door open. He aimed for that. The guards were only ten or fifteen feet behind them.

"In here!" he called out to his team.

He swung through the open door by gripping the closed one, his momentum crashing him into it. The others followed close behind. As soon as the first soldier appeared, he thrust his knife into the man's gut.

The second soldier behind that one got Solel's sword through the chest. The bodies dropped where they died, making it more difficult for the next soldiers in line to get through, giving his team time to take them out. Jacek used his weight on the closed door to keep it from being opened.

Jacek glanced around to see where they were, and his heart sank. It was a grand hall, with a sunken floor in the middle. A dais sat at the far end with a large stone chair on it. Tarken's old throne room.

The sconces were all lit, and the room was clean and tidy. It was obviously still used. Sesk possibly thought of himself as worthy to sit on the giant throne.

There was bound to be another entrance to the hall, possibly behind the throne somewhere.

"Rilaiz, go check for any other entrances in this room."

The young man nodded and headed toward the other end of the hall.

"Make sure to check behind any tapestries!" he called out, pushing back against the door. The soldiers had stopped trying to come through the open door and were trying to push the other one open. "Mular! Get over here!"

The large man rushed over to stand close to Jacek, lending his strength to the effort. The door immediately stopped moving.

Before Rilaiz could get to the throne, a robed figure stepped out behind it. Jacek squinted to see and realized it was Sesk. Good, he could interrogate the man and find out where Aleni was.

But Rilaiz got no further. Sesk held out his hand in front of him, palm out in a stopping motion. Rilaiz seemed to hit an invisible barrier and stopped moving. What? This looked familiar, but it couldn't be.

With a flick of his hand, Sesk sent Rilaiz hurtling off his feet to one side of the hall, finally falling and rolling to a stop. The young man lay there with his back to Jacek, not moving.

Jacek's attention swung back to Sesk, who was now stepping down from the dais and walking slowly toward them. This was not good. He was probably using a stone somehow.

Dunvern made a run for Sesk, his two swords out in front. He let out a wordless yell as he moved. Jacek's stomach curled over. "No! Dunvern!"

But it was too late, Sesk flicked his hand up again and the red-haired fighter flew back directly toward Jacek and Mular.

Chapter Thirty Two

The darkness was cloying. Being in the dark was alien to her. Her eyes could amplify even the slightest light source, but here there was absolutely none. The black wrapped around her like gripping fingers, making her skin crawl. The fear of something coming out of the darkness at her sat foremost in her mind, threatening to take over her body and leave her unable to move.

But she had to keep moving, otherwise she would never get out of here. This tunnel had to lead somewhere, and right now, she didn't even care if it led her right back into the hands of Sesk. At least Sesk wasn't Krodon. She could deal with what the old monk would do to her.

With one hand on the wall to her right, and the other out in front, she took one step in front of the other. Somewhere, there was a bang that reverberated through the stone. The cold air caressed her cheek like a ghost. Her imagination ran wild with possibilities of what could be in the dark ahead of her.

Bit by bit, she made progress. Eventually, her right hand hit open air, and after feeling around, discovered the passage turned to the right. She followed it, not allowing herself to stop.

Her foot came down on something that gave way under her weight, and a splintering sound rang through the passage. She tripped, falling forward to catch herself on her hands.

Something had caught her foot. Heart ramming against her chest, she tried to extricate it. She felt around her ankle with her bare right hand and a coldness fell over her.

Bones. What felt like ribs, broken unevenly off around her ankle, threatened to stab at her leg. They were large enough to be human.

With the fear thrumming through her body, she probed further out. That was definitely a chest bone. Her fingers felt a gap, then more bone and a lot of small ridges. Teeth. Flattened teeth. She jerked her hand back toward her chest. This was a human.

Someone had died in here. Had they been murdered, or had they gotten trapped and died from hunger and thirst? Either situation didn't appeal to her imagination. She had to get out of here. But what if there was no end to this passage? Or if there was a door, it could be locked. She might end up dying in here like the poor person whose bones lay on the floor. Aleni's heart sped up even more at the thought.

Tugging at her foot frantically, she eventually got it free. Her breaths came in short gasps, her chest heaving. Clambering to her feet, she moved forward again, her hands out in front.

After a short while, she heard noises. Shouts, sounds of fighting. It was up ahead somewhere. It was encouraging, because it meant there was an opening somewhere along this passage for the sound to reach her. Aleni hoped the opening was big enough for her to get through.

Then she heard something that made her stop in her tracks. A voice, as familiar to her as her own.

Jacek.

Her heart leaping in her chest, she moved faster, hoping her ears weren't deceiving her.

———

Dunvern came flying toward Jacek and Mular. It forced the two to catch the semi-large man. All three fell in a heap, breath knocked out. Behind them, the door moved inward, pushing against the pile, the strength of the soldiers getting the upper hand.

Dunvern shook his head rapidly and looked slightly dazed. "What in the hells was that?"

"Sesk appears to have magic. We can't fight that." Jacek felt the door moving behind him and knew they had lost the battle there. They would have to make their stand further back.

He pushed at Mular next to him, who rolled out of the way. Jacek sprang to his feet and backed up toward the west wall, monitoring both the door and Sesk.

Solel ran over and joined them, with Mular and Dunvern now on their feet as well. Rilaiz still lay unmoving next to the east wall. Jacek hoped he wasn't dead. Surprising even himself, he liked the young man.

The group continued to back up with the wall behind them.

The door burst open, and the soldiers poured into the room, swords out and menacing. Jacek got his axe in his hand and readied himself for a fight.

Sesk took a few steps back himself and folded his arms. "Get them. But don't kill the Red Hunter. I want him alive. The others I don't care about." He seemed content to let the soldiers take care of business for now. Good. At least swords Jacek could deal with.

The first row of soldiers rushed forward. The line of Jacek's mercenaries met them with a resounding crash of weapons and grunts. Jacek kicked out to push his opponent back and whipped his axe up in a huge backhand swing. The sharp pointed end of the blade sliced through the face of the soldier. The man collapsed on the floor, covering his face with his hands.

More soldiers surged in behind him, pushing in on Jacek's space. He moved with speed to keep them back, blocking blows and moving to keep only one in front of him.

Around him, his team fought with skill. The soldiers greatly outnumbered them, but they had to keep fighting. Solel ducked to avoid a high swing aimed for her head. She returned with a slash to the midsection.

The soldier, who obviously didn't have time to put his armor on in the rush, clutched at his belly as blood gushed out. He fell to the floor, his weapon clanging after him.

Dunvern was a whirling devil with his two short swords. He slashed out in a silent rhythm, moving his arms peculiarly. The soldiers coming at him could not defend against the speed of the swipes.

He was fast, but he would tire quickly. Then they would overrun him. Over thirty soldiers and monks swarmed the room. They moved in on Jacek and his team until eventually they pressed them up against the wall.

There was nowhere to go.

The muscular soldier in front of Jacek stabbed his sword straight out at Jacek's gut. With a parry to the side, he swiped the weapon out of the way. He stepped in and stabbed his knife high into the soldier's side.

The soldier dropped his sword and grabbed at the deep wound. He wheezed and his legs buckled. Jacek let him fall, making it harder for the man behind him to get in closer.

But then a movement on his right had him only just managing to block with his arm. Another soldier had taken the opening and tried to slice into his arm. With his axe arm up, he was open to another strike.

The soldier took it. He lashed out with his fist and drove it into Jacek's injured side. Jacek curled into it to soften the blow. But it still took the breath out of him and shot searing pain through his body.

The fist pounded into him again and again. He felt his ribs creak. Then with a rush of movement, the soldier pushed Jacek up against the wall, slamming his right wrist into the stone. After several blows, his hand gave out and released the axe.

Another soldier moved in and held him from the left. Jacek struggled to move, but they leaned in. It was no use. He was done.

Panting to get the air back into his lungs, he watched helplessly as one by one they overwhelmed his team and pinned them up against the wall too.

Jacek glared at Sesk, watching the older man pace back and forward on the other side of the teeming mass of soldiers. The scar tissue on one side of his face contorted up to allow his mouth to form a smirk.

Jacek couldn't wait to cut it out of his face.

But for now, he was well and truly stuck. They quickly disarmed him of his knife and pouch. There was not much he could do. The two soldiers leaned heavily on him, their breath hitting his cheeks.

But then a blur of movement behind Sesk caught his eye. Being careful not to react, he watched and waited.

Something attacked Sesk from behind, and the old man's feet flew out from under him. Jacek couldn't quite see over the tops of the men's heads, but the commotion moved on to the soldiers.

Another man went down at the back of the group. A sword flashed up and down again, and another fell. A ripple of unease flowed through the crowd of men. They turned toward the movement.

Then they all spread out. Something was coming in and they were eager to get away from it. A gap appeared and Jacek finally got his first glimpse of what was happening.

Aleni darted in and out among the men, moving at full speed. She had a sword in each hand and moved like water. Spinning, kicking, slashing and stabbing. The swords, merely an extension of her arms, were merciless.

Men fell before her attacks like wheat. Scything through the crowd at such a speed that the soldiers had no chance to act.

Jacek's heart felt as if it was going to burst. Relief at seeing her alive accompanied his pride at seeing her use the skills he'd taught her to seek vengeance on these men for imprisoning her.

Cries of pain rang out in the large hall, along with rings of metal and thumps of men hitting the floor. The metallic tang of blood hung in the air.

Bolstered, Jacek pushed out at his captors. Distracted by the commotion among their compatriots, he took the two soldiers by surprise. With a loud roar, he took them both down to the ground.

He wrapped one leg around one man's neck and his right arm around the other's. With a quick bunching of muscles and a jerk with each limb, he broke both necks at once.

He looked around. His team were also using the distraction to act. The soldiers holding them suddenly had additional problems to deal with.

Jacek retrieved his weapons and moved toward Aleni to help.

It seemed she needed little help, as he took out only one man before she felled the last. She came to a stop a few feet from him, still in a fight stance, her chest heaving, waiting for someone else to attack.

But they were all down.

In the quiet following the clamor, Dunvern's voice could be heard speaking to Mular. "She's on our side, right?"

Aleni blinked twice, then her gaze fell on Jacek. A slow smile grew on her face. It took her two seconds to drop her swords and run to him.

She leaped up and into his open arms. Jacek held her tight, never wanting to let go. A part of him suddenly felt whole again.

Eventually he had to let her go and drop her gently to the floor. "Are you alright?" He held her at arms' length, looking her over for any wounds. She seemed unharmed, although her white hair was stained with blood. Like it had been dunked in it. The only other thing of note was that she was missing her right sleeve. "Is that your blood?"

"Uh, it is my blood technically, but I'm unharmed. Now, anyway. He drugged me to stop me using my powers, though. Some of the drug is still in me and it's hard to keep a hold of it. But I'm alright." Her smile faded. "They told me you were dead. I was so worried."

"I nearly was. Someone helped me. I'll tell you later."

"Where's Bandur?" Aleni looked around the room.

"He's with a friend."

Aleni snapped her attention back to him with a jerk of her head. Her eyebrows furrowed. "You have a friend?"

"He has a few, little one." Mular stepped up behind Jacek and gave a bow of his head. "I am proud to help your father find you. No one should ever be taken from their family. This I believe is wrong. Even in Selendria."

Jacek stared at the big man. It seemed there was more depth to him than he thought.

"Thank you, kind sir," Aleni said with a smile. "My father is an independent man, but I think there are still times he needs others to help him. It's a lesson he's needed to learn for some time now." She gave him a sideways look and a smile.

"Look who's talking," Jacek grumbled.

Just then, something made Aleni look around Jacek and toward the stone throne at the end of the hall. Her face drained of any color and her body shook. Her eyes unfocused and she started to back up.

Jacek whirled in that direction. Behind the throne was a door. It had opened and someone had stepped out. Jacek's blood ran cold.

It was Krodon.

Chapter Thirty Three

With only a slight limp that bespoke his past injuries, the former warlord that Aleni had almost crushed to death with her magic over a year ago, walked out onto the dais and leaned indolently on the back of the throne. A wicked smile blighted his face, his dark eyes holding something malevolent that almost made Jacek shudder. His dark hair hung lank and unwashed to his shoulders. Garments made from wolf-pelt had pieces of metal attached in strategic places to create a sort of armor.

He didn't look too worse for wear in Jacek's eyes. He had obviously spent his time well in recuperation. His men must have secreted him out from under the mountain and nursed him back to health.

Jacek tightened his grip on his axe, his teeth squeaking as he ground them. He remembered well the feeling as Krodon's sword had run through his body, nearly taking his life. It was only because of Aleni that he was still here. But then he was brought back to the moment as Solel spoke.

"Hey, is she alright?"

Jacek's attention dragged back to Aleni. She had bumped into Mular behind her and was just standing there, breathing fast with her eyes unfocused. Beads of sweat had broken out on her forehead.

Gut twisting, Jacek moved to stand a couple of feet in front of her, leaning down to meet her eyes and being careful not to touch her. "Hey, come on baby girl, come back to me." But she wasn't there. She was back in a nightmare. A waking nightmare.

"Sesk is awake," Dunvern warned.

Jacek turned his head to see the old man rise to his feet. He backed up, monitoring Jacek's group until he stood near Krodon.

"You see, my lord, I have brought them to you. They are yours for the killing." Sesk clenched and unclenched his fists, as if to test out their strength. Jacek wondered if the power the man wielded gave him extra strength as well.

"Did he do that to her?" Solel asked Jacek in a low voice, pointing to Aleni.

Jacek could only nod. There were no words for someone as evil as Krodon. Having taken Aleni with the ambition of trying to re-populate the world with elves single-handedly, he was a monster. And that was an insult to monsters.

Solel drew her sword again. "Then I'm going to kill him." She started forward, her face set in determination.

Sesk raised his hand. Solel ignored him and kept moving. A wave of force rushed out from him. Solel went flying back. She landed on her feet and rolled backwards to break the impact, unharmed. Her face held a determined look, but she didn't move.

Jacek turned back to Aleni. He had to get her to return to the present. She was too vulnerable like this. He had to get through to her somehow. There was something he could try.

He spoke in elvish, his tone low and gentle, but firm. "Aleni. It's Jacek. Listen to my voice. You are alright. I'm here with you and I will not let him hurt you. Listen to my voice. Come back to me, baby girl. You can do this. You are so strong. He will not defeat you. You can overcome this. He is not hurting you now. He will not hurt you again.

"I need you to squeeze your hand." He looked down at her tiny open hand, waiting to see if she would do it. "Squeeze your hand if you can hear me."

Her breathing continued raggedly, her mouth open and her eyes blank. As if he had some sort of mind power, he tried to will her back to the present. In the past when she had been like this, it had taken a while for her to return. There was no time for that now.

Around him, his team stood protectively, weapons drawn and ready to fight. On the other side of the hall, Rilaiz groggily got to his feet. The young man turned and caught his eye. The two nodded at each other. Rilaiz picked up his sword and crossed over to join the team.

"Cover us," Jacek commanded.

Krodon then made his move, drawing a massive sword and advancing on the group.

"Aleni, it's Jacek," he began again in Elvish. "Listen to my voice." He went on, continuing his coaching as before. Second by agonizing second, he watched her come back to reality. Around them, the crashing of metal and scuffles of feet threatened to burst their bubble of security. At any moment Krodon could crash through the line of mercenaries and kill them.

He turned back to his daughter.

"Come back, Aleni." He said again in Elvish. The hair on the back of his neck rose as he felt Krodon close in.

When Aleni finally squeezed her fist tightly, Jacek's heart gave a leap of joy. "Hey, there you are. Look at me."

Aleni blinked a few times and focused her gaze on Jacek.

He spoke quickly. "You're back. You're in the present, and I'm here with you. Let's take this fucker out once and for all, eh?"

Aleni narrowed her eyes and set her mouth. Then she nodded.

"That's my girl." He handed her the two swords she'd dropped. "You'll need these."

Jacek turned.

A large force crashed into him, taking him to the ground. He only just got his hand up in time to grip Krodon's sword arm. The two grappled, each trying to get the upper hand. Now was their chance to finally fight evenly.

⁓⁓

Trusting that Jacek had Krodon in hand, Aleni turned to Sesk, who was continuing to wreak havoc with this new power he possessed. Her heart still pounded from the flashback. Taking a deep breath in and out, Aleni cleared her head of the last vestiges of the awful memories that had returned unbidden.

She moved in beside the woman with the patchy skin, who still wielded her sword, but braced herself steadily with one foot farther back. When Sesk threw force power her way, the woman bunched her muscles and leaned into it.

Aleni reacted with her own wall of power. Pulling on the magic within her, she let it flow through her unchecked. Gritting her teeth, she pushed out in Sesk's direction. The two opposing forces met in the middle in a battle of wills.

"How do you have this power, Sesk?" Aleni called out over the rushing sound of the two magics colliding.

The old man smiled thinly. "I drank your blood, of course."

Horrified, Aleni turned her head to meet the woman's eyes. She didn't know her name, but the husky woman screwed her face up into an expression of disgust.

Aleni studied the old man again. The scarring on his face looked old. They hadn't changed from earlier, so he must not have her healing power. That must come from some other part of her.

"How did you know that would work?" Aleni asked between gritted teeth. It was taking a lot of effort to maintain the magic. But she knew if she let go, the battle would be lost.

"I didn't. But I had an idea that it might. Now you're not the only person with magic, my dear. It seems to be controlled by will alone. Do you think yours is stronger than mine?" He grinned, baring his teeth in a mix of pleasure and hate.

"Let's see." Aleni drew in her will and pushed out with it.

Sesk's wall of magic fell back under the onslaught. The old man grunted with the strain, holding both arms up as if to ward her off.

She kept on relentlessly. Magic whirled out of her core and toward Sesk, forcing his wall back. Sweat dripped from her brow.

But Sesk seemed to have an iron will of his own. With a growl, he redoubled his efforts. His wall moved back toward Aleni. He had many years of life experience, and going by the scars he bore, probably heartache and pain to go with it. Aleni sensed bitterness and anger in his attack. And sorrow. A lot of sorrow. Aleni knew that pain, but it didn't excuse him from his actions. She certainly didn't go around kidnapping people and slicing them open to drink their blood.

Her wall faltered under Sesk's assault. Slowly it fell back in her direction. With a rush, it came at her. She was lifted off her feet and sent flying.

Hitting the back wall of the throne room, the air rushed out of her lungs and her head hit the unforgiving stone. Pain speared into the back of her head. She dropped to the ground, the room spinning. Trying to breathe in, it felt like there was no air. Her lungs simply wouldn't work. Panic rose as she realized Sesk was walking toward her. Her body slumped without air powering it. She reached up to feel at the back of her head, her hand coming away bloody.

The lady warrior tried to stop his advance, but he merely flung her to the side with magic. She then threw her sword at him. He held up an arm, halting it in midair.

A wicked smile erupted on his grisly face. He angled a hand and turned the sword toward Aleni, blade point first.

Fresh horror clenched her chest. She whacked feverishly at the front of her leather armor as if she could force her lungs to work. But it took precious seconds before her chest untightened and allowed air in. As she gasped in a precious lungful of air, the sword flew at her. She tried to get a hand up to erect a shield. But nothing happened.

Pain erupted in her side as the blade sliced through. She bit back a strangled cry. With a clang, metal hit stone and bounced to the floor. Aleni looked down to find an inch-deep gash in her side. Hot thick blood already began to pool and drip out over her armor.

She reached for her power again, but it felt far away, almost like when she was drugged. But how could that be? She'd just wielded it. She looked down at her hands. One hand covered in blood.

Her head. This had happened for a bit after the head wound on the mountainside with Jacek. This one didn't feel as bad, so all she could hope was it wouldn't last as long.

Powerless, she dragged herself to her feet, clutching her side and leaning heavily on the wall behind her.

Sesk narrowed in on her again, raising his arm.

Another weapon came shooting in at him from the side. Aleni's eyes darted over to see another of Jacek's friend's launch a spear at Sesk.

"No!" Both her and the warrior woman shouted at the same time. But it was too late.

Sesk caught this as well in midair. With growing dread, Aleni braced herself for what was coming. She tried valiantly to grip the magic again, but it was no use. The spear slammed into her shoulder and didn't stop. It spun in place, drilling through her armor and slowly bit into her flesh. She clenched her jaw against the pain, but couldn't stop herself from screaming as the agony grew.

Weariness crept over her suddenly, ushered in by frustration. She had lost a lot of blood not long ago, and then expended a great amount of energy taking down all the soldiers that now littered the room. Bone tired, she realized she was going to die here. She batted weakly at the shaft of the spear, but Sesk held it tightly in place with his magic.

Her magic. *Stolen* magic. Just like so many other things, stolen from her. She couldn't let him steal her life as well. She *wouldn't* let him.

Gritting her teeth against the pain, she channeled it. Channeled the pain and exhaustion into an emotion she had been suppressing for a long time. One she should have let out long before now. One she should have *acknowledged*.

Rage.

Rage at losing her parents. Rage at Krodon's abuse. Rage at nearly losing Jacek. Twice. Sesk kidnapping and nearly killing her. All of it molded into one huge ball of rage. Funneling it all into focus and gritting her teeth, she reached once more for the ball of power within.

Got it.

Her eyes fell on Sesk's scars. Becoming rage incarnate, she burst into flame. Tongues of fire licked over her entire body. Heat blazed through her. But none of it consumed her. She *was* the fire.

The spear dropped to the floor with a clatter. Blood pounded in her ears. With a guttural scream, Aleni clapped her hands together in front of her. An arrow of flame exploded out. Sesk screamed as the fire came at him, and his wall of magic disappeared like it was never there. Jacek was wrong. Emotions had everything to do with her fighting. They were tools for her focus.

Sesk continued to scream, reaching out to her with his hands outstretched. "Please! Have mercy on me! I didn't kill you, I just wanted what you had. Please! Stop!"

But her vengeance would not be denied. She continued, unrelenting. Fire surged out from her body, a roar of unrelenting heat and light. Fueled by rage and focused by pain. But at the edges, weariness crept back in. She had pushed too hard for too long. Her vision darkened. The room was disappearing quickly from her sight. If she pushed too far, would it be permanent? She had no idea.

The smell of burning flesh assaulted her nostrils and made her stomach turn. A sense of horror arose within as she realized what she was doing. But he deserved it for what he'd done. He was going to kill her otherwise. Black smoke rose from Sesk as the flames carried on unabated. His screams rang out until suddenly they cut short. He fell into a heap on the floor.

Only then did Aleni let go of her power. The flames covering her died, her body steaming. Burned out like the body on the floor, she fell to her knees. Her vision was gone. Chest heaving, she was spent.

Her attuned ears heard hesitant steps come closer to her. She reached up for a hand, still unseeing. A female but calloused hand gripped hers and hefted her to her feet.

"Are you alright, little fiery one?" There was a hint of amusement in the woman's husky voice.

Aleni's rage was gone. Harnessed for use, she found herself strangely empty. Where once there was deep hatred, there was now nothing. Almost peace. Not because she had killed him, but because she acknowledged the feeling and allowed it into her.

She smiled. "Yes, I think I am." The hand gave a silent squeeze. An unspoken word passed between them. Whatever this woman had endured, she seemed to understand Aleni's actions.

"What is your name?" Aleni asked. She blinked, starting to see spots of light returning to her vision.

"I'm Solel."

"Thank you for helping Jacek." She squinted up at the women's face, which was starting to coalesce in front of her.

Solel shrugged. "It was the right thing to do."

They turned to where Jacek and Krodon were still wrestling. Krodon's sword was on the ground next to them, with the warlord trying to reach for it. Jacek was holding his arm to prevent him from getting it.

With a deft move, Jacek rolled him over to be on top. He had one arm pinned with both hands, but the other was free.

Aleni took a step toward them, but Solel held her arm. "Don't. Let him do it. He needs to do this. For you."

Aleni understood that. She knew Jacek often felt powerless to help her. Whenever she had a nightmare, or a flashback episode, she knew he wanted to do more. He didn't seem to understand that he already did plenty. Just being there was enough.

But he was a man of action. And Aleni had had her chance to wreak revenge on Krodon already. He must have spent the last year in a lot of pain.

The two men bashed at each other with their fists and elbows. Skin puffed up and broke open. Muscles strained and tendons stretched. Sweat poured down. Armor creaked.

Aleni watched anxiously, not entirely sure who would win. Jacek was good, of course, but so was Krodon.

Krodon was on top when he suddenly reached down and whipped a knife out of his boot. In one lightning-fast move, he stabbed it down onto Jacek's right hand. With a sickening crunch, it sliced through the first and second fingers. Aleni's legs weakened and nearly buckled.

Jacek let out a roar of pain, then gritted his teeth. Blood poured out of the stumps of his severed fingers.

Aleni surged forward, sword in hand, her heart thumping against her chest. But Jacek moved first. He flicked his wounded hand up toward Krodon's face and flung blood right in his eyes.

The warlord tried to turn his face away, but it was too late. It blinded him.

"Throw me a sword." Jacek said in elvish to Aleni, holding out his left hand. His voice strained and his vowels sounded weird, but she understood. She slid her sword along the floor. Jacek closed his hand over it.

In one quick thrust, he stabbed the sword through Krodon's chest. The same spot Krodon had stabbed Jacek in a year ago. A killing wound.

Krodon's mouth fell open. Aleni wasn't sure if it was in surprise or an attempt to breathe in. Either way, she took no small satisfaction in seeing him suffer.

He toppled over, helped in part by Jacek throwing him off. The sword still stuck out of his chest, and he fell awkwardly onto his side, clutching feebly at the blade. In the space of two heartbeats, he breathed his last.

Chapter Thirty Four

Jacek knew pain. He had been injured many times in the past. But this was something else. It consumed him, shooting right up into his head and making his face pound in time with his heartbeat. Noise around him faded away and all he could sense was the pain and his own body.

Still lying on the floor, he looked over at his ruined hand and simply watched the blood pump out. The pain faded as shock hit, and he realized almost a quarter of his hand was missing.

Vaguely, he registered people gathered around him. A thick cloth was pressed onto the wound and wrapped around it tightly. This just made the pain worse, and he screamed again.

Then Aleni was there. Her voice cut through the pounding in his body and suddenly he could hear. She held his face in her hands and stared into his eyes with those icy blues. "Can you hear me? Jacek, hold on. Don't you dare leave me!"

He smiled. "I'm not going anywhere. It's not a fatal wound. Just hurts like a... well, I can't think of a good comparison." He groaned as he sat himself up. Aleni and Rilaiz braced his back to assist. He dragged the mangled hand around to cradle with his other. His breath came out in heaving gasps. His body shook. "I hope you don't mind I killed him."

Aleni looked over at Krodon's still body and stood to face it. She swung her foot back and with a heave of energy, kicked the corpse. She screamed wordlessly at it.

With Mular's help, Jacek got to his feet, cradling his hand close to his body. With his good arm, he wrapped it around Aleni from behind her and held her close. Sobbing, she leant into him.

"It's ok baby girl, he's gone." He kissed the top of her head and looked up at his team, standing off to the side. Rilaiz and Dunvern seemed to find their feet extremely interesting. Mular had a sad look in his eyes, while Solel wore an equally sad smile.

Aleni's breaths heaved in and out, but she slowly calmed.

Then she said quietly, "I don't mind that you killed him. I'm not sure I could have done it myself."

"I think you could have, but you didn't need to. You're already so strong. You didn't need to kill him to heal." He lifted one shoulder, thinking. "But maybe I did."

"I killed Sesk though."

"He was just an asshole who needed to die."

Aleni laughed and turned toward Jacek, who let her go. He was trying not to shake from the shock of his injury, but it was difficult.

Just then, there was a bark, and they both looked around. Bandur came bounding into the room, his tongue lolling out to the side. Thu walked in behind him.

"This place seems to be deserted. Where are the guards?" Thu said.

Jacek glanced around the hall at all the bodies strewn around. "In here. What are you doing here?"

Thu pointed to Bandur, who was currently licking Aleni's face. "He started barking like crazy and scratching at the door. I opened it and he went out but stopped and looked back at me. I think he wanted me to come. So, he led me here, to you." Thu's gaze moved down to Jacek's hand. "And you are injured. Let me look."

Aleni stared at Thu. "Wait, aren't you the guy from the ambush on the road?"

Thu avoided her gaze and unwrapped the cloth from Jacek's hand.

Jacek winced as the movement of the cloth set off fresh lances of pain. "This is Thu, Aleni. Yes, he is the same man from the road. But we've come to an understanding now, and he's been very helpful. The same people who took you, took his daughter."

Aleni continued to stare at Thu, her eyes narrowed. "Is her name Thiri?"

"Her name was Thiri." Thu corrected quietly. He inspected Jacek's hand. "They killed her."

Aleni took in a quick gasp of air, her eyes wide. "No! Oh, I really liked her. I'm so sorry."

"So am I. But she is at peace now. No more suffering, from me or this world."

Jacek watched Aleni, his head floating in a hazy field of blood loss. Sadness fell over her face, but she didn't cry. She was so tough, trying not to show her emotion. He wondered idly if he had taught her that inadvertently. He made a point of never showing emotion, and she copied everything he did. He probably needed to correct that, but how?

"We should get out of here." Rilaiz spoke up.

Jacek looked up at him wearily. The young man had a bump growing on his forehead. "You gonna live?"

Rilaiz grinned. "Ready to fight another day, boss."

"I'm not your boss."

"You better be. No one else is going to pay me for this shit." He looked around at the bodies lying around. He wrinkled his nose. "Let's leave, I don't want to be here when it starts to smell. Well, smell worse," he corrected.

Several days later, Jacek found himself once again standing in Vossler's house. His hand was heavily bandaged and strapped to his torso so he didn't move it too much. He'd spent the last few days laying in bed in the little room at the top of Thu's house. Thu had stopped the bleeding and stitched the skin together over the two stumps of his fingers. The pain had pushed him into an exhausted sleep for an entire day.

Aleni had hovered near his bed, she and Bandur keeping guard over him. She helped Thu make food for them all, and slowly Jacek gained some strength. It comforted him to have her nearby.

While he'd been laying there awake, Aleni had come to him with an idea she'd had. She wanted to do something for the street kids. Find somewhere for them to live. It was too dangerous for them out there.

It hadn't taken him long to think of Vossler. The house stood empty, only the bodies of the guards and Vossler himself still there. None of the locals had known it was empty. Jacek had led Aleni here to lay claim to it, as was the custom in Amathnore. But now they were here, walking around the house and making plans, he still had a sense of unease. Something that sat in the pit of his stomach, trying to get his attention. But he didn't know what it was.

Solel and Thu had helped with getting rid of the bodies, and Aleni rushed around cleaning up the place. It was such a large house, it would require a lot of help to keep it clean and running. A particular person had come to mind for Jacek. He would hopefully turn up soon.

While watching out for him at the front door, Jacek scratched at his bandage.

"Stop it." Thu caught him while walking past. "You must let it heal."

"It itches."

"That means it is healing."

Jacek growled under his breath, but left it alone. At the back of his mind a small but fearful thought wondered whether he would ever hold a sword or his axe in that hand again. He could use his left hand, as he had trained to do, but it wasn't as strong as his right. Would he have to give up being an assassin or mercenary? He shook his head to try and clear the worry.

Shortly, a clean-shaven man and an older woman walked through the snow up the front path to the door.

Jacek nodded his head at the man. "Neran." He turned to the woman. "And you must be his mother."

She nodded. "Cestray. Neran tells me you were kind to him."

Jacek shrugged. "I will repay kindness with kindness. He gave me information freely."

"I helped you?" Neran asked.

Jacek nodded. "Yes. I was looking for my daughter. She had been kidnapped by Vossler." He gestured to the surrounding building. "This is his house. It's now empty."

Neran's eyes widened, looking up at the large manor . "Did he leave?"

"In a manner of speaking. I encouraged it. Needless to say, he doesn't need it anymore. He's donated it to us to use. And I would like to offer you a place here. In exchange for helping us."

Cestray looked puzzled.

Before Jacek could go on, Aleni and Bandur ran up next to him and stopped. Her hair was almost coming out of its braid, but it didn't hide the points of her ears. She now displayed them proudly. Since they had come to the house, she'd had almost a permanent grin on her face. Filled with purpose, her cheeks glowed. It pleased Jacek greatly to see her like that, alleviating the pit in his stomach.

"Hi!" She waved to Neran and Cestray. "I'm Aleni."

"My daughter." Jacek was getting used to saying that to people. It was odd the first few times, but now it was feeling more natural. Especially as Aleni accepted it readily.

"You're not human!" Neran said, pointing at her. "What are you?"

Cestray looked a little embarrassed and held his arm gently. "Neran, that's rude."

"It's alright." Aleni said, smiling. "Yes, I'm an elf. I'm adopted, of course. My parents died a very, very long time ago."

Neran jumped up and down excitedly, flapping his hands. "Mother, a real life elf!"

"Yes, dear. It's very exciting." She gave her son a kind smile.

Jacek spoke up. "So Aleni here had an idea, why don't you tell them?"

Aleni gave an excited bob. "Oh yes! I think this will be a perfect place for the street kids to live. Somewhere warm and safe. And we need people to help with looking after the house and cooking and all that. The kids will help too, but Jacek thought you would be the type of people who might want to help. Especially since your boss is now gone." She gestured to Neran.

Cestray's eyes lit up. "That is a very good idea! It's definitely time people here started helping one another."

"Yes. This is a normal concept for my people. Everyone helps each other. Even my parents served others. This was just the way. It saddens me to see humans treat each other so badly." She lowered her eyes and stared down at her feet. It took only a second, however, for her to snap her head back up. "Anyway, come in and see the house! It's amazing."

Aleni gave them the tour, with Jacek and Bandur plodding along behind. He could feel his cheeks aching from the smile he couldn't suppress. They weren't muscles he was used to using.

"And we could dig garden pits out the back to grow vegetables for everyone to eat and sell any extras," Aleni was saying. Her eyes were alight with ideas. "We can teach some of the kids how to hunt, so they can help provide for everyone. It will be like a little community. Everyone will have a job and a place to belong."

"What about me?" Neran asked, his face also lit up with excitement.

"You can do whatever you like. What are you good at?" Aleni asked.

"I'm good at sweeping!"

"Perfect! And I'm sure we can find other things to teach you so you can help."

Cestray smiled at her son. "I think we can find a good place here. I can cook and teach the children what I know."

Aleni grinned and glanced up at Jacek. "I'm glad to hear Jacek wasn't wrong about you." She paused for a second, something going through her mind. Jacek had no idea what. "Anyway, make yourself at home. Pick your rooms. There are plenty. Bring anything of yours you wish. I will go now to find the children." She started to move off.

Jacek moved quickly to catch up with her. "Should I come with you?" Anxiety danced around his stomach.

Aleni turned and gazed up at him. "I know you're worried about me. But I can take care of myself."

She was right. He had to admit it. He didn't save her from captivity at all. She did that all by herself. In fact, she saved him. Twice. She was more than capable of looking after herself. Strong and resilient, she seemed to have come out no worse for wear. The worst of her traumas were hopefully behind her.

Sure, she would probably still have nightmares and moments of flashbacks, but she persevered. She had a will of iron. A survivor.

"Yes, you can." He motioned to their surroundings. "And you look after everyone else."

"With your help, of course. You've changed a lot, you know."

Jacek was silent at that. Had he changed? He thought back. When she'd met him, he didn't trust anyone. Not even her. Now, he had actual friends. And a daughter he loved with everything he had. He was probably almost unrecognizable from the person he had been.

And it was all because of her.

"Go on, find your friends." Jacek grumbled. He couldn't help himself. He didn't want to let her out of his sight, but he knew he had to. "Oh, one other thing."

Aleni stopped and waited.

"I decided on a name for my horse."

Her eyes lit up, expression expectant.

"Elyon." He smiled.

She grinned. "Perfect!" Then she clicked her fingers to Bandur and the two ran off.

Chapter Thirty Five

Aleni raced through the streets, not quite using her top speed, but not holding back much. Her secret was out now. She was proud of her heritage. There needed to be no shame in it. The only way to change people's view of her was to show them who she really was. There was something freeing about that.

Despite that, she kept her hood up so as not to cause a scene. She certainly didn't want to be mistaken for some goblin offspring.

The mid morning sun was shining down and there was barely a cloud in the sky. But the icy breeze still blew in between the buildings, unrelenting. Together with Bandur, they searched the streets she had seen the youths on before. There was evidence they had been there, but the little alcoves and alleyways were empty. Maybe the market?

As usual, the market was teeming with people. The merchants with their self-importance waited for people to come and buy their essential wares. There was no calling out to draw people in. They wore surly faces and drove hard bargains. It was not a friendly place. Aleni didn't like it.

She weaved her way through the crowd. One of the pickpockets was bound to be here. After a few minutes, she spotted a small body moving in amongst the adults. Catching only a glimpse of an arm, a torso and a leg, she moved toward them.

Bodies pushed against each other, jostling for a place closest to the merchandise. Aleni wormed her way through them, trying to catch the young person ahead. A hand darted in and out of view, and Aleni was almost certain it was a successful lift.

A large man suddenly stood right in her path. Others stood too closely on either side to get around him. She looked up and saw he hadn't even noticed her. "Excuse me please, can I get past?"

He moved his head slowly, bringing his gaze down upon her like she was a flea he couldn't even bother to squash. He wore expensive furs and had long blond hair tied back in a ponytail. "What did you say to me?"

"I said, can you please let me get past?" Her heart beat a little faster, knowing she could get into trouble here, but after everything she'd been through, there was a new confidence deep inside that surprised her.

She stood her ground. Bandur next to her stood tall with his tail erect, his eyes fixed on the man. Aleni placed a calming hand on his ruff. Their connection glowed in her mind and she sent calm but alert signals to him.

"Why would I do that?" The man crossed his arms.

"Because it's not a hard thing to do, and will do neither of us harm. Believe me, it's the easier way out of this."

"Oh really? And what's the other way?"

"Have you heard of Elyon?"

The man scoffed. "The new Arena champion? The one they're saying isn't human? She beat a horde of goblins with ancient magic. My brother saw it with his own eyes." He affected a prideful look.

Aleni refrained from rolling her eyes and pulled back her hood. She attempted to curl any stray wisps of hair back behind her pointed ears.

It took a few seconds, but the man's eyebrows shot up. "You! Are you her?" He took a step back slightly.

"I am. And if you don't get out of my way, I'll have to show you."

He put his gloved palms out in front of him in a sign of surrender, his eyes wide. "I'm sorry, miss. I didn't know. Please, I'll step aside." He moved back and to the side, pushing others out of the way behind him. There were cries of protest, but the man gave them scowls and they left him alone.

Aleni kept her eyes ahead and walked on, her hand still on Bandur's head. As she passed the man, she couldn't help a small smile.

The man stared after her. Soon others noticed. A mumble of awe ran through the crowd. Whispers and murmurings she heard easily.

"Is that the elf witch from the Arena? I thought it was a crazy story everyone was making up!"

"Look at her ears!"

"Do you think there are more like her?"

"Will she kill us all?"

At that, Aleni stopped. If she was to come and go freely, she had to educate them. She turned and faced the crowd. They kept their distance. There was a sizable gap around her.

Lifting her voice, she spoke. "People of Amathnore. Yes, I am an elf. I am not a witch. I simply have inherent gifts that are normal for my people." She held up her right hand and let a flicker of flame dance on her bare palm.

A gasp ran through the gathered people. She let it go out and closed her hand.

"I want you to know that I will never use it to harm you. Unless you try to harm me or anyone I care about. I am the last one of my people. I am not here to exact revenge on you. I simply want to live among you peacefully. Maybe teach you about my people. So we do not forget them."

She let her gaze fall on individuals in the crowd, meeting their eyes. "Do not fear me. But do not think I will lie down if you come for me. You will regret it. You have seen my skills in the arena." She decided not to mention Jacek. She could stand on her own reputation. Those who were there knew there was some connection to him. Let them think about that.

They continued on, Bandur at her heels. The crowd parted for her, revealing a couple of kids standing on the far side of the market. They both had shocked looks on their faces and were staring at her incredulously. She came to a stop in front of them.

"Hello. Do you remember me? I was friends with Thiri."

"Yeah, we remember you. But we didn't know who you were. Are you really Elyon?" One boy, a blond-haired, blue-eyed kid of about eleven years, spoke.

She leaned down and cupped her hand around her mouth, whispering. "It's my secret identity." She gave them both a knowing smile.

"Wow!"

"So I have a surprise for you. For all the kids who live on the streets. I want to help you. Will you help me gather everyone? I don't know where to find them."

"Alright! Come with us!" The two boys ran off out of the market. Aleni and Bandur kept up behind them.

For the next half hour, they rounded up all the street kids. Aleni talked to them and introduced herself, then explain that she had a surprise for them. Not all were trusting, but they listened to their fellow street kids and eventually followed along.

Nearly twenty-five youths and kids trailed behind Aleni and Bandur when she arrived back at the large manor. Eyes widened and mouths dropped open when she led them up the front path.

Turning to the group, she addressed them. "This is your new home, if you want it. The previous owner has generously donated it to you."

More mouths dropped open and stared up at the grand building.

Jacek stepped out just then and joined her on the front step. He placed his good arm over her shoulders and looked out at the group of kids.

"This is my father, Jacek. If he gives you an instruction, you will need to listen to him. He is here to help as well." She gave him a quick side squeeze around the waist.

Whispers grew among the group, all looking in awe at Jacek. They obviously recognized him. Aleni felt a sense of satisfaction at that. They didn't believe her back when she told them he was her father. But she didn't blame them. It was a bold claim, after all.

"Please, come inside." She waved her arm to gesture toward the door.

The kids moved carefully around Jacek, but once they were past, they ran inside, cheering and whooping.

Jacek, his arm still draped over Aleni's shoulders, turned with her and followed them in.

"I'm proud of you, you know. This was a good idea."

"Well, it's just the redistribution of resources, right? There are vast resources here, and many who are in need. If this world is to move ahead, it must stop living in the past. You're not the criminals you're descended from. That must stop. People need to look after each other. It's the only way Selendria will grow and thrive."

Jacek studied her face, his own unreadable. "You are a treasure, you know that?"

"I sure do!" She gave him a cheeky smile and wriggled out of his arms and ran off after the street kids.

This would be her new legacy.

Epilogue

Several days later, a cloaked man boarded a ship headed for the south. The sun was out, but the biting cold was a constant companion. Seagulls circled above the three masted ship, squawking and watching carefully for any food dropped. The ship was filling with people escaping the fallout of the Brotherhood disintegrating after Sesk was killed. Many had been monks in the sect, but former devotees also filled the hold. The air was thick with the feeling of defeat.

The cloaked man found a seat next to a former devotee, his heart heavy with regret. He had been a key component of the whole operation. He'd kidnapped the girl with the magic. Without her, Sesk wouldn't have become so powerful. If he'd known then what would happen, he wouldn't have done it. He would have walked away sooner.

"You looking to start a new life in the south too?" The man next to him said.

Icas lifted his head and slid the hood off. "Yes, I hope to." He needed to make up for what he'd done. The poor girl had suffered greatly, and nearly died. Being part of that was not him. He just gathered information. But there was something about Sesk that made Icas want to please him.

He shivered at the thought now. What had come over him?

The man next to him spoke again. "I can't believe I was duped into thinking there was power in the stuff that old monk said. I had a stone, I was promised protection. But it was all a lie."

"I'm sorry." Icas knew what it was like to be on the wrong side of things.

The man narrowed his eyes at Icas. "You're not one of them, are you?"

Icas winced. "Not quite. But I did work for Sesk. But no more. I'm going to do better. Try and make up for what I did by helping others."

"Maybe you can join us in the south. I heard about this village, Riveracre, where they live well and help each other."

Icas perked up with interest. "Riveracre you say?"

As the ship sailed away toward the south, Icas had a renewed sense of hope. He couldn't undo what he'd done, but maybe he could do some good. Maybe, just maybe that would be enough.

Acknowledgements

Thankyou to everyone who has helped in the making of this book. To my developmental editor, Kimberly Hunt, thank you so much. Any mistakes or grammatical errors in this work are all mine. As a note to the readers, I tried to write this in US English, even though my native language is British English, so if there's anything that doesn't make sense that's on me! To my beta readers, Darla, Andrew, Rosie and Mum. To Wim, thank you for the beautiful cover once again. My friend I am at a loss for words. To everyone who encouraged me on this journey, I thank you.

About the author

J.A. Gates lives and works in New Zealand, where they work in IT. Their hobbies include gaming, puzzles, making models, and various arts and crafts projects. They previously studied mixed martial arts, which they use to bring authenticity to the fight sequences in their novels.

Check out their website at www.jateswrites.com and on Facebook for author updates!